"I'm terribly sorry to walk in on you like this—"

"Since you're here," Rocky drawled lazily, "you might as well make yourself useful and scrub my back." He drew his right arm back in a passer's motion and threw the cloth-wrapped oval of soap toward her. Startled, she jumped, bringing her hands up at the same moment to make an easy reflex catch. "That's the least a good Revelers fan like yourself can do, don't you think?"

Before she could recover from her spurt of surprise, he was sliding down lower into the bubbling water, leaving only his head sticking out. With a deep sigh of pleasure, he closed his eyes, a faint smile of amusement on his lips.

"That's not the kind of scrubbing I do," Kitt snapped irritably, and hurled the wrapped bar of soap into the tub.

Dear Reader:

Romance offers us all so much. It makes us "walk on sunshine." It gives us hope. It takes us out of our own lives, encouraging us to reach out to others. Janet Dailey is fond of saying that romance is a state of mind, that it could happen anywhere. Yet nowhere does romance seem to be as good as when it happens *here*.

Starting in February 1986, Silhouette Special Edition will feature the AMERICAN TRIBUTE—a tribute to America, where romance has never been so wonderful. For six consecutive months, one out of every six Special Editions will be an episode in the AMERICAN TRIBUTE, a portrait of the lives of six women, all from Oklahoma. Look for the first book, *Love's Haunting Refrain* by Ada Steward, as well as stories by other favorites—Jeanne Stephens, Gena Dalton, Elaine Camp and Renee Roszel. You'll know the AMERICAN TRIBUTE by its patriotic stripe under the Silhouette Special Edition border.

AMERICAN TRIBUTE—six women, six stories, starting in February.

AMERICAN TRIBUTE—one of the reasons Silhouette Special Edition is just that—Special.

The Editors at Silhouette Books

CAROLE HALSTON
Surprise
Offense

Silhouette Special Edition

Published by Silhouette Books New York

America's Publisher of Contemporary Romance

SILHOUETTE BOOKS
300 E. 42nd St., New York, N.Y. 10017

Copyright © 1986 by Carole Halston

ISBN: 0-373-09291-1

First Silhouette Books printing February 1986

Books by Carole Halston

Silhouette Romance

Stand-in Bride #62
Love Legacy #83
Undercover Girl #152
Sunset in Paradise #208

Silhouette Special Edition

Keys to Daniel's House #8
Collision Course #41
The Marriage Bonus #86
Summer Course in Love #115
A Hard Bargain #139
Something Lost, Something Gained #163
A Common Heritage #211
The Black Knight #223
Almost Heaven #253
Surprise Offense #291

CAROLE HALSTON

is the wife of a sea captain, and she writes while her husband is out at sea. Her characters often share her own love of nature and enjoyment of active outdoor sports. Ms. Halston is an avid tennis player and a dedicated sailor.

Chapter One

Using some vague excuses that, fortunately, everybody was having too good a time to question, Kitt managed to slip away from the wedding reception early. She had an easy time with traffic on the I-10 expressway since it was Sunday in New Orleans, and then sped north across the Lake Pontchartrain Causeway connecting greater New Orleans to the North Shore. If she'd been stopped by a causeway patrol officer, it would have been awkward, especially for a woman dressed in silk, to admit the reason for her hurry: she wanted to get home and watch a football game on TV!

And not even a game that was being televised live. The New Orleans Revelers, sharing the Superdome with the Saints in the former's first season as a pro football franchise, had played the Atlanta Falcons earlier in the day in Atlanta. The game was being replayed on a cable station. Kitt already knew the outcome and the score—the

Revelers had lost—but she was still eagerly looking forward to seeing for herself how the new team had performed on the field.

Her timing was close. The game was scheduled to be shown at six, and it was five minutes of six when she walked in the door of the house she shared with her business partner and good friend dating back to college days, Ellen Parity, and Ellen's five-year-old son, Andy. Since they weren't home, she assumed they were somewhere with Bob Bailey, whose years of secret devotion to Ellen were finally making his dream of being more than just a friend to her come true. Kitt couldn't have been happier for him. She and Bob had been friends since high school when they formed a "Mutt and Jeff" duo, Kitt at five feet ten inches topping him by a good four inches.

As much as she loved all three of them, Bob, Ellen, and little Andy, and enjoyed their company, Kitt was delighted to have the house to herself, at least until she could get settled in watching the game without any protest from Ellen, who happened to be one of those stereotypical female types who detested football. She considered Kitt a traitor to her sex because she was such an avid fan of a macho man's sport.

"How can you enjoy watching a mob of oversize, padded dumbbells bump and push each other?" Ellen would demand with sincere exasperation. "Most of the time I can't even figure out where the ball is until everybody's all piled up, and there it is on the ground."

"You just don't understand the game," Kitt would point out good-naturedly. "If you did, you'd like it. You'd appreciate how complex every single play is. Twenty-two highly trained athletes on the field, all with a different job to do."

The conversation always took the same course. Kitt would try to enlighten her friend with some basic insight into the game of football, and Ellen would keep her mind steadfastly closed. "Sometimes I think you wish you'd been a man so that you could play that stupid sport," Ellen had accused recently, with a kind of shrewd insight.

Kitt had grinned sheepishly, admitting that Ellen had hit upon a near truth. "I've never really wished I was a man. After all, I had my share of fun playing women's team sports in high school and college. But if I had been a boy instead of a girl, you're darned right I'd have played football. I'd have been a wide receiver and a doggone good one."

Clowning, Kitt took a few steps backward like a wide receiver fading for a catch and then leaped up for the imaginary ball, tucked it securely against her chest and took a few loose-jointed steps across the carpet of the den. Ellen giggled appreciatively along with her son.

"Dana Kittredge! What am I ever going to do with you!" she scolded fondly. "A woman who likes football. And you would have been good, too," she mused. "Remember all those sportswriters in college who said you'd have been a certainty to go on to pro basketball if you'd been a man instead of a woman?"

"Sure, I remember," Kitt said cheerfully and nimbly changed roles, dribbling an imaginary basketball and then passing it to the delighted Andy. "Shoot! Shoot!" she shouted and then took the rebound off an imaginary goal when he complied, convulsed with giggles. "Bad luck," Kitt sympathized. "The ball rolled right off the rim, but you managed to get yourself fouled, anyway. You get a free throw, big buddy."

"Aunt Kitt, you're not like a grown person," Andy declared admiringly. "You're fun."

Kitt took the remark for the compliment that it was and flopped down on her stomach on the carpet next to Andy to watch the football game that had started the whole exchange with Ellen minutes earlier. Ellen stood there a short while and watched what was a long-since familiar sight to her by now: Kitt totally engrossed in the action on the screen, as though she were right in the middle of it all. "Pass the ball! *Pass the ball!*" she would scream and then pound the carpet with elation when her advice was taken and worked or groan with disappointment when she was ignored or the play wasn't executed successfully.

It was all a total mystery to Ellen that anyone could get so involved in a mere game played by strangers, but then that was the way Kitt did everything, with one hundred percent of her body, mind and soul. She moved through life somewhere between a fast walk and a lope, eagerness on her open, friendly face, a thirty-year-old tomboy with a sixteen-year-old's spirit. She seemed so vulnerable at times like this that Ellen felt as fiercely protective toward her as she felt toward her small son. Yet, Ellen had to remind herself that Kitt, not Ellen, was the real force behind their successful and growing business, a cleaning service that employed a couple of dozen women glad for the opportunity to work at a job that allowed flexible scheduling of work hours. Kitt had, in effect, rescued Ellen three years ago at the lowest ebb in her life, financially and emotionally. With a little shake of her head, Ellen went off to another part of the house to do the laundry, not just hers and Andy's, but Kitt's, too.

On this Sunday afternoon Kitt made a beeline for the den, intending to turn the TV up good and loud so she could hear it while she hurriedly shed her finery and changed into jeans and a sloppy, comfortable shirt. Her first thought when the ringing of the telephone brought her up short was that it had to be Ellen, through some uncanny sense of timing calling to give her a hard time about watching the game!

"H'lo." As she spoke into the receiver, her mind was busy marshaling reasons she couldn't come right over to Bob's place for steaks or hamburgers or whatever he might be cooking on the grill. But it wasn't Ellen. It was Betty Boudreaux, one of Kitt's and Ellen's most hardworking and dependable employees. A widow raising a teenage son and taking care of an ailing mother who lived with her, Betty wasn't dependent upon the money she earned working for The Magic Broom cleaning service, but she liked getting out of the house and the extra money certainly came in handy. No sooner had she spoken to identify herself, distress making her Cajun accent more noticeable than usual, than Kitt knew her plans for watching the Revelers' game were in peril.

"Kitt, it's Betty. I've been trying to get you all day. Mama's been having one of her bad weeks. My sister Sophie was supposed to come over from Kenner and sit with her today, but then she called this morning and said she wouldn't be able to come. It put me in a real bind since I always clean 1-A over in Mariner's Village on Sunday afternoon. That's the only day it's always supposed to be okay to go in there. I couldn't leave Mama with Joey, not with her too weak to get up and go to the bathroom. When I couldn't get you or Ellen on the telephone, I was fit to be tied, not knowing what to do. Even if I could have gotten somebody else over there in my place, I didn't know if it'd be the right thing to do...." Betty's worried voice trailed off.

"You did exactly right, Betty," Kitt assured her quickly, knowing that she herself had impressed upon Betty the fact that only someone Kitt really trusted would be assigned to cleaning the eight units in the luxury condominium complex in Mariner's Village. The management agent Kitt had dealt with in negotiating the cleaning contract had explained that the occupant of 1-A had bought the whole complex and was renting out the individual units to wealthy important people who put a high premium on privacy. In most cases, they would be using the condos as weekend or vacation homes or perhaps as guest accommodations. It was important that The Magic Broom use cleaning personnel who were not only extremely capable but discreet.

Kitt got the man's message that the condos might now and then be the scene of some higher echelon hanky-panky, but that was none of her concern. The terms of the cleaning contract were most generous, and she grabbed it. That had been six months ago, and so far there hadn't been a breath of complaint from the management agent.

And now this glitch. It was unfortunate that the condo Betty hadn't managed to clean was the owner's, who, as luck would have it, wasn't just any Mr. Well-Heeled Joe Citizen. He was Rocky Players, pro football superstar, signed by the new Revelers' team for an exorbitant sum, far more than Kitt thought he was worth, since he was a running back and not a passer or a wide receiver. The very fact that he specified Sunday as the day when his condo would be unoccupied and could be cleaned indicated something about the way his mind worked. He didn't sound like the considerate type who would listen to perfectly reasonable excuses.

"Don't worry about a thing, Betty," Kitt ordered cheerfully, glad that she was able to conceal her concern. There was absolutely no point in making the other woman feel any worse than she already did. "I'll dash over there right now and clean the place myself. I'm here all by myself anyway." Her most generous instincts couldn't draw out the lie that she had nothing to do.

"But, Kitt, Sunday night's not a coast-clear time for 1-A. Not after 6:00 P.M.," Betty pointed out worriedly.

"Yes, but the Revelers played in Atlanta today. That game wasn't over until after four. The whole team will probably be spending the night at a hotel in Atlanta and flying home tomorrow morning, don't you think?" Kitt's voice was distracted on the last words because she was beginning to feel a sense of hurry. She'd better get over to Mariner's Village pronto and get the place cleaned before it got too late, since she had no way of being sure the Revelers would stay overnight in Atlanta. The "magic broom" was supposed to sweep unobserved. It wouldn't do for Rocky Players to walk in and catch her in the middle of scrubbing that swimming-pool-size whirlpool tub of his!

It didn't look as though Rocky Players had even been there since Betty had cleaned the condo a week ago. There wasn't a used cup or glass to be found anywhere downstairs in either the kitchen or the great room, no disarray of sofa pillows or personal clutter to give the place a lived-in look. Kitt had the same feeling she'd got the only other time she'd been in the condo—well, naturally she'd been curious to see the habitat of a sports superstar!—that it gave no hint of Rocky Players's personality, unless that personality was totally bland. One look was enough to tell that the condo had been furnished by a decorator supplied with general guidelines to make the place comfortable for a man.

Upstairs there wasn't a wrinkle in the navy and maroon spread on the king-size bed, no faint trace of a water ring or a telltale body hair in the immense whirlpool tub, again no personal clutter anywhere, not even a wisp of feminine lingerie to give credence to Rocky Players's reputation as a lady's man. At thirty-two he was still a bachelor, despite much-publicized romances with several heiresses in the jet set.

After she'd checked the condo downstairs and up, Kitt wrestled with the powerful temptation just to skip this week's scheduled cleaning, since it truly wasn't needed. Rocky Players would never know the difference. She could zip on back home in time to catch most of the tape of the Revelers' game.

"Oh, crap!" Kitt muttered irritably when her feet, comfortably shod in running shoes, refused to budge. Her conscience must be located in her feet and not her brain because they seemed to know that no amount of rationalizing would allow Kitt to do what she could never sanction in the behavior of her cleaning workers, who were never sent out on any job, small or large, with the instruction to "clean what needed cleaning." Instead they were given a list of specific tasks, depending upon the individual contract, which were to be done and done thoroughly, in a recommended order for speed and efficiency. Through her own experience Kitt had evolved a system that she taught her workers.

How could she as co-owner of The Magic Broom violate those principles of reliability and thoroughness on which she and Ellen had built their thriving little cleaning business? She could hear her own cheerful voice mocking her. "The broom sweeps in dark corners as well as in the middle of the room," she always firmly impressed upon new employees. "It sweeps in both places whether those places seem to need sweeping or not, because that's what the broom is paid to do."

Blowing out her breath in philosophic defeat, Kitt decided that she could at least listen to the game while she worked. With the volume on the TV as loud as she dared make it, she headed back up the stairs, carrying a plastic caddy of cleaning supplies in either hand.

There was no prohibition against wielding the "magic broom" fast, especially over smooth, clean territory, and move it fast she did, stopping now and then to catch a few words of commentary on the football game. She had to grin at the irony when she would catch Rocky Players's name. All she had asked was to watch the man's team play ball, and here she was cleaning his bathroom instead!

By the time she had finished the upstairs and then all of the downstairs except the great room, the game was in the final quarter. Kitt had long since lost any sense of unease about being there in a customer's home during a time he hadn't approved for cleaning service. With no imprint of that owner's personality, the condo seemed more like a high-price chain hotel suite than someone's private home, anyway.

With everything done but the vacuuming, Kitt had no qualms about sitting down and watching the last minutes of the game, secure in her belief that Rocky Players was somewhere in Atlanta, probably being the life of some big party. She had already loaded up her cleaning supplies into The Magic Broom minivan parked outside and would do the vacuuming, using the built-in vacuum system, as soon as the game was over.

As usual with football games, the final minutes were stretched out by time-outs and maneuvers to stop the clock. In spite of the fact that she already knew the outcome of the game, Kitt threw herself into each play, offering frequent coaching advice followed by praise or blame as they were deserved. With the TV still turned up quite loud and her own voice joining in with the voices of the commentators and the background noise of the crowd, she didn't hear the quiet sound of the electrically operated garage door of 1-A as it slid open to accommodate an early-model Mustang. She didn't hear the final rev of the engine, the slam of a car door or a door opening from the garage into the kitchen.

Totally engrossed in the action on the screen, Kitt was secure in the belief that she was all alone. With just a minute left in the game, the Revelers had the ball on the Falcons' forty-nine. It was third down with two yards to go for a first down. "Fool 'em and go for a long pass, a bomb," she urged loudly, knowing in her bones the call would be for a running play, and sure enough it was! The quarterback faked a handoff and then gave the ball to Rocky Players, who went charging through the middle into an impenetrable wall of Atlanta defense, quite obviously expecting the play.

"That's right, try to run the ball!" Kitt shouted in disgust. "There's Peronski back there free and clear, just waiting for a touchdown pass, but we have to do just what the whole Falcon defense knows we're gonna do: give the ball to Players, who couldn't find a hole in the middle if his *life* depended on it! Why do you think the Vikings let him go, for cripes' sake!"

In her excitement during the play, she had jumped to her feet. Slapping her thighs disgustedly, she remained crouched forward, totally unaware that her eyes weren't the only ones in the room watching the huge pile of Atlanta defense giants get up, one by one, to reveal the prone, still figure at the bottom. Behind Kitt, Rocky Players's face had a wincing expression as he watched himself being helped up from the ground by his teammates. That play had gone like dozens more before it. His blockers just hadn't done their job today. He'd gotten killed every time he carried the ball. He ached in every muscle and joint of his body. That's why his movements had been slow and weary as he came in just now, and why he hadn't made any noise, even though he'd made no effort to be quiet and slip in unnoticed.

The sight of the cleaning service van parked outside his condominium had caused both puzzlement and irritation, since Sunday evenings were not a time he had okayed for cleaning service. Most Sunday evenings during football season he was in this same condition: exhausted, stiff and sore. Right now all he wanted was to take a couple of pain pills and crash, preferably in his bed if he could muster the energy to get up the stairs. He felt like he could sleep for a week while his battered body healed itself. The last thing he wanted was to see or talk to anybody, but he braced himself to be patient and civil in getting rid of whoever was inside, someone forced by circumstances to earn his or her—probably her—living cleaning other people's houses.

Rocky Players had come up the hard way himself. He'd seen his own mother dish up food in a school cafeteria line and come home exhausted during the summers when she would clean other people's houses. Resentment of life's basic inequities and anger at his own helplessness to correct them during his growing-up years had made Rocky as hard as his name and deserving of his reputation for toughness, but there would always be a soft spot inside him for any woman forced into menial service. It was a hang-up, he knew, that as much as he traveled and stayed in hotels, the sight of a uniformed maid trudging tiredly along a corridor pushing a cleaning cart could touch off a Pavlovian response, and he would feel again the frustrated anger and shame of his youth, quickly soothed by the reassurance that the days of servitude were gone forever for his mother. He'd seen to that. He could die tomorrow and she'd never have a financial worry.

Predisposed as he was toward dismissing the cleaning woman inside his condo as fast and yet as pleasantly as possible, Rocky wasn't prepared for what he found in either the person or the situation. He had expected to find her in the midst of some cleaning task, not sitting in front of his TV with the volume at an ear-splitting level watching, of all things, a taped telecast of the game he'd played that day in Atlanta.

Rocky heard her voice before he actually saw her and confirmed that it belonged to a female, but other than that, the scene was all wrong. The vigor and youth hit him like a revitalizing current. As he paused in the entrance of the great room behind her, he could see only the back of her head and shoulders. From beneath a bright turquoise kerchief, a thick tawny braid hung down her back, glossy against the turquoise fabric of what Rocky assumed to be her uniform. The van parked outside featured the same vivid color in the design painted on its sides.

When she came up out of her chair, wailing her dismay that the quarterback had given him the ball and hadn't passed, Rocky could see more of her. She wasn't wearing the standard kind of uniform at all, but a loose overblouse and jeans. Even crouched over as she was, he could tell that she was very tall and lanky of build. Rocky's instant perceptions of the stranger in his living room had already undermined his ready-made sympathies for one in her situation. She didn't seem to require any sympathy. Then came her tart criticism of his football playing abilities, combined with the fact that there wasn't a cleaning aid in sight to substantiate her presence there in his home. He found himself feeling none too tolerant.

"That cleaning outfit you work for had better have a magic broom, from the looks of things," he declared sarcastically.

Kitt gave a startled little yelp and whirled around. For a second she just stared at the man standing there, comprehension of his presence bringing a quick flood of emotions that Rocky could read easily in her clear gray eyes and expressive features: recognition, dismay, embarrassment, curiosity.

"You're supposed to be having a wonderful time at a party in Atlanta," Kitt joked weakly, with a little grimace. "I really can explain...." It was the closest she had ever come to experiencing mortal embarrassment. If Rocky Players had walked in on her thirty minutes ago when she was doing her job, it wouldn't have been so bad. But to be discovered making herself thoroughly at home, mouthing off abuses of his football ability! If it hadn't been so hysterically funny as well as tragic, Kitt thought she'd probably have just died on the spot.

"I'm sure you can explain," Rocky replied with deep irony, surprised at the provocation he heard in his own voice. That was no way to get rid of her. Wincing at the effort of putting his stiff joints and muscles into action, he walked carefully over to the sofa and lowered himself down on it. With a groan he stretched out full length and closed his eyes as fatigue closed in.

Kitt was watching him the whole time with intense interest. Despite the extreme embarrassment of her situation, she was surprised to find herself reacting like any ordinary person seeing a celebrity close up, in person. No doubt about it, it was a thrill!

She'd seen Rocky Players on television and in the sports pages numerous times and never felt the impact of his physical presence. At six feet two inches, two hundred and twenty pounds, he didn't look big on the field with the other players, a giant among bigger giants, but standing just a few yards away from her and dressed in slacks and a long-sleeved shirt, with his tie loosened at the neck, he looked big and powerful and dangerous. She felt a little jolt inside all the way to her fingertips and toes as she fleetingly visualized him in his runner's crouch, head down, ramming straight into the defensive line looking for a hole to wedge through.

Following fast upon that strange little reflex sensation came the surprise of seeing him move with all the flexibility of an eighty-year-old man across the room to the couch. The deep weariness on his face as he lay down, his eyes closed, brought her sympathetic nature to the foreground and caused her to relax her guard.

"The woman who always cleans your condominium on Sunday afternoon couldn't get over here today. You see, her mother, who's very old and lives with her, was sick, and Betty couldn't leave her." Kitt's voice faltered as she noted a twitch in his features that might possibly be a sign of irritation. At the same time the TV screen drew her attention. In the back of her mind she'd been listening to the commentators the whole time. Only ten seconds of play remained, and the Revelers had the ball, with no chance at this point of tying the score, since they were eleven points behind at 14-3. There was still time enough for a touchdown, though.

"All right! Let's pass the ball!" she burst out approvingly, when the quarterback dropped back in the pocket formed by a tight ring of his teammates whose task was to protect him from the opposing team's rushing defense. "Get rid of the ball!" she urged as seconds passed. "You'd better pass the ball, Carrington, or you're gonna get sacked!" The dire outcome she warned the quarterback against became a thudding reality on the final word, as an Atlanta defensive man broke through the quarterback's blockers and sent him crashing to the ground.

Only when the play was over, along with the game, did Kitt come back to the present and realize she was under scrutiny. Rocky Players had opened his eyes and was watching her.

"Sorry," she apologized sheepishly. "I'm one of those football fans that get carried away."

"So I see," he said dryly. "I take it you favor a passing game."

Kitt felt a telltale flush rising in her face and grinned engagingly. "I have to admit I do." It was both a relief and a disappointment to see his eyelids drop again. She had been about to confess her deep-seated wish that she could have been a pass receiver herself. "I just have to do the vacuuming, and I'm all finished," she offered tentatively when seconds went by and she didn't know whether he had fallen asleep or not.

"Don't bother," came the deep, weary reply.

Kitt took the opportunity to look him over thoroughly, noting the powerful shoulders and arms and chest, the trim waist and hips and long muscled legs. It was hard to reconcile the brutal, driving energy she'd seen

on that screen within the past thirty minutes with this totally inert, spent man on the couch. He didn't look as if
he would ever move again, and yet he couldn't be comfortable, fully dressed like that, even wearing his shoes.
The thought of helping him take off his clothes made her
feel deliciously strange.

"Can—can I do something for you?" she offered hesitantly and felt instantly foolish when his heavy eyelids
lifted a little. She hoped he hadn't been able to read her
thoughts.

"Turn off the TV."

Something in his voice, which was deep and drowsy,
made her heart beat ridiculously fast. Kitt hurriedly carried out his request, for it had been that, not an order,
and left the room, unable to resist one last look over her
shoulder. His eyes were closed again, but there was a hint
of a smile on the mouth that had been tense and hard.

Rocky Players lay there, wondering if he would find
the energy to get up and haul himself upstairs. The whole
encounter with the cleaning girl had an element of un-
reality. No one brimming with liveliness and intelligence, as she was, would be reduced to earning her living
with low-paying, menial work. Watching the expressions play across her face and listening to her voice, especially when she was lost in the football action on the
screen, had been oddly refreshing for him, like taking in
a fresh, tangy breath of lake breeze. She had a delightful
blend of youthfulness and spontaneity that was a matter
of spirit rather than age, because Rocky had never experienced it and probably never would. And yet she was
poised and ultimately unthreatened, even at the height of
her embarrassment.

No, he was quite certain she was a figment of his
imagination, and equally certain that he wouldn't make

it up the stairs at this point. He'd just stay right here with all his clothes on and sleep forever. In a year or two when he finally woke up, he'd realize that he'd dreamed the whole thing. He hadn't come home and discovered some wholesome, outgoing cleaning service Cinderella watching his TV and giving him hell for getting creamed when he carried the ball!

As he drifted deep into sleep, his ears rang with an eager, vibrant voice and his brain held the image of clear gray eyes and a mobile, expressive face. Like any weary war veteran, Rocky was grateful for a pleasant diversion to distract him from painful recollections. It was a fairly rare occurrence in his life to fall asleep, as he did now, with a smile on his lips.

Chapter Two

The encounter was all too real for Kitt as she drove home, thinking of the possible repercussions. The owners of The Magic Broom cleaning service would undoubtedly be hearing from Rocky Players's real-estate management agent in the next day or two. Fortunately, Players hadn't even bothered to get Kitt's name and was so uninterested in talking to her that she hadn't had an opportunity to divulge her real identity. When the complaint was lodged, she and Ellen could simply promise dire punishment of the nameless malingerer Rocky Players had caught lounging on his premises! More likely, whoever took the call would entertain the agent with the truth and assure him that Mr. Players would have no such cause for complaint in the future.

Kitt couldn't wait to tell Ellen and Bob about the incident. They would both howl with appreciation of her embarrassing predicament. Ellen would declare gleefully that it couldn't have happened to a more deserving person than Kitt, who wouldn't know a thief was stealing the chair she was sitting on during a football game on TV.

There wasn't any doubt that this incident would become one of those treasured anecdotes in the "most embarrassing moment" category. While the businesswoman in Kitt hoped it wouldn't cost The Magic Broom a very good contract, she wouldn't lose any sleep worrying about the outcome. Life was too short for regrets when no serious harm had been done.

Since it wasn't worry that kept the incident fresh in her mind for days afterward, Kitt supposed she must be as susceptible as anyone to the novelty of encountering a celebrity in the flesh. Certainly Rocky Players had made a powerful physical impression. When she visualized him as he had stood there looking larger than life in street clothes, his explosive power harnessed now that he was off the field and in the realm of ordinary humans, she got this funny, weak little sensation in her middle. But then she got the very same feeling when she remembered the way he had looked lying on the couch, a Samson stripped of his power.

Kitt didn't confide these feelings to Ellen or Bob because she knew darned well that they'd tease her about going through belated adolescence and getting a big crush on the star football jock at school. In Kitt's case, it would be a belated experience because she had been something of a star herself in high school and college and known all the big jocks without ever suffering the first tremor of girlish awe. She had been friends with most of them and dated quite a few of them casually, but then "casual" was a keyword in describing Kitt's dating life. She'd never had any lack of dates—she was too outgoing and too much fun for guys not to seek out her company—but she always ended up being a friend and not a sweetheart.

"Your problem, Kitt, is that you won't take a man seriously," Ellen had warned as far back as their sophomore year at Louisiana State University in Baton Rouge. "Their egos are fragile. You can't make a joke of everything, especially when they try to say nice things to you!"

Kitt hadn't doubted that Ellen knew what she was talking about, since every guy Ellen dated seemed to fall desperately in love with her. Men instantly wanted to protect her, but then Ellen was just a shade over five feet, and weighed one hundred and five pounds, all arranged into perfect little curves. It seemed to come naturally to her, even now after her marriage had ended in bitter disappointment and she was espousing feminist views, to let a man open a door for her or help her into her coat. Kitt could play along with those little niceties, but what she referred to as the "candlelight and roses routine" always made her ill at ease, and she invariably ended up lightening the situation with humor.

Maybe that was the reason that at age thirty none of her relationships with men, not even those few that had become sexually intimate, had ripened into a grand passion. Kitt was more than a little skeptical that such a thing would ever happen to her, or indeed that it really existed at all, outside of romantic lore and wishful thinking. If romantic love weren't just myth, she'd jokingly declared more than once, it was probably reserved for cheerleaders and homecoming queens, not for girl jocks like herself. Perspiration would kill romance every time!

Lack of faith in the notion of falling in love was partially responsible for Kitt's business success, although other factors were involved, too. Three years ago she had been living in the French Quarter and working at her latest colorful but dead-end job, just as she'd been doing since she'd graduated from college. The man she was seeing regularly was considerably older and quite wealthy. Kitt liked him well enough and enjoyed his company, but she envied him his thoroughbred horse farm located north of Covington in the rolling hills of Folsom.

It hadn't really occurred to Kitt that she was being seriously courted, and there was no calculation whatever in her resistance to his physical advances. She had never made a habit of casual love-making, and he simply didn't turn her on. His proposal of marriage took her completely by surprise, but her own reaction to it was even more surprising—and appalling. She found herself thinking that he was a nice enough man and she could probably put up with being married to him because of all that he could give her!

About this same time, she came home one night and, as was more frequently than not the case, had to park several blocks away from her apartment. All the parking was on the street, and she couldn't afford to rent a parking space in one of the hotel parking garages, as wealthy French Quarter residents did. What well-meaning friends had been warning her about for years finally happened, and she was attacked. After a violent struggle, she managed to get away from her assailant, losing only her handbag and her peace of mind in the process.

Suddenly, Kitt knew that it was about time she stopped living day to day and made some decisions about her life. The French Quarter scene had been fun, but she was tired of the congestion and grime, tired of the roaches, tired of the centuries-old smell. Working at jobs that offered more in novelty than pay had been fun, too, but she was ready to earn a decent income so that she would never again be even fleetingly tempted to "sell" herself and give up her freedom in marriage to some man, however good he might be, just because he could give her material things.

In this state of mind Kitt drove across the lake to have lunch with Bob Bailey, who had opened a law practice in Covington. She thought she knew why he had chosen St. Tammany Parish when he practically opened the conversation with the news that Ellen was recently divorced, extremely unhappy and having a hard time of it trying to keep up her house payments and support her two-year-old son on her elementary schoolteacher's salary. Her ex-husband had skipped town and wasn't contributing a cent.

Kitt would have been more sympathetic to Ellen's plight and Bob's secret hopes if she hadn't been so absorbed in her own problems. As soon as she could, she got the conversation around to herself and poured out her dissatisfactions. Bob was as good a listener as he had always been and just as prompt to cut through the camouflage of emotion and bare the clear-cut answer underneath.

"You need to move somewhere safer where you can draw a clean breath of air—and you'll have to go into business for yourself if you ever want to make any money. You can't make real money working for somebody else."

"But how can I go into business for myself when I don't have a penny saved?" Kitt wailed despairingly. "I'd have to get a job over here before I could quit the one I have in the city and give up my apartment—" She broke off, as Bob's thin face lit up with inspiration.

"Why don't you dust off the old 'magic broom,' Kitt? If there was ever an area that was wide open for the business entrepreneur, it's St. Tammany Parish, especially at this end. Everywhere you look, there's new construction, commercial and residential. To my knowledge there isn't a real professionally run cleaning service over here, just a few outfits with several housewives getting together and working part-time. Say, I'll bet Ellen would be glad to have you move in with her and help pay the house note. She might even be interested in going into business with you!"

Before the weekend was over, The Magic Broom cleaning service was reborn. Bob and Kitt had gotten together with Ellen and they had relived those wonderful six months following their college graduation five years ago. The three of them and Carrie Johnson, the fourth in their close-knit little group, had traveled the length and width of the United States in a van, seeing America before they settled down to what they had all referred to rather grimly as "real life."

The idea for a big postgraduation trip was born in their senior year at Louisiana State. It was agreed that everybody would contribute to a common fund, sacrificing birthday and Christmas money and chipping in whatever extra they could pick up from part-time jobs. Kitt, of all people, hit upon the source that became their gold mine. With a father who was a highly paid corporate executive and a child psychologist mother with permissive ideas about child-rearing, Kitt had grown up with maids and housekeepers and had never been required to pick up after herself or make her own bed. Yet she was the one who hit upon the idea of cleaning other students' apartments in her own apartment building to earn money.

She had made notices and stuck them on all the doors. The response was so overwhelming that she'd had to call in the others for help. Over pizza and beer they decided they really should dream up a name for their cleaning business and devise eye-catching uniforms, too. By the time the evening was over, they were The Magic Broom Cleaning Specialists. Ellen would make harlequin outfits for the four of them.

By graduation they were known as the campus entrepreneurs, having earned enough money to buy a second-hand van and have its sides painted with The Magic Broom logo designed by Kitt, the commercial art major in the group. The colors were fanciful, befitting the name: pink and turquoise and gold. The four good friends and business partners would postpone "real life" for six months to a year. They'd take to the open road and wield their magic broom along the way when opportunity and necessity were combined.

They'd had some wonderful adventures and would never have had to curtail their trip for shortage of money, since along the way they discovered another gold mine—cleaning large newly constructed buildings. But after six months, real life beckoned, and they had retired the magic broom. Ellen had gotten married and returned to her hometown of Slidell to teach in elementary school. Bob had gone on to law school at Louisiana State. Carrie Johnson had gotten a sales job with a pharmaceutical company and was now an assistant district manager. Kitt had gone to New Orleans to live in the French Quarter and work for a tour company, where she'd done about everything except drive a horse and buggy around Jackson Square!

Resurrected, The Magic Broom fast became visible and successful. Kitt and Ellen both worked hard, determined from the first to establish themselves as a full-time business, not a brainstorm by a couple of women to earn extra money. They advertised even when they couldn't afford it and borrowed to buy a small van and have its sides painted with their whimsical logo.

Bob was there to give encouragement and shrewd advice and even to pitch in and work on big jobs some weekends and evenings. A year after the partnership was begun, Ellen was able to quit her teaching job. And now two years after that, she rarely did any of the actual cleaning work at all. It suited her much better to run the office and attend to paperwork. Kitt liked to be out on the job, training and supervising and, more often than not, jumping right in and working, too.

That's what she was doing on the Monday afternoon, one month following her first encounter with Rocky Players, when she came face to face with him again, under circumstances even more embarrassing. She was working with a large cleaning crew in a new office complex on Causeway Boulevard in Mandeville, up on a ladder cleaning fixed-plate glass windows, when Ellen called from the office.

"Kitt, I've been trying to get in touch with Betty Boudreaux over at Mariner's Village. I have an important message for her. It's not an emergency, but she's supposed to call Dr. Clanton's office before five. He has the report back from the orthopedist in New Orleans about the X rays on Joey's knee. You know, he was hurt at football practice at the junior high—"

"I know," Kitt broke in quickly, before Ellen could get started on her views about allowing young boys to play football and risk injuring themselves for life. "Did you call the number at the condo she's cleaning?"

"I called, and when she didn't answer, I called her house. I must have woke her mother up from a nap. She was a little vague but seemed convinced that Betty should be over at Mariner's Village. I would just keep trying the phone at the condo, but I have a dental appointment in Slidell, and Susie's going to have her hands full with me out of the office. I'd feel better if you could take care of this. Maybe you could send somebody over to track Betty down."

"I'll take care of it," Kitt assured. "Give me the telephone number in Mariner's Village, and I'll try it again in a few minutes. She might have been cleaning the shower or running the vac when you called and couldn't hear the phone. Give me her home number, too." Kitt wrote down the numbers. "Which condo is that?"

"Just a minute. Let me check."

During the brief pause, all of Kitt's senses sharpened. She could feel the dampness at her armpits, hear the traffic out on the busy four-lane highway, smell the pungent aroma of ammonia. *Betty wouldn't be cleaning Rocky Players's condo on a Monday afternoon. She cleaned it on Sundays.*

"Kitt, she's cleaning 1-B." Ellen giggled and lowered her voice knowingly. "Isn't that the one right next to you-know-whose? You'd better not go over there yourself looking for Betty. If a certain famous person happens to catch sight of you, you might jog his memory!"

The reason for all the double-talk was that they weren't supposed to publicize the whereabouts of Rocky Players's residence in Mariner's Village. To keep from slipping, they made a habit of not mentioning his name.

"Nah, he's probably forgotten the whole thing," Kitt scoffed. "Go on to your dental appointment and I'll see that Betty gets her message."

The phone call completely shot her concentration on the job at hand. Instead of climbing back up on her ladder and resuming the task Ellen had interrupted, Kitt walked around restlessly, checking on the crew until ten minutes had crawled past. Then she dialed the number of the condo where Betty was supposed to be. When it had rung five or six times and there was no answer, she hung up decisively, her mind made up. Mariner's Village was only five minutes away, and she could use a break, anyway.

On the drive over, Kitt derided herself for the adrenaline pumping through her veins. There wasn't a chance that she would run into Rocky Players, and even if she did, he probably wouldn't recognize her or give her a second glance. Evidently he hadn't complained about her to his management agent, since a whole month had passed and there hadn't been a word from the agent about anything.

At first Kitt had been relieved, but as time went on, she had to admit to herself that she was vaguely disappointed, although she would have been hard put to say exactly what it was she would have had happen. Knowing Players's reputation with women, she hadn't expected him to be intrigued with her and come seeking her out.

There was little doubt that she had been intrigued by him, to the extent that football had become a whole different game, at least when she watched the Revelers play. Now when the team's offense was on the field, she kept her eyes trained on Number 38. In TV close-ups of his face she noted the grimness and hardness and wondered if she hadn't imagined that little ghost of a smile on his lips that night.

Not for anything would she have admitted that now there was a little thrill in watching him interviewed by sportscasters. His voice had a special familiarity since she'd heard it addressed to her. She hung on to every word, noted rather proudly that he talked well for an athlete and approved the fact that he was always patient and cooperative with the sports journalists, even when they stuck their microphones in his face as he trooped off to the locker room after a hard, losing game.

Trust Ellen to notice this new concentration when Rocky Players's face appeared on the TV screen, put it together with the sudden absence of critical remarks about overpaid running backs and come up with her own conclusion. "I think you've got a crush on Rocky Players," she had teased. Kitt pretended to be indignant for just a moment and then grinned.

"You know, I'm beginning to think the same thing myself." She held her head thoughtfully to one side. "Lately I've had to fight this urge to cut his picture out of the sports section and tape it up on my dresser mirror."

It was an ingenious defense Kitt had perfected over the years, agreeing to the accusation and then undermining the admission with ridicule. Ellen had laughed and dropped the subject after that. Kitt was left to wonder in privacy if she really did have a crush on Rocky Players and concluded that if she did, it was perfectly harmless and she definitely wouldn't let it cause her any worry.

The condominium complex that Rocky Players owned comprised four two-story buildings each facing the lake, with two units in each building. Each condominium had its own two-car garage and private driveway. Plus, there was a central space for visitor parking shared by the two units in each building so that the driveways would not have to be blocked unless someone was having a big party.

When Kitt arrived at the complex, driving a Magic Broom van, she immediately saw that Betty's station wagon, with magnetic Magic Broom signs on each side, was parked in the visitors' space shared by 1-A and 1-B. Kitt parked next to the station wagon and sat there a moment before she got out of the van, gazing at the closed garage door of 1-A, which gave not a clue as to whether its owner was home. It wasn't likely that he was, not at this time in the afternoon. What difference did it make, anyway?

None, quite obviously. She gave the van door a brisk slam and went about her business, striding up the bricked walkway to the door of 1-B. After punching the lighted button and hearing distant chimes from inside the condo, she waited a full minute, expending nervous energy by rising up on her toes and then up on her heels.

"Betty, are you in there?" she called loudly, punching the button again.

There was no response to the doorbell just as there had been no response to the telephone. Kitt stood there, frowning in puzzlement. Where the devil was Betty? She had to be around somewhere since her station wagon was parked right in plain sight. Was it possible that she wasn't cleaning 1-B, as they thought, but 1-A?

With a shrug Kitt wheeled around in her tracks, took a shortcut across the grass to 1-A's bricked walkway and without giving herself a second to stop and think of somebody besides Betty answering the door, she punched an identical lighted button and waited, her heart doing a little tap dance. Again there was no response.

Where the hell was Betty? Had the woman been kidnapped in broad daylight? In this puzzled and half-worried state of mind, Kitt reached out and tried the doorknob, certain that the door would be locked. Lots of ordinary folks in Mandeville and Covington didn't bother to lock their doors in daylight, but these condominiums weren't the residences of ordinary folks.

To her surprise, the knob turned easily in her hand. The door wasn't locked. Pushing it open several inches, she called out cautiously, "Betty?" and listened. No answer, but a sound. With her heart definitely beating hard now, Kitt took a few steps inside the foyer, poised for quick retreat. "Betty? Are you in here?" she called out and relaxed as she located the source of the sound and identified it. Water running upstairs in the master bathroom. So Betty was cleaning this condo and not the one next door. She hadn't come to the door just now or answered Kitt's voice calling her because she hadn't been able to hear anything over the noise of the running water.

Not wanting to walk in on the other woman unwares and startle her, Kitt called out Betty's name several times as she mounted the stairs and made her way directly to the bathroom. When the sound of running water stopped, to Kitt's surprise the whirlpool motor began to hum. Why would Betty turn the whirlpool on? Maybe she'd hit the switch by mistake and didn't know how to turn it off.

"Betty—it's me, Kitt." Kitt noticed as she breezed through the large master bedroom that it showed signs of occupancy today, a man's clothes draped across the armchair, the bedspread a little crooked and not perfectly smooth. Betty obviously hadn't gotten around to the bedroom yet. "Why don't you answer—" Kitt was demanding with a touch of impatience as she crossed the roomy dressing area, automatically noting the neat male clutter on the onyx marble countertop next to the sink. The words died in her throat as she skidded to an abrupt halt in the open doorway of the bathroom.

"Oh, no!" she muttered weakly, the enormity of her error sinking in and bringing a kind of paralysis of shock.

The person running the water in the bathroom was Rocky Players himself, not Betty! He was lying naked in his huge whirlpool tub, regarding her with a calm mixture of amusement and recognition. Somewhere in Kitt's brain it registered that he wasn't surprised. He had heard her calling out for Betty.

"You should have *said* something—" she began accusingly and stopped to watch in fascinated disbelief as he proceeded to soap up a washcloth as though her presence didn't interfere in the least with his bath. "I thought you were Betty," Kitt explained foolishly.

Rocky stopped rubbing the oval bar of soap on the washcloth and glanced over at her, his eyebrows lifted in openly feigned thoughtfulness. "To my knowledge, there's no Betty here." Giving in to a devilish impulse, he carefully wrapped the washcloth around the soap bar while she watched uncomprehendingly.

"Well, I'm sure you would know," Kitt joked lamely, glued to the spot. Now that it was quite clear that Betty wasn't here and Kitt had walked uninvited into Rocky Players's home and disturbed him in the middle of taking a bath, she couldn't seem to make herself turn around and leave! She just stood there staring at him, caught up in some spell of fascination! Part of the problem was that he showed no curiosity in the reason for her presence. Kitt felt the need to explain.

"I'm terribly sorry to walk in on you like this—" Kitt gestured with her hands and then was distracted for a moment with the problem of what to do with them next. She hung them down by her side and drummed her fingers against the taut denim covering her thighs. "You see, Betty Boudreaux is supposed to be cleaning 1-B next door. I have an important message to get to her, and when she didn't answer the phone over there or the doorbell, I thought she might be in here instead." She shrugged to emphasize the undeniable logic of her thinking, her gaze dropping from his face to skim again over his bare upper torso, which was wet and sleekly powerful. The covering of dark hair on his chest and forearms, she was pleased to discover, was not abundant. She didn't like hairy men. Kitt had to fight the most incredible urge to step closer, right up to the edge of the tub, and continue her inspection of Rocky Players's nude body!

Rocky noted her absorption and was surprised to find himself mildly amused by the whole situation. After ten years of playing pro football, he was used to being looked over like a stallion by women and no longer got any ego thrill from the open sexual advances. But this was different, somehow. There was absolutely no coquetry in that clear gray gaze, no seductive offering, just intense, very natural female curiosity.

"Since you're here," Rocky drawled lazily, "you might as well make yourself useful and scrub my back." He drew his right arm back in a passer's motion and spiraled the cloth-wrapped oval of soap toward her. Startled, she jumped, bringing her hands up at the same moment to make an easy reflex catch. "That's the least a good Revelers fan like yourself can do, don't you think?"

Before she could recover from her spurt of surprise and settle upon one of several possible reactions, ranging from outrage to laughter, he was sliding down lower into the bubbling water, leaving only his head sticking out. With a deep sigh of pleasure, he closed his eyes, a faint smile of amusement on his lips. Kitt eyed him in disgruntlement. It was obvious he had only been teasing her. There was no need even to put him in his place. She found it highly offensive, this tendency of his to take her presence so casually that he could doze off, right under her gaze.

"That's not the kind of scrubbing I do," she snapped irritably and hurled the wrapped bar of soap into the tub. It landed with a plop and brought his eyes open, as she'd intended, but with a changed expression that took her aback. Gone was the male teasing and the amusement. His dark eyes were apologetic and vaguely pitying. Kitt stared into them with some confusion. Why on earth would Rocky Players feel sorry for her?

The obvious, humiliating explanation jerked her to her senses. She'd been standing there gazing worshipfully at his body, like some new addition to the harem gazing longingly at her lord and master. It probably showed in her eyes that she was dying for a closer look, and the idea of scrubbing his back had had an instant, crazy appeal! Still, he had a hell of a lot of nerve to look at her with that sympathetic expression, as though she might die of disappointment because she didn't interest him.

"If you'll excuse me," she said with all the bored contempt she could feign, but then ruined any illusion of nonchalance by wheeling and marching out stiff-shouldered. She didn't dare stick around, she thought, because she'd probably push his swelled head down in the bubbly water and try to drown him.

"Hey, don't go. Please—wait a minute!" Rocky called after her, switching off the whirlpool motor and climbing out of the tub. Kitt heard a loud splash and a curse and concluded with satisfaction that he must have slipped.

With every opportunity to escape, she found her steps lagging out in the bedroom. "What do you want?" she called out resentfully and then stopped and turned around, her heart pounding expectantly as she watched the door of the dressing room, waiting for him to appear.

Rocky took in her alert stance and felt his compunction threatened with a new onslaught of amusement. She stood there, like a fleet-footed prey pausing to let the hunter get a little closer and thus make the chase more interesting. He could see in her face that she had expected him to come out naked, not modestly and very securely wrapped in a large maroon towel. The fact that she was every bit as disappointed as she was relieved brought a resurgence of the impulse to tease her. Fortunately, the kerchief and overblouse she wore, pink today rather than turquoise but embroidered with the fanciful logo of the cleaning service that employed her, served as a firm reminder to Rocky that it would be unkind of him to tease someone in her position, who had a job to worry about. He was a big client, and she was undoubtedly aware of that fact.

"I'm sorry," he apologized, picking up a tube of Ben Gay salve from the top of the dresser and unscrewing the cap. "I was only kidding you about scrubbing my back." A smile threatened the corners of his mouth as he resisted the urge to add that back there in the bathroom, she had looked as though the idea of scrubbing his back might appeal to her.

Kitt quite frankly looked him over from head to toe as he walked over to the bed and sat down on the edge with a little grunt. Big-headed he might be, but this was still her first opportunity to view a famous pro football player almost naked, in the flesh. What she saw was pleasing to her woman's eyes. He wasn't brawny and he didn't bulge and ripple with muscles like a weight lifter, but he was broad at the shoulders, powerfully contoured in the chest and narrow of hip with long legs. He looked hard and rugged and superbly fit, except for the way he moved.

Just out of the whirlpool, he wasn't as stiff-jointed as he had been on that Sunday night, but it was obvious to Kitt that he was aware of aching muscles and joints with every movement. For some reason, his limited mobility served as a kind of compensation for her injured woman's pride, enough at least for her to stay awhile and observe him.

He didn't seem to object to her scrutiny as he applied himself to squeezing a glob of Ben Gay from the tube onto his right palm and began massaging his left shoulder. Involuntarily the fingers of both her hands curled into her palms.

"I don't mind being kidded," she offered cautiously, the smell of Ben Gay pungent in her nostrils. It mingled with the clean scent of his soap. She watched his features wince as he reached up and massaged the muscles in the curve connecting neck and shoulder. With his arm lifted, she could see bruises on the underside of it and from his armpit down to his waist.

"You're covered with bruises," she announced as though he would be as interested and concerned by her discovery as she herself was.

Rocky's grin was good-naturedly cynical. "In case you haven't noticed, sweetheart, pro football is a rough game. The guys playing defense tend to be big, strong fellows. Any time a ball carrier gets through a game with bruises instead of broken ribs and concussions, he has to call himself lucky." He held his right arm aloft and scrutinized his bared side. "This looks like Angel O'Brien's cleat print right here." He touched a purplish spot with tender fingers. "Down here's an imprint from a Ram helmet." He dropped the arm and without any warning of his intentions, tossed the tube of salve in her direction, partly to disrupt her concentrated gaze and partly just to watch her catch it, as he knew she would. She made an instinctive flinching motion and caught the tube simultaneously, impressing Rocky again with her quick reflexes. "Be a good sport and rub my back, would you?"

As he stood up, turned around toward the bed and eased himself facedown on it, Rocky couldn't hold back a low groan as his sore muscles and stiff joints complained. He had been only half serious in making the request. A rubdown, even an inexpert one, would have been welcome, but he expected her to throw the Ben Gay at him the way she'd thrown the soap and make an indignant departure. It was one way of bringing to an end a situation he didn't quite know how to handle, despite all his experience with women.

Kitt watched him in considerable indecision, sensing that he expected a refusal. There was no doubt that he could benefit from a rubdown. She could empathize with how he felt right now. She'd had her share of sore, stiff muscles herself, in her days of high school and college basketball. Well, why not? It wouldn't be her first time to give a guy's back a rubdown with Ben Gay, she reasoned, making her decision and approaching the bed. Those other times the prospect just hadn't been quite so enormously appealing, and she was afraid he might know it. As she crawled up on the bed and knelt close to his waist, her heart was tripping a little faster and all her nerve ends were on alert for pleasure.

If her hands had been less eager for their task, Kitt would have been gentler, but she didn't want him to think he was giving her the big thrill of her life. As her palms settled upon his firmly muscled back in brisk circular motions, she felt the involuntary flex of resistance. Rocky's low groan was half complaint for her roughness and half gratitude for the mixed pleasure and pain of her touch. Within seconds Kitt could feel him relaxing and giving himself over to her expert ministrations. She could relate entirely to his gradual surrender to knowledgeable hands. Well could she remember the pure bliss of a thorough rubdown after a hard game.

"God, you're fantastic," he murmured once or twice.

With this kind of appreciative response, Kitt warmed to her task and took her own pleasure in attending to every square inch of hard-muscled shoulder, back and arms with the aromatic salve. When she had finished, she gave him a little trainer's slap, not just to signal the end but to banish her own reluctance at severing the physical contact, and then got up from the bed. Rocky let out a long sigh of total relaxation and stayed motionless for several seconds before he mustered the effort to roll over. He lay there looking at her, the expression on his face friendly and curious.

"Maybe you could go to work as a trainer instead of cleaning other people's houses," he suggested lazily and then seemed to hear his own words and wish he could retract them.

Since there was nothing offensive in his words or his tone, Kitt couldn't fathom any reason for his vague discomfort unless he just didn't like the idea of treating someone who cleaned house for a living as an equal. She'd run into that attitude before and usually wasn't bothered by it as she was now.

"I could do a lot of things if I wanted to, but I'd rather clean houses," she informed him briskly and pitched the half-used tube of Ben Gay at him. He made a reflex motion as though intending to catch it, but then let it drop to the bed.

"Sorry—I didn't mean to sound as though there's anything *wrong* with being a...with doing cleaning for other people," he finished up awkwardly.

The clumsy apology seemed to confirm Kitt's suspicion that he considered her his social inferior. She drew herself up to her full height, her face indignant. "Of course, you didn't," she said scornfully. "You also didn't mean to imply that rubbing and pounding big, dumb athletes was preferable to cleaning up their messy condominiums. Now if you'll excuse me, I really do have to go and—" For a moment she hesitated, trying to remember what it was that she had to do that was quite urgent. Remembrance of the forgotten mission erased irritated pride and brought dismay flooding into her face.

"Goodness! I forgot all about Betty—" She glanced down at her watch and then puffed out her breath in relief when she saw the time.

Rocky had watched the swift transitions in emotion with some fascination. He'd never seen expressions change so fast and so vividly. Her face and eyes were like a screen reflecting every thought, every feeling, and watching the spontaneous flow somehow brought him pleasure. It had been the same, tired as he was, that Sunday night a month earlier when he found her watching his TV instead of cleaning his condominium. Slowly he sat up, picked up the Ben Gay, squeezed a blob of it onto his palm and began massaging his chest.

"Betty?" he prompted, for no other reason than to keep her there a while longer. To his amusement and subtle delight, she had to fight a momentary abstraction as she watched the circular movement of his hand on his chest. He was tempted mightily to ask her if she didn't think she should finish the job herself.

Kitt read his amusement and took herself firmly in hand. "Betty Boudreaux is the woman who usually cleans all eight of these condominiums that you own," she explained crisply. "According to the work schedule, she was supposed to be cleaning 1-B, next door to you, this afternoon. I have an important message to give her. She has to call her son Joey's doctor and find out whether an orthopedic specialist in New Orleans recommends surgery on Joey's knee. He injured it last week in football practice at the junior high."

The look on Rocky's face was grim and disapproving at that final bit of information. Kitt didn't give him an opportunity to say what he was so obviously thinking.

"I'll bet your mother let you play football in junior high, too," she pointed out with quick belligerence, taking up Betty's case before he could condemn her for allowing her son to play a rough contact sport in junior high school.

His quick grin took her by surprise and his answer confused her with its unexpected gentleness. "You're right. She sure did. She didn't want me to play, and she worried about me every single game, but she let me play because it was what I wanted more than anything else in the world."

Kitt was touched right to the core by the reminiscent light in his dark eyes and the timbre of love in his voice. Tender emotion was so incongruous with all her physical impressions of Rocky Players, who on the field and off seemed as hard as his name and deserving of his reputation for toughness. But apparently even tough, violent football players had memories of being nurtured by protective, loving mothers.

"I guess I'd better go and find Betty," she said reluctantly as he dropped his gaze and concentrated on rubbing Ben Gay into a muscular thigh. Kitt watched, involuntarily sucking in her breath as his palm pushed the edge of the maroon towel higher. It had loosened a bit and was sagging lower on his hips.

There seemed nothing relevant to say in parting. She wasn't at all sorry that any of this had happened, just sorry that it was going to end so unsatisfactorily.

"See you around," she said, starting for the door.

Rocky had every intention of letting her go. He fought against giving in to her reluctance to leave until she'd had time enough to reach the door, and then the words to stop her came of their own accord.

"Say—you haven't even told me your name."

Kitt easily checked her motion and came to a stop.

"You haven't asked me."

Rocky had to twist his body around toward the door so that it wasn't a strain on his sore neck muscles to see her. In swiveling his hips, the towel almost came completely free. He glanced down to confirm that he was still modestly covered and then looked up to see that she was making the same inspection. Once again, her frank interest in his body didn't turn him off. He felt the same kind of mild flattery and indulgence he might have felt if she were the best friend of a kid sister: cute, fun, but off-limits. In actual years she probably wasn't that much younger than Rocky, but he felt a hell of a lot older and riddled with invisible scars of experience.

"I'm asking you. What's your name?"

"Kitt. Actually my name's Dana, Dana Kittredge, but everybody calls me Kitt."

"Glad to meet you, Kitt." Rocky was silent after that, surprised that someone who'd had to settle for cleaning other people's houses would have a classy name like *Dana*. There'd been a girl named Dana in his past. He remembered her as someone totally unattainable for him at the time. She was the daughter of the leading doctor in Shreveport, where he'd grown up. She was cute and blond and fluffy and drove a sporty little car to school. She flirted outrageously with Rocky just as she flirted with all the star athletes at school, but Rocky had never had the nerve to ask her for a date because he was too aware that she was out of his class, too afraid she'd turn him down. It wasn't just that he was dirt-poor and lived in a shabby part of town with his mother and four younger brothers. That was part of it, as was the fact that his mother was a cafeteria worker. The real point of embarrassment was that his mother did cleaning for the doctor's wife. It had always seemed degrading to Rocky to clean up other people's personal filth.

After he had made it big in pro football, Rocky enjoyed his share of Danas. Every high-society debutante and heiress to which his name had been linked had been a Dana. To some extent they made up for the inaccessibility of the first Dana in his life. Kitt didn't seem at all like a Dana to Rocky, but then she didn't seem like anyone who should have to work their way up from the bottom, either. She was definitely something of a puzzle to him, a most appealing puzzle.

From Kitt's point of view, the conversation had lagged to another unsatisfactory close. She gave Rocky's faraway expression and his superb athlete's body, darkened with purplish bruises, a parting glance and turned away to leave.

"So long, Rocky."

The casual farewell was fully resigned to the inevitable, but the faint wistfulness caught Rocky's attention and prompted him once again to stop her, against his common sense.

"What do you do on Monday nights, Kitt?" he asked reluctantly, as though he had been forced into conducting a survey.

Surprise and skepticism were written all across Kitt's face. Nothing had prepared her for such an inquiry, not even one spoken in a tone too unenthusiastic to foster hope. Her reply was automatic.

"What everybody does on Monday night—I watch 'Monday Night Football' on TV." Curiosity flashed in her gray eyes, and she sought to satisfy it without stopping to think. "Do pro football players watch 'Monday Night Football'—when they're not playing the game, I mean?" Halfway through the question it had occurred to her how she must sound, as though she were angling for an invitation. It was too late to stop and by the time she'd finished, she was turning over in her mind the very tempting thought of watching a football game with Rocky Players.

"Why don't you drop over tonight and see for yourself? You seem to like my TV, anyway." Even as he issued the dry proposal, Rocky had serious second thoughts. Just as he'd expected, the notion had instant and enormous appeal for her, and he suspected he had spoken just to witness her reaction. However, her expressive features had no sooner bloomed with delight than they drooped with chagrin at some reminder.

"I'd love to watch the game with you," she mused regretfully, "but I don't know what to do about Andy— he's five...." On Monday evenings during football season, it was taken pretty much for granted that she would baby-sit Andy since she would be home all evening anyway, watching the game, and would just as soon have

Ellen somewhere else enjoying herself and not making cracks about stupid football games. Tonight, though, Ellen would just have to understand and either get a sitter or change her plans. Kitt wasn't giving up the one opportunity she would ever have to watch "Monday Night Football" with the Revelers' star running back himself. No, indeed.

When her eyes began to brighten and her features grew firm with determination, Rocky steeled himself to balk at what he just knew she was going to suggest: bringing five-year-old Andy, presumably her son, along with her. Rocky had come to his senses with a crash and couldn't believe he had actually invited her over. She was a total stranger to him, a cleaning woman, for chrissakes, who'd cleaned his own condominium. Aside from that fact, there was no telling what kind of domestic mess he might be getting himself into. Kitt wore no rings on her hands, but five-year-old Andy had to have a father. All Rocky needed to make his life perfect was to have some irate ex-husband or live-in boyfriend show up in his pickup truck at halftime of "Monday Night Football."

"It's probably just as well you can't make it." Rocky forgot the towel as he stood up and had to clutch it for modesty's sake. "Nine times out of ten, I'll be sound asleep by eight o'clock, anyway. Maybe some other time."

Kitt waited while he wrapped the towel firmly around his loins. As he looked up and caught her expression, Rocky was taken aback to see that in addition to the disappointment he'd expected, there was a reflective curiosity that quite unexpectedly put him on the defensive.

"Why did you change your mind?" she asked him bluntly.

"I didn't change my mind," he lied. "You said yourself you couldn't leave your little boy—what was his name, Andy?—at home by himself."

Kitt looked vaguely surprised and then threw back her head and laughed merrily. "Is that what you thought? Andy's not my little boy," she explained cheerfully. "I share a house with his mother, and I usually baby-sit him on Monday nights. But if you've changed your mind..." She shrugged her shoulders to indicate both regret and philosophic acceptance and turned again for the door, this time with a purpose.

"I haven't changed my mind," Rocky denied forcefully to her back.

Kitt paused and looked questioningly back at him. Rocky felt her direct, clear gaze sweep him from head to toe and back up again. He had to resist the ridiculous urge to look down and check the status of his towel.

"Well, what do you say?" he pressed, impatient of his own suspense. Who'd have thought he'd be afraid she *wouldn't* come over, for chrissakes?

Whatever reassurance she had been looking for, Kitt must have found it. "I'll be here," she declared and then flashed him a candid, abashed grin. "I wouldn't miss it for anything," she confided ruefully. "I've never watched a football game with a pro before. It ought to be fun. Like going out to eat with a chef," she added gaily.

Her unaffected enthusiasm came at Rocky in a fresh, invigorating wave, washing away his reservations about inviting her over that evening and infusing him with an anticipation he found totally mysterious. The last thing he would ever expect to look forward to on a Monday night following a hard game on Sunday was watching a pro football game on TV. It would be the same as a car mechanic working twelve hours on Friday and then going down to the garage on his Saturday off to watch a fellow mechanic do a routine engine installation.

But Rocky thought he might surprise himself and stay awake during the game, just to watch her watching it. He remembered her animated involvement in the football action on the field that night he had walked in on her in his living room. She'd been addressing herself loudly to the screen and hadn't known another person was anywhere around, though he had made no effort to be quiet.

"There's one condition," he said, remembrance causing a smile to tug at the corners of his mouth. He shook his head almost reprovingly as she instantly came alert to the possiblity of a sexual innuendo he hadn't intended at all. "Not that, believe me," he said dryly. "If you come over here tonight expecting to be ravished, I'm afraid you're in for a big disappointment. No insult intended, but on a Monday night it would take quite a woman to turn me on." He smiled teasingly, noting with secret amusement that she was irked by his words. "I just meant that you're going to have to take it easy on the running backs tonight in my presence and tone down your compliments for the wide receivers."

Kitt's smile grudgingly forgave him for not finding her sexy enough to stir his slumbering libido on a Monday night. "I promise." No sooner had she spoken than her eyes widened and flashed with an urgent remembrance of the present that took precedence over any thought of the evening ahead.

"I've got to go and find Betty!" she exclaimed. "See you later."

She was gone, leaving Rocky with an impression of long-limbed agility he could envy in his present state of semimobility and a final glimpse of a thick tawny braid bobbing against a jaunty pink back. In an incredibly short time, he heard the closing of his front door. Only then did he dare to loosen his towel and let it drop to the floor.

Chapter Three

It was the first time Rocky had seen her not engulfed in the loose overblouse of her cleaning service uniform, but he'd known she would be small-breasted and slim. Dressed in jeans that hugged the lean curves of her hips and thighs and a long-sleeved print blouse, she was just a shade away from being too thin, her figure quite unexpectedly bringing to his mind the attenuated build of the fashion model Rocky had been rumored to be engaged to a couple of years ago.

But unlike the model, Kitt didn't have a practiced elegance of movement, and she didn't have that gaunt, semistarved look, either. From the way she eyed the open can of mixed nuts on his coffee table and helped herself to a handful, Rocky doubted that she dieted to keep herself thin.

"Could I get you something to drink?" he offered after she'd settled herself on the sofa and immediately fixed her attention on the pregame show on the TV. "I'm afraid the choices are limited. I have beer, several kinds of fruit juice and water. That's about it."

"Beer's fine," Kitt said promptly, helping herself to another handful of nuts. He obviously hadn't gone to any trouble on her behalf, but that realization failed to take the edge off her anticipation. She was looking forward to the evening.

"You're moving a lot better than you were this afternoon," she volunteered when he came back into the room carrying two tall beer glasses, one filled with beer and one filled with orange juice. She also thought he looked as masculine and virile in his jeans and open-throated knit shirt as he'd looked wrapped in a towel, but she discreetly kept that opinion to herself.

Rocky didn't answer until he had handed her the glass of beer, sat down at the opposite end of the sofa and toasted her with his tall orange juice. Then he addressed only the spoken observation, not the frankly admiring assessment in her eyes.

"I'll be up to a light workout on Wednesday. By Thursday and Friday, I'll be ready for some intensive practice, and Sunday I'll be ready to play." He set his glass on the end table at his right and sprawled comfortably lower into the sofa cushions with his long legs stretched out in front of him.

Kitt sipped her beer, eyeing him over the rim. "Then next Monday you'll be stiff and sore and full of bruises again," she prophesied sympathetically. She didn't think she'd like to go for months on end with the certainty of acute physical discomfort and often pain.

Rocky's grin was cheerfully cynical. "It's not so bad when you consider some of the alternatives. Beats the hell out of waking up in the hospital on Monday mornings."

Aware of her absorbed, quite thorough scrutiny searching out all the places in his anatomy where he might possibly suffer injury, Rocky took a drink of orange juice and glanced over at the TV screen. He didn't know if he could withstand several hours of this kind of intensive surveillance!

Kitt sipped her beer and crunched another handful of nuts. A beer commercial featuring several former pro football players gave her the perfect opening she was looking for.

"Don't you like beer?" she asked, casting a curious look over at the glass of orange juice. It was a surprising choice of beverage for a man with a reputation for being one of the biggest party goers in professional football. "If you don't, you'd better not let the news get around or you won't be asked to do beer commercials after you retire from the game."

Rocky knew he was being probed. It came with the territory of being a media personality to have football fans and nonfans alike follow up an introduction with questions they wouldn't dream of asking just any new acquaintance. *Is it true?* was the common preface to a whole range of personal inquiries into his habits and tastes regarding everything from food to sex. At this stage in his football career, Rocky figured he had fielded all the possible questions with most of the possible answers, depending upon his reaction to person and situation. He was amused by Kitt's transparent effort at subtlety and indulgent of her perfectly normal curiosity.

"You're not an undercover agent for the Miller beer company, by chance," he teased and was rewarded by her appreciative grin. "No?" He blew out an exaggerated sigh of relief and grinned back at her. "Sure, I like beer, and I'd be having one now if I hadn't taken a muscle relaxant. Drinking a small amount of alcohol on top of it wouldn't be dangerous, but it wouldn't help me stay awake, either." Rocky picked up his orange juice and made a toasting gesture. "I thought you'd rather drink alone than listen to me snore through the game."

Kitt was pleased with the friendly tone of the explanation, but possibly even more curious than before. Could this be the Rocky Players of that legendary bar brawl some years ago? He and a half-dozen of his teammates had taken on all the patrons in the bar and, before it was over, the city police force. The bar premises had been wrecked, and there'd been huge fines. It had been the kind of scandal that delighted the most law-abiding football fans, who accepted the fact that any player worth his salt had to raise a little hell now and then. The newspaper reports had made Rocky Players the ringleader, this calm relaxed man sipping a tall glass of orange juice!

Thoughtfully Kitt reached toward the can of nuts again, but instead of taking another handful, she picked up the can and offered it to him.

"Do you take mixed nuts with your orange juice?" she asked jokingly.

Rocky detected the faint note of disappointment and guessed that the reality of Rocky Players didn't measure up to the media legend. "Just cashews," he countered and added with good-natured irony, "I always eat cashews with my orange juice. If I read that in *Sports Illustrated* next month, I'll know who the leak was." He fished out several cashew nuts and crunched them with relish while she watched. Her eyes also followed his hand as he wiped his fingers carelessly on his thigh. Rocky wasn't sorry when she switched the spotlight of her gaze over to the TV screen, where the two team lineups were being introduced. He relaxed too soon, though.

"Number 81, offensive guard, Darryl Hanson...." the loudspeaker was blaring out.

"I don't suppose he's really a member of AA," Kitt announced out of the blue. "I guess more than half the stuff they print about football players isn't true. It's just all a part of hype, to add color to the game."

Rocky was caught red-handed holding his glass of orange juice when she looked over for confirmation of this unenthusiastic bit of insight. He was amused by his own defensiveness.

"Darryl is a member of AA," he hastened to assure her. "Willie Freeman does drive that fleet of sports cars he owns like a demon. It's true that he got drunk and drove one of them all over the practice field one afternoon. Scott Baylor really is a video game freak. He must own a hundred of them, and he can't pass one up, not even when he's rushing to catch a plane in an airport." Rocky set his glass of orange juice down on the end table. "Probably the majority of the things you read about pro football players is true. We live under a lot of pressure, and every now and then, we have to blow off steam. When that happens, there's usually a reporter around with a camera. We work harder than most people, and when we play, we play harder, too, but there's definitely more work than play. Any football player who doesn't live by the training rules won't be in the game long."

Rocky hadn't meant to get terse and preachy. "So who are you picking for the winner tonight?" he asked conversationally to change the subject.

"The Cowboys," Kitt replied, following his gaze to the screen, where the first quarter of the game had begun. She was reluctant to drop the conversation, but the action immediately engaged her attention. The Dallas Cowboys took the kickoff and then began their offen-

sive drive toward their opponent's end of the field. On
first down and ten, when the Dallas quarterback dropped
back into his protective pocket of blockers, Kitt slid forward to the edge of her seat, waiting for the pass, which
was high and spiraling. She was crouched forward with
her weight free of the sofa cushion when the ball made
contact with the receiver's hands and then spurted free
into the sidelines.

"Did you see that?" she cried, settling back disgustedly. "The ball was right *there*. It was all but in his
hands! He should have caught it!"

"He would have if his feet hadn't been knocked out
from under him," Rocky pointed out. "It's hard to catch
a ball when you're being hit by a moving brick wall."

Kitt glanced over at him, sheepish at having let loose
in front of him that way. "You just said I had to be easy
on the running backs," she reminded him teasingly.

Rocky was watching the shaken wide receiver pick
himself up off the ground with the help of the free safety
who'd hit him hard, just as he was supposed to do.
"Those guys are lucky to stay alive," he mused grimly,
shaking his head. "They have to keep their eyes on the
ball every second, or they don't have a prayer of catching it. That makes them sitting ducks for the secondary
man guarding the zone."

Kitt was silent as she watched the replay shown first at
normal speed and then in slow motion, seeing something totally different after his comments. Instead of
keeping her eyes trained on the ball and the wide receiver's hands, as she had before, she watched the speedy
approach of the free safety and sucked in her breath at
the explosive impact.

"Why did he have to hit him so hard?" she protested.

"That's his job to hit the receiver hard," Rocky replied patiently. "He wants to impress upon the wide receiver the danger of straying into his zone. The more worried the receiver is about pain the less likely he is to catch the ball and hold onto it. Football's a game of intimidation. As a football fan, surely you must know that."

"I'm glad Ellen's not hearing this," Kitt declared, her eyes straying back to the screen. "Then she'd *really* give me a hard time for watching football. Ellen hates football . . ."

Rocky's grin went unnoticed. "Maybe Ellen's a sensitive person," he suggested to her rapt profile and couldn't detect any hint that she'd heard him.

Kitt had heard, but she waited until the play was over to make an impudent retort. "It's a good thing for you there are a lot of insensitive people like me in this country. If there weren't, you football players wouldn't be earning those huge salaries, would you?" Kitt was a little amazed at her own temerity, which even in the heat of good-natured retaliation didn't quite extend to asking him point-blank if the astronomical contract terms bandied about by the sportswriters and TV commentators were really true.

"Right you are," Rocky agreed promptly before she could finish gauging his reaction and decide whether to risk getting down to specifics. Actually the high numbers mentioned in the press weren't far from the truth, and Rocky wouldn't have minded confirming that fact for her, but he didn't want to get into a discussion of his move to the Revelers. It had been thoroughly discussed by every sports journalist in the business. The decision hadn't been an easy one, but Rocky knew that at the age of thirty-two, he didn't have but a few good years left to

play, if he was lucky enough not to sustain a serious injury. Why not go for the money while he could? That had
been his pragmatic reasoning.

"You just missed the best play of the game so far," he
declared, nodding his head toward the screen. "Look at
the replay on Donaldson ripping off fifteen yards straight
up the middle. You don't even notice running plays, do
you?" he jeered lightly.

His tactic worked perfectly. Kitt's attention snapped
back to the game. "He's got some good moves," she admitted, watching the running back swivel and fake and
make lightning changes in direction as he charged his way
through the opposition's defense.

"He's got some good blockers, too," Rocky put in.
"You don't think that hole opened up by accident, do
you?"

Kitt listened in awed attention as he briefly described
exactly what had happened in the play, calling all twenty-
two of the men on the field by name. He hadn't even
seemed to be watching the play closely and yet it was as
clear in his mind as though he were seeing it replayed on
the screen.

"How do you see all that?" she asked admiringly.

When halftime came, Rocky was surprised that the
time had passed so quickly. He hadn't dozed off once,
even though the game wasn't especially good. It was
watching the action through Kitt's eyes that had entertained him and kept him awake. He got a kick out of her
abandoned involvement in the action, but it was obvious very soon that she was not only enthusiastic but
quite knowledgeable about the game.

Before he realized what was happening, she'd lured
him into the role of analyst and teacher and was such an
apt pupil that he'd actually followed along with her ea-

ger suggestion that he diagram some of the more complicated plays for her. He was impressed with her quick grasp and aware that there was a hint of hero worship in her attentiveness. It didn't make him uncomfortable, though, because even hero worship in Kitt seemed wholesome and natural. Somehow she had passed through the years of innocence and managed to remain spontaneous and uninhibited and in love with life. For Rocky, who looked upon himself as a kind of battle veteran, it was refreshing and utterly relaxing to be in her presence.

"How about another beer?" Rocky offered, remembering his duties as host when the two teams had trooped off to their respective locker rooms, leaving the commentators with some time to kill.

"I'd love one," Kitt accepted promptly and sat back with a little blissful sigh as he left the room. The evening was a total success in her estimation. His tutoring her in the complexities of football was enjoyable on more than one level. She really did love the game and was learning more in a couple of hours than she'd learned in years of watching it.

But she wasn't fool enough to think she'd be this fascinated by the instruction of just any man. There was a special thrill in sitting close to one of the biggest pro stars in the game and having him analyze the individual plays and the overall game strategies. Maybe it was the "sitting close" that she enjoyed more than anything else, Kitt admitted gleefully to herself. That had been a stroke of genius on her part to ask him to diagram some of the plays for her! It meant they had to move closer together on the sofa.

By now there wasn't a single doubt in her mind that she had a high school crush on Rocky Players. Never had she

felt so intensely physical toward any member of the opposite sex. Everything about him pleased her senses. She
liked the way he smelled, just kind of clean and masculine. She loved his low-pitched voice, whether it was sincere or dryly humorous, and as for his body, it was next
to impossible to keep her eyes off of him when looking
at him was sheer pleasure. He was definitely a hunk, a
candidate for a male centerfold, and nice, to boot. Too
nice, she reflected with a rueful sigh. He'd warned her
ahead of time that it would take quite a woman to rouse
him on a Monday night, and she obviously didn't have
what it took.

Kitt was amused at her own train of thought. She
hadn't come here to be ravished by Rocky Players! Why
the big disappointment because he didn't make a pass at
her? She was having a great time and wouldn't have
changed places with anybody at the moment.

When Rocky returned with her beer, he also had one
for himself.

"I see you couldn't resist the temptation!" Kitt teased.

They sat companionably, giving idle attention to the
halftime prattle. To fill in the time, a network sportscaster was giving a recap of Sunday's pro games and
showing film clips of key plays. When he came to the
Revelers' game, Kitt paid closer attention and was rewarded with the sight of the man beside her in football
garb on the screen. *I just can't believe I'm here with you,
like this,* she felt like murmuring aloud.

"How does it feel to see yourself on TV?" she asked,
the wonder there in her voice for him to hear.

"Sometimes good, sometimes bad. Depends," Rocky
replied indifferently, raising his glass of beer to his lips.
It tasted cold and good going down. Tiredness had begun to close in upon him now. Even with the muscle re-

laxant he was aware of all the aches and sharp twinges every time he moved.

The game commentators were back on screen now, filling up the last few minutes before the game would resume. They were praising several of the players in tonight's game who had recently suffered injuries and yet were in the lineup, playing because they were tough, the way pros have to be if they're going to survive, and also because they loved the game of football.

"He *wants* to be out there on that field, not sitting on the bench," one of the commentators, a former pro player himself, declared of a defensive lineman who was playing with a cracked rib.

"Bullshit."

The calm crude expletive took Kitt totally by surprise. "Are you saying it's not true?" she asked curiously. "I know pro football players are paid well for playing, but don't they—don't you—really like the game? I've always heard that."

Rocky drained the rest of his beer, put the glass down and sank down a little lower so that he could rest his head on the back of the sofa. It was becoming too great an effort to hold it up. The beer on top of the muscle relaxant was hitting him now like a half-bottle of Scotch. That's why he'd let his guard down. He had to smother a yawn before he answered her, and stringing the words together intelligibly was an effort.

"Asking a pro ball player if he likes the game is like asking him if he likes to breathe and eat. He can hardly remember a time when he didn't play football. He probably played neighborhood ball and couldn't wait to get on the team in junior high. Then four years of high school ball. If it was a big football school, he got into intensive training there and got a taste of the pressures of the game. Then off to college on a football scholarship. Four more years of living and breathing football, putting in as much as forty to sixty hours a week. The big football colleges are like pro training camps.''

Rocky had to smother another yawn. His voice when he continued was drowsy and he was fighting to keep his eyelids from lowering. He turned his head sideways and focused upon her face. Her expression was so solemn that he tried to lighten his tone.

"Read some statistics recently. Over a million kids play high school football. Forty to fifty thousand play college ball. Less than two thousand players in pro ball." Rocky shifted a little and winced at the pain. "Problem is that once a guy's made it to the pros, his worries are only starting. He knows he has to stay healthy and fight to hang on to his place. Because for every one of him, there's at least a thousand top college players who'd love to do his job and earn his salary."

Rocky sighed and gave up on keeping his eyes open. "Sure," he murmured sleepily. "I guess most of us do love the game. It's in our blood. But the reason we walk out on that field and play when we're injured and hurting is that we can't risk letting some other guy show the fans he can take our place. The fans love us today and forget us tomorrow...."

Rocky Players was sound asleep under the tender gaze of one particularly ardent football fan. Kitt had to battle the strong urge to touch her fingertips to the hard features, relaxed now in sleep. She wanted to lay her palm very gently across his brow as though to ease away all thoughts that might trouble his rest. It was ridiculous, she knew, this swell of protectiveness inside her as she looked upon her sleeping football giant. She felt oddly privileged to see him that way, oddly content.

It didn't occur to Kitt not to finish watching the game. She turned down the volume and restrained her usual reactions, looking over often at the sleeping man beside her. His breathing was deep and regular and his expression utterly peaceful until he would shift his body, and then there would be a grimace and occasionally a soft groan.

When the game was over, she had no excuse to linger any longer. She turned off the TV set, using the remote control, and sat there a moment in indecision, looking at him. Should she just leave or should she wake him up and say good-night? Her inclination toward the latter was bolstered by the commonsense knowledge that he would be far more comfortable sleeping in his bed than sprawled on the sofa.

"Rocky, wake up." Gently she grasped his shoulder and then gave a little shake. "The game's over. Time for you to go up to bed."

Rocky moaned and stirred, flinging out one arm. Kitt went stock-still when it settled laxly across her lap. Very tentatively she stroked the muscular forearm and smoothed out the fingers of his hand. Her breathing was coming very rapidly and she had a strange stirring sensation deep in her stomach.

"Rocky—please—wake up," she begged him.

Somehow her voice must have penetrated this time: perhaps it was the thin note of desperation. Rocky jumped and his eyes flew open. He stared at her a moment in total confusion and then blinked.

"Kitt. For a minute there I didn't know who the hell you were." His voice was husky with sleep and played across her nerve ends like the stroke of a feather. He took in their positions and saw his arm resting across her lap. "Sorry." He straightened up very slowly and carefully, his features tight as he flexed stiff, sore muscles. "I warned you I'd fall asleep on you." His hand settled familiarly on her denim-clad thigh, gave it a friendly squeeze and then stayed there while he smothered a huge yawn with the other hand.

"I can't promise you that it won't happen the next time," he declared cheerfully, rising to his feet and slowly flexing and stretching in preparation for seeing her to the door.

"Yes, you did warn me." Kitt heard the lilt in her voice. He'd said "the next time"! "You didn't miss a whole lot in the second half, anyway. Neither team could seem to figure out how to score."

"Dallas win?"

"Naturally. Didn't I tell you they would?"

"So you did."

Rocky chuckled as he slipped his arm around her shoulders companionably and walked with her to the door. "Drive carefully, now," he admonished her. "We can't afford to have any accidents to football fans like you."

"I will," she promised cheerfully. "Thanks, Rocky. It was fun."

He gave her shoulders a squeeze that let her feel his strength. "It *was* fun. I'm glad you barged in—" He stopped and casually dropped away his arm. "Hey, I forgot to ask you if you ever found Betty this afternoon."

"Yes, I found her. She was down the street, playing good Samaritan. One of your neighbors' little pet dog had gotten out and wandered off. Betty saw it and was afraid it might get out to the highway and get run over. It was wearing a collar with the address, so she took it home. The owner was an old lady and so beside herself

Betty was afraid to leave her before she'd calmed down. Betty ended up making her a cup of tea."

During the explanation, Kitt could feel the change in him. He was suddenly uncomfortable and anxious to be rid of her. No sooner had she finished speaking than he had the door open, and there was a stiff perfunctoriness now about his good-night pleasantries.

"Thanks for coming over, Kitt. Be careful driving home."

"Night, Rocky."

He stood in the open door and watched her walk to her car, parked in the exact place where she'd parked the Magic Broom van that afternoon. Kitt's thoughts matched her long, quick strides. He'd changed the instant he remembered who she was: a cleaning woman! The question about Betty had been the first mention of anything to bring up her job. She certainly hadn't avoided the subject; there had been just too many other topics of more interest, mainly football and Rocky Players himself.

Kitt turned and waved to Rocky just before she slid behind the driver's seat of her Toyota. With eighty thousand miles on it, she kept thinking she would have to get a new car soon, but it hummed along so faithfully she hadn't begun to look yet. When she had the engine running, she sat there several moments looking at the closed door to Rocky's condo.

As much as she didn't want to think it of him, she had to wonder if Rocky Players wasn't a snob. That afternoon he had acted vaguely apologetic over the subject of the work she did for a living. It hadn't come out that Kitt didn't just clean houses for people; she was co-owner of a profitable cleaning service. She hadn't deliberately withheld that information, but had been too embarrassed and then too intrigued with the circumstances to think about introducing herself.

Would he have treated her any differently tonight had he known she was a successful businesswoman and didn't have to do any actual cleaning at all if she chose not to? Kitt pondered that question almost hopefully as she drove home. Thinking back over the news coverage of Rocky's personal life, she couldn't think of a single woman he'd been linked to who wasn't either high society or a celebrity in her own right. Would he ever have spent a Monday night sleeping on the couch next to the corn flakes heiress or the high fashion model?

Kitt thought not. Somehow the realization just couldn't dampen her spirits, maybe because she hadn't really minded in the least having Rocky sleep peacefully next to her. It was hard for her to reconcile the media legend and the man. To some extent, she had to admit to being a little disappointed that he had seemed so human, so almost ordinary, when she knew he wasn't ordinary at all. He was one of America's highest paid athletes. A superstar.

And he had invited Kitt to his home, served her beer and nuts out of a can, explained in patient detail the first two quarters of a mediocre game on "Monday Night Football," and fallen sound asleep beside her. As unexciting as it was in the telling, Kitt could only admit the truth: *It felt like the greatest darn night of her life!*

Chapter Four

Kitt couldn't believe her own obsession with Rocky Players. It was too obvious to hide from Ellen and Bob. She took their ribbing good-naturedly and continued to fix her attention hungrily upon any mention of Rocky in the newspapers or the TV sports news. It was almost more pleasure and agony than she could stand now to watch the Revelers' games in their entirety or even the film clips on sports programs. Pleasure because she basked in the compliments and the glory of watching him play. Agony because now that she'd seen the bruises covering his body, she couldn't bear to see him hit hard by blockers anymore and end up beneath the huge piles of the opposing defense.

It was three weeks following the night at his condo that her fears seemed justified. In the fourth quarter of a game played away from New Orleans, Rocky remained a crumpled figure on the ground when one by one his attackers peeled off the mound. Kitt was watching the live telecast on a cable station and had to wipe desperately at the tears of utter dismay that blinded her as a stretcher was brought out on the field and he was carried off, unconscious.

"Oh, no!" she protested, heartbroken. "Oh, no, not Rocky!"

She wouldn't venture away from the television after that, afraid that there would be some report of his condition and she might miss it. On the evening sports news the Revelers' head trainer was quoted as saying that Rocky's injuries were "fortunately not serious." Rocky had a slight concussion and a cracked rib, injuries that "might" keep him out of the lineup the following Sunday, but probably not longer than that.

"Might keep him out of the lineup!" Kitt shouted at the TV screen. "*Might* keep him out of the lineup! I've never heard anything so asinine! The man has a concussion, for heaven's sake!"

She fumed and muttered at some length and flipped around the various channels, tuning into every single sports news program. When Ellen came home, she took one look at Kitt's appearance and distraught manner and was instantly concerned.

"Kitt, what's wrong? You look like a wild woman."

"It's Rocky. He's been hurt," Kitt replied and explained what had happened during the game that afternoon.

Ellen hesitated, but friendship was stronger than discretion. "Kitt, don't you think you're taking this Rocky Players thing too far? You're a grown woman, not some little kid with a case of hero worship about a football player."

Kitt's expression was the closest she had ever come to telling her friend of more than a decade to mind her own business. For the next two days, Kitt scoured the New Orleans and Baton Rouge newspapers and found them disappointingly lacking in any further news of Rocky's condition. On a wild impulse, she called Rocky's rental management agent with the pretext of wanting to know if there would be any change in the cleaning schedule for Mr. Players's condo, since he was injured and might be convalescing at home. The call was not only totally unproductive, the man's callous and knowing attitude infuriated Kitt.

"Nobody's notified me about any change, little lady. Don't worry your head over him. You can't kill those pro football players. They're not flesh and blood and bone like the rest of us ordinary folks. They're made out of some tougher stuff. Players is probably living it up somewhere with one of those sexy girlfriends of his."

Kitt thanked him curtly right in the middle of his male chuckle and hung up before she could volunteer a highly uncomplimentary opinion about his personality and character.

"Stupid ass!" she blurted out angrily and then slumped in her frustration. She so wanted to find out if Rocky was really all right. It hurt to think of him suffering. How could she get the message to him that she was concerned and cared?

The answer came immediately. Kitt didn't waste an instant acting upon it. She went shopping for a humorous get-well card, called Rocky's unlisted number at the condo to make sure the coast was clear and then drove over to leave the card some place in the condo where he couldn't fail to find it. After some indecision she left it taped to the refrigerator door. Inside the card she had scrawled her name, telephone number and a message she tried to make as casual as possible: *Call if I can be of help. Anything to get a key man back in the game!*

Ellen' answered the phone when Rocky called that night. "Kitt, it's for you. A man," she added and arched her brows. "A man with a sexy voice."

Kitt grabbed the phone away from her, heart pounding with hope and disbelief. She hadn't really expected Rocky to call. She had hoped, of course.

When her voice came over the line, Rocky was standing in his kitchen with Kitt's card in his hand. Calling her had been an instant impulse. The little half smile on his lips broadened in response to the hesitancy and the eagerness she managed to get into that one word, "Hello." The picture of her face came vividly into his mind, and he wasn't so aware of the dull throb in his head or the tight bandage encasing the ache in his rib cage.

"Hello, Kitt. Rocky Players here. Thanks for the card."

"Rocky, I'm so glad you called! I was worried about you. How are you?" The words with their honest note of concern tumbled out eagerly.

Rocky drew in a deep breath as though to draw in the vitality that bubbled out of her so effortlessly and was reminded of the constricting tape around his chest.

"I'm okay," he assured her offhandedly. "Only a headache and a couple of cracked ribs. I'm just thankful it wasn't my knees. Knee injuries can end a football career quicker than anything else." Rocky hadn't meant to confide that very real personal horror so he made fun of it. "Every time I get knocked out, I wake up saying, 'Is it my knees, Doc? Tell me it's my hard head or my ribs, but not my knees.'"

Kitt's laughter was a refreshing balm.

"Silly, you had a concussion. That's nothing to joke about." Her voice sobered as she continued. "I was watching the game when it happened, Rocky. I got sick to my stomach when you didn't get up off the ground...."

Rocky had heard numerous women say the same sort of thing through the years of his football career, but voiced by Kitt, the sentiment was genuine and touching. He was grateful for her concern even as he jokingly derided it.

"You can't let yourself get upset every time a pro ball player doesn't pick himself off the field. It'll spoil the game for you. You know what the commentators say about us pros: we're tough. We can take the punishment."

Kitt's silence had a stubborn kind of eloquence. Just because he hadn't been permanently maimed this time didn't mean her worry hadn't been justified. He was human and, for all his ruggedness and strength, fragile. She'd seen him walk like an old man and wince with pain.

"Thank you for being worried about me, Kitt," Rocky said quietly. "But, seriously, I'm fine. I won't make this week's game, but I should be able to play the following week."

"But you have a concussion!" Kitt protested disbelievingly. "You can't play with a concussion. It would be dangerous! Not to mention cracked ribs. What if somebody butts a helmet right into those cracked ribs?"

The vigor of her voice reinforced the altogether likely hazard she was pointing out. Rocky grimaced, knowing what she might not realize. His injured rib cage would be a prime target, not an accidental one. That's the way the game was played. He knew that when he walked out on the field with a publicized chink in his armor, his opponents—the enemy—would be aiming to exploit the weakness.

"I've played with cracked ribs before." The throb in his temple had grown insistent again, the tape around his chest was tight, and he was tired of standing up. "Thanks again for the card, Kitt."

His sudden distance made Kitt clutch the phone tighter in a spurt of panic. Once the connection was broken, she'd be cut off from him again. "Can't I do something for you, Rocky? I could come over and fix you something to eat. I'm not much in the cooking department, but I can manage something easy—"

Rocky was damned tempted to let her come over and fuss over him. Then he remembered that she had probably been working for other people all day, mopping and dusting and scrubbing up their filth. His mother had come home tired, with her legs and back aching, but she'd always had enough energy left over to make sure her boys had a hearty meal.

"It's damned nice of you to offer, Kitt, especially since you're probably dead tired." He paused, awkward at mentioning what she did for a living. "You've probably been on your feet all day. Actually I ate before I left the city tonight. If I get hungry, I can always heat up something in the microwave."

Kitt had sensed his slight wavering and could guess from his vaguely uncomfortable refusal what had happened once again. He'd remembered that she did cleaning for other people and quickly drawn back, as though what he assumed to be her livelihood disqualified her from being his friend. Such an attitude, even based upon a misconception as his was, disturbed Kitt in principle, but it wasn't something she wanted to discuss at this time, over the telephone.

"I'm not usually very tired at all at night," she declared strongly. "But since you've already eaten, why don't you let me feed you tomorrow night? I'll bring over some take-out fried chicken." Her voice projected a very genuine enthusiasm for her suggestion. Kitt was a self-proclaimed fast-food gourmet. Ellen and Bob amended that descriptive tag to addict and teased her about being unable to go for more than a couple of days without a fast-food fix.

"I love fast food, don't you?" she rhapsodized. "Nobody—I don't care how good a cook they are—can make home-made fried chicken as good as a take-out place."

Rocky didn't have it in him to turn her down. There was such generosity of spirit in her offer of a fast-food dinner and such childlike greediness. It reminded him of long-ago days when the infrequent restaurant hamburger, french fries and Coke seemed the ultimate treat. When he was twelve years old, he had sworn to himself that when he was a rich and famous pro football player, he'd eat all the hamburgers and french fries he wanted every single day!

"Sure, I like fried chicken," Rocky agreed indulgently. Of course, he meant to pay, but he didn't want to risk insulting her by mentioning it in advance.

"Dark meat or light?" Kitt demanded and then second-guessed him. "I'll bet you like dark."

"You're right. I'm a leg man." The words were out before Rocky could stop them. He hoped she didn't take the remark in a suggestive context because he wouldn't dream of making a pass at Kitt. Fortunately, she seemed as intent on planning the meal as though she were catering a banquet.

"What else do you want? French fries? Slaw? I'm having the red beans and rice," she informed him, as though her own preference might influence his. "I don't know if you've tried them, but they have a delicious smoky flavor."

"No, I haven't tried them, but at your recommendation, I will. Whatever you want will be fine, Kitt."

Kitt detected the weariness and was instantly sympathetic. "You'd better get off the phone and rest, Rocky. And, remember, if you need something, call me. I'm just fifteen minutes away."

Rocky wondered fleetingly what sort of place she lived in. She had mentioned living with some other woman with a child, probably a divorcée friend who couldn't afford a decent place on her income either. Even as he made this conjecture, Rocky had that recurring sensation that things just didn't fit where Kitt was concerned. There was a mystery there somewhere.

After he had hung up, Rocky realized they hadn't settled upon a time, but it didn't really matter. He'd just gotten out of the hospital today and was under orders to stay home tomorrow and rest. He'd be here whatever time she arrived with her bags of take-out food.

Just what the doctor ordered, he mused, the thought of Kitt breezing through the door, all arms and legs and open smile bringing a ghost of a grin to his lips. She was like a tonic. Every time he had been in contact with her, even just now on the phone, he felt as though he'd been given an infusion of her own eager zest for life. Rocky thought of her as he climbed the stairs to the master suite, took off his clothes and eased himself wearily into bed. The feelings inside his battered breast before he drifted off to sleep were warm and pleasant and pure.

He was glad Kitt would be coming over tomorrow night. In as tactful a way as possible, he would probe a little into her circumstances. Perhaps there was some way he could help her, preferably without her knowing since she already had a case of hero worship that he didn't want to make worse. Somehow hero worship in Kitt was nice because it was undemanding, despite her frank admiration of his athlete's physique. Her inexperience in the feminine art of seduction relieved him of that all too familiar pressure to perform sexually. Women just didn't seem to realize what the schedule of a pro football player takes out of him, physically, mentally and emotionally.

Especially a veteran pro football player like himself, who after ten years in the game had experienced the full glory of battle, sampled all the rewards of dedication and valor and was torn between yearning and dread as he looked ahead to retirement. It seemed that football had been his whole life, with endless training and striving and constant reaching out for the next goal. There had been making the first string in junior high, then high school, landing an athletic scholarship to a big football college, making a name for himself and being drafted into the pros, where he found himself still under constant pressure. He had to earn more yardage in a season, make more carries to a touchdown, give the fans the entertainment they were paying for and gain leverage in the process to negotiate bigger contracts with more frills. Always, too, there was the fear of having it all end in a single instant by a disabling injury.

What would it be like without all that, the pressure and the locker room cameraderie, the adulation and the annoyance of being in the public eye? Who was Rocky Players when he wasn't Rocky Players, Pro Football Superstar?

These were questions that didn't trouble Rocky as he fell asleep, thanks to the pleasant diversion of his conversation with Kitt.

"I got carried away," Kitt admitted first thing when Rocky opened the door and eyed her laden arms with mild astonishment. "I bought enough to feed an army, but that always happens when I'm starving. I hope you're hungry, too."

Rocky caught a whiff of the food as she breezed by him and sniffed appreciatively. "Hmm. Smells good." He was suddenly hungrier than he had been a moment ago.

Kitt went straight into the kitchen and proceeded to open cabinet doors and find serving dishes.

"Sometimes I just rip open the bag and eat right out of the paper containers," she confided. "But tonight we'll eat in style." She inhaled deeply and breathed out a sigh of pure ecstasy as she opened the bucket of crispy fried chicken and placed the pieces on a platter. "Here, you can put this on the table, but no snitching," she instructed, handing the platter to Rocky, who was leaning on the counter nearby, watching the whole procedure with amused interest.

By the time Rocky returned, she had emptied the containers of steamed rice, red beans and coleslaw into separate bowls and was getting together plates, utensils and paper napkins. She was obviously intent on not wasting a moment in delay.

"You really did buy enough for an army," Rocky commented, picking up a bowl in each hand.

"I almost bought biscuits," she told him, as though the fact that she hadn't was proof of some kind of restraint.

Kitt didn't bother with any chitchat until they were seated at the table in the dining area of the great room and had helped themselves amply to the food. She bit immediately into a crispy wing and crunched noisily while she eyed Rocky's rested appearance approvingly. Her eyes rested an extra moment on his forehead and his chest, searching for evidence of his injuries.

"You look good," she announced as soon as she had swallowed and then wasted no time taking another bite of chicken.

"I feel good," Rocky told her, a smile in his voice. He did feel quite rested and relaxed.

That was the extent of the conversation until Kitt had polished off the wing and made inroads into her red beans and rice and coleslaw.

"This is so good I can hardly stand it!" she declared with a sigh, taking out a moment to apply her napkin to her mouth before she resumed eating at a more leisurely pace. "Do you like the red beans and rice?" she inquired anxiously.

Rocky nodded, but had to wait to answer her until he had swallowed his mouthful of food. "You were right. They're very good." He laid down his fork and tried not to be obvious while he watched her eat. "Where I'm from, in north Louisiana, red beans and rice is something only poor people eat. That's not true of this area, is it?"

"Goodness, no," Kitt managed to get out despite a full mouth but waited until she had swallowed to make an expanded reply. "There's nothing in the world better than good red beans and rice. You probably just don't know how to cook them in north Louisiana. You can go to some of the best restaurants in New Orleans on Monday and find red beans and rice on the menu. Monday's traditional red beans and rice day."

Rocky digested the statement about the best restaurants with some interest, but didn't follow up on the source of her knowledge of such things. Television was a great equalizer of the experiences of rich and poor. He ate several bites of red beans and rice, thinking to himself that the dish was something he never ordered in a restaurant on Monday or any other day. It was associated with days when his mother had had to feed five growing boys on a meager income. He thought Kitt was right, though. The red beans and rice of his childhood hadn't tasted this good.

"How do people here in south Louisiana cook red beans to make them so tasty?" he asked Kitt with a kind of double-edged curiosity. He wanted to get her to talking about herself so that he could learn something about her background.

Kitt had cleaned her plate by now. She sat back with a little sigh of happiness to take a rest before she served herself seconds.

"I've never cooked them myself, but I do know that you have to use a lot of seasoning, onion and garlic and, I think, red pepper, too. You cook them a long time over a slow heat with bacon or ham until the beans are all to pieces and the gravy's thick." The description had her mouth watering again, so while she was talking, she heaped a spoonful of rice onto her plate and drowned it generously with red beans.

"Don't you cook at all?" Rocky inquired casually. Last night she had disclaimed any cooking skill when she offered to come over and fix a meal for him.

"Not much," Kitt admitted, busy selecting another piece of chicken and wondering if she could manage a whole breast at this stage, when she was almost full. "Cooking seems like entirely too much trouble to me when it's so quick and easy to pick up something and bring it home. The truth is that I'm one of those people who actually likes fast food better than home cooking. I like fried chicken, hamburgers, Tex-Mex, pizza,

Chinese...." She smiled at him happily as he took second helpings, reassured that he was enjoying his repast, too.

Rocky was thinking that a frequent diet of fast food must get rather expensive for someone with her type of job. It was also odd to him that she should have grown up in an environment that taught her housekeeping skills and hadn't learned how to cook.

"I suppose with a cleaning service it's different," he commented hesitantly and almost lost his nerve when she looked at him with a new alertness. "I mean, lots of time someone who does cleaning for other people is also called upon to cook. I guess you don't have to..." She had gone utterly still and was waiting for his next word. The easy atmosphere had become awkward and tense. Rocky wished like hell now he hadn't gotten started with this because he saw where it was leading. In some strange way, he felt obligated to make disclosures about his past that he found painful and didn't discuss, not even with close friends.

"When I was growing up, my mother used to do cleaning for some of the well-to-do people in Shreveport." His mouth twisted in a humorless smile at some private thought. "The leading doctor in town, for example." The one who had a blond angel of a daughter named Dana. "She worked for his wife on Saturdays during the school year—my mother also worked in the high school cafeteria—and twice a week during the summer. The doctor's wife always expected my mother to cook several meals that could be warmed up and served later, while she did the cleaning and the laundry."

"Your mother cleaned for other people." It was a kind of awed statement, not a question.

"It's not something I'm proud of," Rocky said harshly and then realized how tactless his words were. "I'm sorry, Kitt, I don't mean there's anything wrong with doing housekeeping," he apologized tersely. "It's just that I felt totally powerless at the time, even though I worked at odd jobs during the summers. She wouldn't let my brothers or me work during the school year. She insisted we had to get the most out of school."

"She sounds like a wonderful mother, Rocky," Kitt mused softly. She was beginning to understand now the attitude that had puzzled and disturbed her before.

"She was—is a wonderful mother," he corrected himself. "I felt so damned guilty putting all those hours into football when I knew I should be working after school and earning money to help out. I told myself it would all equal out in the end. I'd make it up to her. And I have," he said with grim satisfaction. "She won't ever have to lift a finger to do anything she doesn't want to do. She won't have to 'yes, ma'am' anybody or put up with their nitpicking grief."

Kitt had a very clear view now of Rocky's opinion of domestic service. He saw cleaning as a demeaning kind of work and considered his mother used by those with greater means. By extension he saw Kitt in the same light. That explained why he was uncomfortable any time he was reminded of her occupation. His was a strange kind of guilty by association thing.

With all this insight, she was in a ticklish situation. She guessed instinctively that he never would have made those revelations about his background if he'd known the truth about her, that she wasn't a poor cleaning girl, but part owner of a cleaning service and making a very decent income. She'd grown up in a household where there was usually a live-in maid, not just a cleaning woman who came in once or twice a week.

Perhaps the best preparation for telling him was to point out very tactfully the narrowness of his view that there was something shameful about a service occupation. It was fortunately a subject she could warm to easily.

"You shouldn't be ashamed of the fact that your mother worked for other people, Rocky. They probably appreciated her more than you realized. She probably made their lives a lot more enjoyable by doing the things she did." Certainly a housekeeper in the Kittredge household was not just appreciated, but catered to. When she went on vacation, chaos set in. Kitt's mother had a doctorate in child psychology, but she couldn't seem to master the intricacies of operating household appliances, and cooking the simplest dish, like scrambled eggs, became a complicated process with inedible results. Any one of her children finding her peering abstractedly at the washing machine control panel or taking ingredients out of the refrigerator would immediately insist, in a panicky voice, "Let me do that, Mother!" Unfortunately, Kitt dared not give this personal testimonial to bolster her thesis.

"I just don't understand why the so-called white-collar worker has more status in our society than somebody who works with his hands and performs a valuable service. Garbage collectors, for example. Look at what happens to any big city when the garbage collectors go on strike, and yet what little kid is conditioned by his environment to grow up wanting to be a garbage collector? What mother says proudly, 'My son's a garbage collector'?"

Rocky didn't look in the least convinced and he wasn't amused by her mimicry of a proud mother's voice. His gaze was narrowed and concentrated on her animated features and clear intelligent eyes.

"What I don't understand," he said slowly, "is why someone who can build up a defense like a lawyer is cleaning other people's houses. You can say what you want about appreciation, but it's a poor substitute for a decent income."

Kitt could feel the guilty expression marching across her face and made a desperate attempt at evasion to gain a little more time. "You haven't been hearing a word I've said, have you?" she demanded. "You're bound and determined to be narrow-minded about the way people make a living."

"Who are you?" he asked with deadly quiet. "You didn't make sense the first time I saw you, and you don't make sense now." Suspicion hardened his features, and Kitt felt a definite skitter of uneasiness up her backbone. "You're not some undercover journalist getting an inside story on me, are you? Because if you are—"

Kitt drew back from the unstated threat, her eyes wide with a kind of fascinated fright. This was a glimpse of the mettle that took Rocky Players onto the football field with cracked ribs. For the first time, she perceived the capacity for violence that was an element of that brutal contact she accepted as a part of the game of football. For a breathless second she wondered exactly what he would do to her if her answer were yes.

"No, I'm not a newspaper reporter!" she denied with such passion that the sheer melodrama of the situation struck her as funny and she couldn't keep back a nervous giggle. "You should see your face!" she gulped, fighting the onslaught of more giggles. Rocky looked as though he didn't know whether to throw her bodily out of his house or call the local mental hospital and have her committed.

"I don't see what's so damned funny," he said curtly. "I'm still waiting to hear just who the hell you are. How is it that you have a key to this place and can come and go at will?"

Kitt struggled unsuccessfully to swallow one last nervous chuckle and shrugged in helpless apology. "Sorry," she said contritely and then plunged headfirst into the explanation he was impatiently awaiting. "Honestly, Rocky, I really am in the cleaning business. That night you found me here in your condo, I had finished cleaning it except for doing the vacuuming. The only thing I haven't told you—and believe me, there was never any deliberate intention not to tell you—is that I don't work *for* The Magic Broom cleaning service. My friend Ellen Parity and I *own* it."

She eyed him anxiously, awaiting his reaction. On TV closeups she'd seen that same grim-jawed expression that said he'd take the football and crash his way through the wall of muscled defense giants, one way or another. When he nodded and the hard mouth twisted into a parody of a smile, it was obvious that he hadn't taken the news well. The biting sarcasm of his voice came as no surprise, but it still made Kitt want to flinch.

"No wonder you think it's noble to clean other people's houses. That's a handy way of not seeing things the way they really are. You're making a profit off poor women like this Betty you mentioned—women like my mother—without any education or job training to go out and get a decent job."

"You make it sound like I'm exploiting them!" Kitt protested hotly. "And I'm certainly not! There is absolutely nothing shameful about doing honest work with your hands! I've done hours and hours of cleaning work myself and felt a pride in what I was doing. You've just got some weird hang-up—that's all!'' Overcome by her exasperation, Kitt jumped up from the table as though to assume a more aggressive stance for what had become as much attack as defense. She stood with her hands braced on her hips and her feet apart.

"The women who work for me make as good a wage as they would earn working nine to five as tellers in some bank or checkout clerks in a supermarket, and they don't have to punch a clock. They get together with Ellen and me and set up a work schedule that suits them. Any time there's an emergency with a member of their families, they know we'll understand and manage to cover for them somehow. That's why I was here that Sunday night. I was covering for Betty. And they never have to 'yes, ma'am' anybody or take any 'nitpicking grief,' because that's what Ellen and I are for—to handle any flak.''

Kitt had to stop for a quick intake of breath. It infuriated her that he was obviously completely unmoved by anything she was saying. That much-touted mental toughness of his could be translated into blockheadedness, as far as she was concerned.

"And another thing,'' she rushed on heatedly when he just sat there, taking no advantage of her pause. "Speaking of taking advantage of people, I don't suppose it occurred to you when you put down Sunday afternoon as the preferred time for cleaning your condo that some 'poor soul' would have to give up that time with her family?''

Kitt knew she had gone too far. She could see him struggling to control his anger and prayed for his success. He was still seated at the table, but every muscle in his body was readied for immediate, explosive action.

Kitt watched with fascination the isolated movement of a tensed arm as it extended in the general direction of the door.

"Just get the hell out of here and take your leftovers with you," he ordered coldly. "I intended to reimburse you, but that was before I knew you could afford the expense."

"You can keep the leftovers," she retorted. "Frankly I hope you finish up the chicken and choke yourself on a bone!"

"I'm sure you don't mean that," Rocky taunted swiftly. "You wouldn't really want me out of the Revelers' lineup permanently, now would you, Miss Cleaning Lady Boss? You're much too faithful a football fan."

His arm relaxed and lowered and he sat back in his chair regarding her with a cool contempt that made Kitt's temper zoom up to the danger zone. For one wild, dangerous second, she considered crowning him with the half-empty bowl of red beans. With that urge subdued, she was suddenly no longer angry, just terribly, terribly disappointed and hurt.

"Have a good evening," she told him bitterly. "If it makes you feel any better, you sure managed to spoil mine."

With that she was gone. Rocky half turned his head in the direction of his front door and waited tensely for a shattering slam, but there was only a solid click. It seemed to unleash the violence he'd kept under control. He half rose up in his chair, looking at the remains of the take-out repast and her still partially filled plate.

"Damn it!" he shouted, slamming his fist down onto the table with such force that the chicken platter went crashing into the bowl of red beans. Kitt's fork clattered against her plate. Rocky eyed it viciously as he dropped back down into his chair and rubbed his fist. In a grim monotone he strung together every curse word he knew.

Chapter Five

Rocky, I want to ask a favor of you."

"Sure, Doc," Rocky agreed without any hesitation, able to guess the nature of the favor even before the orthopedic surgeon confirmed that he had a young patient he wanted Rocky to visit in the hospital. The surgeon knew that even though Rocky didn't publicize the fact, through the years of his career he had been readily available to hospital staffs for visits to the children's wards, especially at holidays when pangs of homesickness were likely to be the worst.

Dr. Gardener filled Rocky in on the details of Joey Boudreaux's case. He was thirteen years old and had injured his right knee in football practice at the junior high school he attended across the lake in Mandeville. The damage was serious and had required surgical repair. Here the surgeon went into some technical detail, knowing that football players tend to be extremely knowledgeable about bones and joints and muscles.

"Will he be able to play football again?" Rocky asked soberly, already fairly sure of the answer judging from the injury. Rocky hadn't been kidding when he told Kitt that his big fear had always been injuring his knees.

Dr. Gardener shook his head negative. "He's taking it hard, too. Football's his big love, as it is with so many boys that age. Apparently he showed a great deal of promise. I've talked to his coach, who's been very supportive through the whole thing, sat with Joey's mother at the hospital during the surgery and has been to visit Joey every day."

Rocky had been listening sympathetically, remembering his own junior high coach who'd been the most important person in his life at the time. "Where was Joey's father?" he asked with a sudden intuition.

"Joey's father died when Joey was just a baby. He doesn't remember him at all."

Rocky's father had died when Rocky was eleven, leaving his eldest son with little reason to grieve the loss. Clayton Players had been a brutal, heavy-handed man, quick to cuff both his sons and his submissive wife. He had been driving home drunk in his pickup truck one night and veered off the road into a tree. He left his family with no money in the bank and not a nickel's worth of life insurance. In his more mature years, Rocky decided that it was probably all for the best that his old man had died when he did because even at the age of eleven Rocky had harbored murder in his heart. Sooner or later he would probably have killed the mean bastard when he came in drunk and abused his wife.

"Sure, Doc, I'll be glad to drop in on Joey in the hospital. Where is he—Oschner's?"

The surgeon nodded and told Rocky the floor and room number. A perceptive man as well as a surgeon of national reputation, called upon frequently to attend to the complicated injuries of top sports figures, he'd noted the hardness in Rocky's face at the mention of Joey's father and guessed that there was probably a sad story deep in Rocky's past. Fleetingly he wondered if much of Rocky's oft-mentioned toughness wasn't built on emotional scar tissue.

"I think you'll enjoy meeting this kid, Rocky, and I know it'll do him a world of good. By the way, you ought to know going in that you're his idol. He wanted to grow up and be another great running back from Louisiana, like Rocky Players."

Rocky shook his head sadly. "Poor kid. What a rotten break." The dark eyes that had been flint hard a moment ago with memories of his dead father were filled with pain now for a kid he hadn't even met.

He dropped by the hospital that same afternoon dressed in sport jacket and tie and encountered glances of recognition followed by frankly curious stares on the way to Joey's room. Several members of the hospital personnel, including a doctor and nurse or two, stopped him and asked him if he wasn't Rocky Players. He good-naturedly pleaded guilty and signed whatever was thrust at him, including one cute young nurse's arm.

"I won't ever wash it again!" she promised with an engaging smile and then continued on her way with a twitch of white skirt around shapely calves.

There had been a time when he had felt slightly overwhelmed with this type of attention and then another period when he'd been impatient with it and wished people would leave him alone. Now he simply accepted it as a part of his occupation and considered himself obligated to be pleasant to the public that supported the game of football. Without their fascination with the sport and the players they made into superstars, Rocky wouldn't be where he was today.

The greeting he received in Joey's room made Rocky feel humble. The boy's face lit up with adulation and he was so struck with shyness in the presence of his hero that he couldn't speak a word. The woman sitting next to Joey's bed, who Rocky assumed to be the boy's mother, rose and came forward. Her Louisiana French background was immediately evident in the musical cadences of her voice.

"Mr. Players, it was so good of you to come and see Joey. He's one of your biggest fans."

Rocky took her hand and appreciated the strength in its grip. She was a small, dark-haired woman with a compact build, her face kind and plain. The gratitude in her voice and eyes was mixed with a mother's anguish over the suffering of a child.

Rocky gave her hand a reassuring squeeze before he released it. "My pleasure entirely, Mrs.—" In sudden embarrassment he realized he didn't remember Joey's last name.

"Boudreaux," she supplied with quick graciousness. "Betty Boudreaux, and call me Betty. If you don't mind, I'll just slip out and get a cup of coffee while you and Joey have a little visit with each other." Her smile toward the youth in the bed was knowingly tender. "I'll just bet you two can find something in common to talk about."

Rocky looked after her as she left the room; he couldn't imagine why her name had stirred a vague recognition.

"How are you, Joey?" he inquired, stepping up closer to the bed. It didn't take a close scrutiny to determine that the boy had been recently crying and that he was terribly afraid Rocky would notice. Rocky tactfully directed his gaze toward the injured knee, encased in plaster. "I understand from Dr. Gardener that you've got a bad injury there," he said soberly, making no effort to inject a false cheer into his voice. "That's a real tough break, one that every football player dreads to have happen to him. Every time we walk out on the field, though, it's a possibility, along with some that are even worse."

Joey swallowed hard. His voice when he spoke was husky from the tears he'd shed. "Dr. Gardener says I won't be able to play football anymore...."

The pathetic effort at skepticism brought a giant lump to Rocky's throat. Joey was a big husky boy just like Rocky had been at his age. It was too painful even to conjecture what it would feel like at thirteen to be lying there in that bed wearing Joey's skin. Yet the accident had happened. There was no changing it. The best Rocky could do for Joey was to help him accept a bitter reality and then try to give him something else to take his mind off of it.

"Dr. Gardener is one of the foremost sports orthopedists in the whole country, Joey. He has tended me a number of times, even before I came to New Orleans with the Revelers. He wouldn't tell you anything that he wasn't absolutely certain about." Rocky gave Joey a few seconds to deal with those words while he readjusted the position of the chair Joey's mother had been sitting in and sat down before he continued in a lighter tone.

"The good news is that you won't be crippled. It's going to take a while, but you'll be able to walk normally again. Think of what a drag it would be to spend the rest of your life on crutches or even limping. I know this probably won't make you feel much better right now, but I can tell you some stories about kids who'd think they were really lucky to be in your shoes.''

Rocky went on to tell Joey about several heartbreaking cases he'd encountered in his visits to hospitals. When it was obvious that he had told Joey enough to at least get him thinking that his misfortune might have been worse, Rocky changed the subject.

''Enough about that. You probably have some things you'd like to ask me about football.''

Joey probably had at least a hundred things he'd like to ask Rocky, but he was a little shy at first. When his mother popped her head into the door thirty minutes later, her face beamed at what she saw and heard. Joey was laughing and talking animatedly, looking like anything but the heartbroken youth he had been when she left.

''Mom, guess what?'' he demanded, catching sight of her. ''As soon as I'm able to get around, Rocky's gonna take me down to the Revelers' practice field one day and introduce me to all the other players. I can't wait to get out of here. The guys at school are gonna be *green* when I tell 'em.''

''I bet they are,'' Betty agreed in her Cajun tones.

When Rocky left about fifteen minutes later, Betty walked with him a distance down the hall. ''I just can't thank you enough,'' she told him gratefully. ''Joey means the whole world to me. I didn't want him to play football in the first place, but you know how it is with boys. They want to play so bad. I just didn't have the heart to say no.''

Rocky knew all too well how it was with boys with the urgent desire to play football. The mother's sentiments

Betty expressed struck a deep chord of reminiscence. His own mother had voiced those exact feelings. It occurred to him that this personable woman and his mother had a number of things in common, including full responsibility for rearing their sons, the difference being that his mother had had five and Betty only one.

"I haven't really advertised the fact, but I live over in Mandeville, too," he told her. "I'd like to keep in touch with Joey. He's going to have some ups and downs for a while."

"I know you live in Mandeville," she replied in a stage whisper accompanied by a broad grin. "I wasn't sure whether I should mention this, what with your living over there being such a big secret and all, but since you bring it up yourself, I guess it's okay to tell you. I'm the one who cleans up your condominium there by the lake. From now on, don't be surprised if you come home and find a fresh-baked apple pie. If I do say so myself, I make a good apple pie."

Rocky stared at her as he repeated her name aloud. "Betty Boudreaux. I thought there was somethimg familiar about your name." She was gazing at him with a warm, expectant expression, pleased as punch for him to know she cleaned his condo. "Er, your boss—I can't remember her last name just now—came by my place one afternoon looking for you, and she mentioned your name. As a matter of fact, she wanted to get a message to you about Joey."

Betty was nodding happily. "You mean Kitt. She's the kind of person whose last name most people don't remember. She's just Kitt to everybody. I know the afternoon you're talking about. When she came looking for me and didn't find me, she got all worried, thinking I'd been kidnapped in broad daylight." Betty chuckled and shook her head. Her voice was fond as she continued. "That Kitt, she's one of a kind, she is. I never seen anybody who can clean up a place as fast as she can and do it good, too. That girl can work rings around the rest of us and hum a tune while she's doing it. Maybe she got fast playing all that basketball in college. She was a big star at Louisiana State, you know. Usually they don't write up girl basketball players in the paper the way they did her." Betty paused only minimally and determined from Rocky's expression that he either knew or else wasn't surprised at Kitt's athletic stardom.

"You won't find a nicer person to work for, that's for sure. I couldn't hope to work a regular job because my mother lives with Joey and me, and she's getting old and has a lot of ailments now. When she's having one of her bad spells, Kitt arranges to have somebody else do my cleaning jobs, or she does them herself. I remember one Sunday not too long ago she cleaned your place for me. I can bet you didn't have any complaints about the job she did, either."

"No complaints at all," Rocky put in quickly and made some hurried excuses about having to run. He could sense that if he gave Betty free range to discuss what was apparently a favorite topic, he'd be there for hours listening to praises of Kitt, the Super Boss. Certainly he'd never run into a happier employee than Betty Boudreaux. Her attitude toward doing cleaning work for other people seemed to match that of her boss. There hadn't been the first hint of embarrassment in telling Rocky that she was his cleaning woman.

For the next week Rocky found himself thinking often about Kitt. Now that he'd had some time to adjust to who she really was, he went back over each encounter with her and realized that her mistaken identity was mainly his own doing. He didn't think Kitt had deliberately misled him. Those first two times they'd come face to face, the circumstances had been disconcerting for both of them. Rocky had to smile as he replayed the scenes in his mind. Without any undue conceit on his part, he knew Kitt had been bowled over with her opportunity to look Rocky Players over, in the flesh, quite literally the second time, in his bathroom.

Despite her speech and her easy poise—clues that she wasn't a local woman of limited education and experience—he had assumed she was a simple cleaning woman because she wore the cleaning service uniform and was caught in the act—well, *almost* in the act—of cleaning his condo. Now after the dinner fiasco and the conversation with Betty Boudreaux, Rocky suspected that Kitt was thoroughly at home in that uniform and thought it not at all strange that an owner of The Magic Broom cleaning service should do menial work. Actually, the concept of menial probably didn't exist for Kitt. She had simply been herself, a "one of a kind" person, to use Betty Boudreaux's expression.

Rocky arrived at a reluctant state of mind where he knew he would have to contact Kitt and admit to her that he'd been a total ass. Once he made up his mind, the idea grew so steadily appealing that he realized he was looking forward to talking to her again. No, he didn't just want to talk to her; he wanted to see her in person. If he was any judge of people at all, he could depend on her not holding a grudge. Besides, he had just the white flag to wave at her and signal truce. He'd call and invite her out to the fast-food restaurant of her choice!

The evening Kit had arrived at home after her confrontation with Rocky, she told Ellen and Bob about the horrible scene, and her account was highly emotional. Her friends were reduced to awed silence as the normally unflappable Kitt stormed up and down the den, waving her arms and giving vehement emphasis to every other word. At the end she declared that the whole incident had been so disillusioning for her that she thought she might abandon all interest in the game of football.

Ellen and Bob looked at each other and then quickly away so that they could suppress skeptical grins. Their remarks were tactfully sympathetic and soothing. Ellen's woman's intuition warned her that Kitt's disappointment might be deeper than Kitt even realized.

For more than a week Kitt kept her word and didn't watch a single football game. She would even switch to another channel when the sports news came on, which was devoted almost entirely to football this time of year. Along with this change in viewing habits came a change in personality that everyone who knew Kitt found disturbing. She just wasn't her happy, buoyant self.

When Ellen found Kitt in the den watching a football game on a Sunday afternoon, she had to restrain herself from a delighted outburst. It seemed to be a sign that things were back to normal: that and the fact that Kitt didn't even realize she was no longer alone in the room. On closer look Ellen wasn't so reassured when she took note of the fierce intensity with which Kitt stared at the screen.

Struck by an uneasy intuition, Ellen dropped down on the couch to determine what two teams were playing, not an easy task for her since football players all looked alike dressed in their silly uniforms, and the background commentary was usually a meaningless babble blending in with the crowd noise. She had barely focused her concentration when suspicion was confirmed.

"...Players's first time back in the lineup after his injuries two weeks ago in San Francisco. What do you think, Jim? Is he fit?"

Ellen didn't get a chance to hear Jim's reply because Kitt drowned him out.

"Of course he's not fit!" she cried out impatiently. "You don't recover from cracked ribs and a concussion in two lousy weeks! But who cares? I don't. I hope he finishes off the job and gets himself killed!"

"Kitt!" Ellen reproved, shocked both at the callous sentiment and the fierce emotion. "You don't really mean that."

Kitt was watching from her favorite position, lying stomach down on the carpeted floor in front of the TV. She glanced around abstractedly and looked mildly surprised when she saw Ellen.

"Oh, hi. I didn't hear you come in." Immediately she returned her attention to the screen, where the Revelers' offensive team was taking the field.

Ellen stayed a few minutes, long enough to see Kitt hold her breath for long moments and murmur "Oh, *no,*" then go limp with relief when a play was over and the two teams sprang briefly into their huddles again. It didn't take long for a perceptive friend, even one with so little knowledge of the game of football, to figure out that every play was agony as long as Rocky Players was out there on the field. When the ball changed over to the possession of the opposing team and the Revelers' defensive squad trooped out to replace the offense, Kitt sank into the carpet like a rag doll.

"You really are a vindictive, hard-hearted person, Kitt," Ellen remarked with fond irony. "I can see that you're holding your breath hoping that Rocky Players gets killed."

Kitt rolled over on her side and propped her head on her hand. Her face was glum and honest.

"Can you believe that this is happening to me, Ellen? Me, who's gone all these years without a real crush on any guy?" She made a disgusted sound and then went unexpectedly alert. As usual, she had been keeping track of the game action even while not seeming to.

"Oh, God, not an interception!" she moaned, strange words indeed for an ardent Revelers' fan. Flopping back on her stomach with a lithe twist of her long body, she watched the Revelers' offensive team troop back onto the field, the expression on her face resigned.

"Enjoy your game," Ellen said with sympathetic irony as she got up and left the room. She didn't expect an answer and didn't get one.

It was the longest football game of Kitt's entire life. She was exhausted and relieved when it was finally over and she and Rocky both had managed to survive the ordeal. She knew it had to be an ordeal for him, but, thank God, he had gotten up from every single pileup and walked away when the game was over. Actually he had played only about half the time the offensive team was on the field, but even when he was sitting on the bench, she was braced for him to come into the game any second.

What must the wife of a pro football player go through? Kitt wondered, picking herself up from the floor.

Watching the football game had a restorative effect on Kitt, perhaps because it had provided an honest outlet for emotions she had been trying to deny to herself. That evening Ellen and Bob noticed at once that Kitt was her old self again. "Welcome back, Kitt," they told her, and she grinned in immediate understanding.

"Guess I'm just a late developer," she said cheerfully. "I never could understand in high school or college how a girl could mope around over some guy, or vice versa." She shot Bob a confidential glance and then frowned thoughtfully. "It always puzzled me that some of the guys my friends had crushes on were such jerks. Seems like I would have fallen for a nice guy, don't you think?"

"It's probably his body you're in love with," Bob quipped, his lugubrious expression as he surveyed his own wiry five feet six inches, bringing instant smiles.

"You could be right," Kitt agreed promptly. "Rocky Players probably has the world's hardest head, but there ain't no denying he's got an out of sight body." She rolled her eyes lasciviously. "I know. I've seen most of it!"

That led to uproarious laughter as they all joined in to reconstruct Kitt's bathroom incident with Rocky Players. Kitt was happy in the company of the two old, true friends, who would eventually get around to marrying, she knew. But she didn't worry about the changes that event would bring into her life any more than she worried about the unfamiliar little sensation that sprang up in her breast when she thought about Rocky. It had germinated entirely on its own, like an alien plant sprouting up in a garden. Exposed to the bright sunshine of open inspection and ridicule, it would soon wither and go away.

The following evening Kitt drove over to New Orleans to visit Joey Boudreaux in the hospital, not suspecting that her "jerk theory" of Rocky Players's character was about to be smashed to bits. Joey and his mother Betty could talk of almost nothing else but Rocky's visit three days earlier. They kept interrupting each other, but Kitt still managed to get the picture that Rocky had managed to change Joey's world from dismal black to dawn with a promise of sunrise.

"Kitt, he's gonna introduce me to all the Revelers players. Can you imagine that?"

"Ah, Kitt, he's a handsome man in person, isn't he? So tall and the shoulders so broad in his sport coat. He must have stayed here talking with Joey a whole hour."

"He told me about all these other kids he's visited in different hospitals who are a lot worse off than I am."

"You should have seen his face how surprised he was when I told him I'm the person who most of the time cleans his condominium...."

"I can just imagine," Kitt put in dryly, the first words she'd managed to sandwich into the mother and son conversational duet.

"I didn't bring it up until he mentioned to me that he has a place in Mandeville and would like to keep in touch with Joey after he comes home from the hospital!" Betty hastened to explain, lest she be accused of indiscretion. "Joey didn't even know before that his mama was cleaning up after such a famous football player, did you, Joey?"

"Wow, no. I promised Mom I wouldn't let on to anybody where Rocky lives in Mandeville," Joey promised Kitt gravely.

"I appreciate that, Joey. It's part of our contract agreement with Rocky that we don't advertise the fact that he has a place there in Mariner's Village. If the news gets out, he wouldn't have much privacy and might end up moving."

Even as she reinforced the need for discretion, Kitt was thinking of Joey's reaction to the news that his mother did cleaning for his football idol. As far as she could tell, there wasn't a hint of embarrassment. If anything, Joey seemed to consider his mother privileged! It was such a healthy attitude and one his hero could well afford to develop.

Kitt left the hospital with praises of Rocky ringing in her ears, not surprising since she'd heard every one of them at least twice. *So what if he did visit a kid in the hospital?* she told herself in a futile effort at cynicism. *Big deal. He's still a pigheaded snob who was ashamed of what his mother did for a living.*

All across the causeway, Kitt found herself visualizing the scene with Rocky and Joey and Betty, and the feelings in her breast weren't at all cynical. They were by turns poignantly warm and amused, the last when she imagined Rocky in the clutches of the voluble Betty. The woman had a heart of gold, but she could talk your head off.

It might be true that Rocky had done nothing more than give an hour of his time, but he had lightened the personal tragedy of a young boy and eased a mother's worry, something he'd apparently done other times in the past. Had he seen the parallel between Joey and himself, both with a passion for football and the good fortune to have a wonderful, devoted mother who did housecleaning for other people?

Kitt was sure that Rocky had seen that parallel. He might be pigheaded, but he wasn't stupid and he wasn't insensitive. So much for her bafflement at falling for a jerk instead of a nice guy. It made little difference that her instincts had served her right. She knew she wouldn't be hearing from Rocky or seeing him again, not if he had anything to do with it anyway.

A half mile from the north end of the causeway, Kitt looked over to her right and saw lights along the shore-line that marked the location of the condominium complex Rocky owned. Monday night. If he was home, he'd probably be lying on the couch or up in his king-size bed, asleep or drowsy with painkillers, resting his bruised, battered body so that it could regain its strength and agility and take him out on the field again the following Sunday. Against the background of the fans' roar, once again he would take the ball with those strong, long-fingered hands, tuck it close against his chest and lower his head and shoulders as he charged and twisted and dodged, seeking some passageway through the forward surging wall of defensive muscle and brawn.

Kitt's shiver was a combination of a new fear and an old exhilaration. The game of football had been changed for her, perhaps forever. The thrill in the speed and daring and contact was still there, but now a human element had been added, making her hypersensitive to the enormous physical and mental demands the game made upon its players.

The undefined sensation in her breast that was there when she thought of Rocky spread out a little, taking in more territory. It was warm and odd, bringing together joy and sadness in a marriage Kitt hadn't experienced before. If she'd had to describe the feeling, she'd have said it made her feel like laughing and crying at the same time. She wanted to nurture the feeling and savor it; she wanted to banish it totally and go back to the way she had been before she ever met Rocky Players.

Arriving home in this disconcerting state of mind, she was greeted by Ellen with news that did nothing to restore her normal equanimity.

"Rocky Players called while you were gone. I told him you'd be home later, but he said he wouldn't call again tonight. He was going to bed. He'd try to get you tomorrow night." Ellen paused, a fond smile playing with her lips. "I told him that as far as I knew, you'd be home."

After her initial surprise, accompanied by a wild leap of gladness, Kitt adjusted almost instantly to the news of Rocky's call and put it glumly in perspective. She thought she knew why he had called: probably to apologize. That run-in with Betty had probably made him realize his accusation that she exploited the women who worked for her was ridiculous. In the meanwhile she wasn't building up any false hopes, and she definitely didn't intend to make any overtures toward seeing him again. Pride demanded that if she had to worship him, she would at least worship from afar.

"Of course, I'll be home. I told you I'd baby-sit Andy tomorrow night while you go to that bank opening with Bob." The firmness of the reminder reflected Kitt's thought processes.

"But, Kitt, you don't have to—"

"I'm baby-sitting Andy tomorrow night, and that's that," Kitt stated flatly, as she led the way to the den and plopped down on the couch. "Rocky Players is welcome to call if he wants to."

"I see."

The two women looked at each other in one of those long, wordless exchanges of close friends.

"How was Joey?" Ellen inquired briskly, thinking that she was changing the subject. When Kitt's face instantly assumed a pensive expression, Ellen understandably assumed that the news wasn't good. "That nice kid isn't going to be crippled, I hope."

"No, Joey's going to be fine," Kitt hastened to assure her. "Joey's fine. Betty's fine." Kitt drew in a deep breath and blew it out. "Ellen, you're just not going to believe this...."

Ellen listened and when Kitt had finished telling her about the visit to the hospital, shook her head in commiseration.

"Poor Kitt. That just makes things worse, I guess. Rocky Players isn't such a total jerk, after all, is he?"

"Nope. Isn't it the pits, though?" There was a cheerful finality about these words. Yawning, Kitt got up from her place on the den sofa and announced that she was going to bed. At the doorway she stopped and looked back.

"You know what, Ellen?" she confided softly. "I never really thought Rocky was a jerk. I just said that to try to make myself feel better."

"I know, Kitt."

"Night, Ellen."

"Night, Kitt." Ellen gazed at the empty door a second or two after Kitt had gone. Her expression was soft with fondness and sad with the wisdom of a sage. "Sweet dreams, Kitt."

Chapter Six

Rocky called much earlier than Kitt expected. It was only six-thirty, and Bob hadn't even arrived yet to pick up Ellen, who was in her room getting dressed.

"Hi. How are you?" Kitt inquired impersonally after Rocky had unnecessarily identified himself. "Ellen mentioned that you had called last night."

"I'm okay." Rocky decided to dispense with the preliminary bullcrap. "Kitt, I called to apologize for being an ass that night you were nice enough to bring dinner over and serve it. I said some things I had no right to say."

"I suppose you came to that conclusion after you talked with Betty in the hospital a few days ago." Kitt didn't know why there should be a little ache of disappointment. She'd known darn good and well he was just calling to apologize.

"Yes, well, I guess I did." If Rocky's admission sounded faintly grudging, it was because he didn't appreciate having her shortcut him like that. He wasn't surprised that she knew about his visit to the hospital and conversation with Betty Boudreaux, but she could have let him tell it himself in his own way. After all, this was *his* apology.

"Apology accepted. Don't give it another thought." Kitt wasn't even aware that she sounded less than sincere. She was undergoing an inner struggle where feminine pride wrestled with her spontaneous self. *It's up to him to strike up a conversation, Kitt. Remember what being friendly has gotten you so far. Insults, that's what.* In the end, pride was too much of an upstart to change a lifetime habit of speaking generous thoughts. But it managed to make her voice so unnaturally aloof that she hardly recognized it as her own and afterward wished she'd kept quiet.

"I watched the Revelers' game on TV Sunday afternoon. That was quite a win. Congratulations."

Rocky ignored the stiff little conversational offering, his mind still on the whole business of the apology. It was irritating that she had already accepted it, in the most casual manner, before he even had a chance to complete it! There were things, difficult things, that he wanted to say, but it would be awkward as hell now to backtrack. There was nothing to do but wait and then bring up the subject later in the evening when they were talking face-to-face. In this state of mild frustration that the phone call hadn't gone according to his plans, Rocky issued his invitation.

"Since I spoiled your dinner that night, I was hoping you'd let me make it up to you by buying you dinner tonight at the fast-food restaurant of your choice."

So that's why he had called so early. Every joke Kitt had ever made to a love-struck friend about heart palpitations came home to her now as her own heart performed intricate little tap dances in her chest. She took a deep breath, telling herself unconvincingly that it was probably all for the best that she couldn't accept what sounded like a rather grudging offer anyway.

"Sorry, but I can't go anywhere tonight." She did her best not to sound disappointed and braced herself philosophically for him to bring the conversation to a close, his conscience having been adequately salved.

During the brief silence, Rocky wrestled with a male pride that wasn't an upstart in his life, but an old companion. He won, for mostly selfish reasons. He had been looking forward all day to going out somewhere casual and having a meal with her. If she wanted a little coaxing, what the hell, he'd coax. It just came as a surprise and a disappointment, too, for her to play by the same old female rules.

"I didn't think you'd be the kind of person to hold a grudge, Kitt."

"I'm not holding a grudge," Kitt denied quickly, surprised at the turn of conversation and instinctively defensive at the undeserved accusation. "I can't go anywhere tonight because I'm baby-sitting Andy. You can take me out tomorrow night, if you really want to." The swift challenge would call his bluff, and meanwhile she had to cope with more new cardiovascular knowledge. Heart palpitations were nothing compared to a heartbeat that felt like a whole herd of runaway horses. *Was there a chance he* had *wanted to take her out?*

"I wouldn't have asked you if I didn't want to," Rocky countered, but he was considerably cheered to learn that she had a legitimate excuse not to accept his invitation.

He didn't like to think that Kitt would stoop to age-old feminine tactics like playing hard to get. What had delighted him about her from the first was her refreshing directness combined with a quick sense of humor and a nimble mind. She was probably the only woman since his mother he'd sensed he might be able to trust.

"I thought maybe you just felt like you *should* do something to make up for being such a jackass," Kitt explained tentatively. "If that's the case—I mean if you don't really want to, I'd just as soon you didn't—if you know what I mean."

Rocky had a grin threatening the corners of his hard mouth by the time she had come to an awkward stop. Somehow her blunt honesty made it all the more urgent that he see her tonight, one way or another.

"What time of night does Andy go to sleep, anyway?"

"Somewhere between seven-thirty and eight." Kitt's reply was prompt and tinged with relief. She was more than willing to drop the subject of motivations, if he was. If there was anything she didn't enjoy, it was analyzing every word and gesture. Life was so much simpler and so much more fun if people just did and said what felt right.

"Why don't I pick up something to eat and bring it over? Do you think Andy would object to a third party?"

"I know he wouldn't object to *you*. He'd be thrilled. He's a real little football fan already."

The loving warmth in Kitt's voice as she spoke of the child assigned to her care made Rocky faintly envious. *Lucky little devil to grow up with Kitt as a nursemaid and playmate.*

"What would you like for me to pick up to eat? Hamburgers? Tacos? Chinese? Pizza?" He paused while they both thought of the obvious unmentioned choice: chicken.

"Pizza, I think," Kitt said thoughtfully. "Yes, definitely, pizza. My mouth's beginning to water just thinking about it. I hope you like lots of stuff on yours because I like everything—Italian sausage, pepperoni, mushrooms, onions, black olives, green pepper... I can take or leave the jalepeno peppers. You can suit yourself."

"I think I'll leave them," Rocky put in hastily before she could change her mind and take the choice away from him. He thought the combination she'd mentioned would be sufficient challenge to any healthy digestive tract without the fiery hot peppers. "I'll call and order the pizza right away. By the time I get there, it should be ready, and then I'll drive over to your place. You'll have to give me detailed directions. I'm not very familiar with this area at all."

Kitt explained the simplest route to the house that she shared with Ellen and Andy and then added, as though it were a last-minute thought, "I think you'd better get a large pizza, Rocky. It's always better to have too much than too little. If there's some left over, it can always be warmed up later."

"Large, it is," Rocky agreed and then couldn't resist teasing her. "I think you're taking advantage of a good thing and planning ahead for tomorrow morning's breakfast."

"How did you know that!" Kitt demanded and chuckled before he could reply. "You should see Ellen's face when I get up and pop a slice of pizza into the microwave at six-thirty in the morning. It totally grosses her out. Really, how did you guess?" Kitt was oddly pleased at his insight into her eating idiosyncrasies.

"Actually, I suspected it the minute I saw you watching my TV and giving me hell for not making any yardage. Now here's a hard-hearted girl who eats pizza for breakfast, I told myself."

"Speaking of that night, did anybody ever tell you that you should keep some snacks in the house? I couldn't find a thing to munch on."

One remark called for another equally as inconsequential. When they brought the lighthearted exchange to a somewhat reluctant end and hung up their respective phones, they both were smiling.

Rocky didn't have any trouble locating the house, which was located in one of the more modest subdivisions without a country club and the requisite golf course and tennis courts. It was a one-story ranch style house with brick exterior set back from the street. The lot was wooded and attractively landscaped with shrubbery.

As he pulled into the driveway that led to a double carport, Rocky remembered how he had conjectured about Kitt's living circumstances when he thought she was a mere employee of her cleaning service. He had guessed that she probably lived in some rundown rental house. Instead she lived in conventional, middle-class comfort. Compared to the house that Rocky grew up in, this one was a mansion.

"Pizza Man here," he announced when she opened the door.

"Come in, Pizza Man," she welcomed him gaily.

They were both just a little ill at ease, looking each other over and trying not to be obvious about it. Kitt was overwhelmed all over again with his physical presence. She was keenly aware of all six feet two inches, and two hundred twenty pounds of him as she took the flat pizza carton out of his hands and made a production of sniffing in the delicious aroma, which had some stiff competition for her senses tonight.

Rocky noted with a satisfied glance that she probably hadn't changed clothes after he called and invited himself over. She was wearing old jeans faded and softened by many washings so that they molded her slim hips and long legs. Tucked into the waistband was a Revelers T-shirt that wasn't snug, but it fit closely enough for Rocky to know without even taking a second look that her small breasts were bare underneath it. He quite consciously didn't take a second look, concentrating instead on her face with its attractive glow of health, her gray eyes alight with the flurry of emotions she was experiencing, the pale sheen of her hair pulled back and braided into the single plait.

Rocky found her appearance altogether pleasing and her attention to his anatomy as mildly disconcerting as ever.

"Has Andy bit the dust yet?" he prompted.

"Not yet. Actually he's still going strong." Kitt led the way to the door of the den, where she and Andy had been watching TV and playing a game at the same time. "Why don't you go on in and introduce yourself. I'll put the pizza in the kitchen. We can eat later after I've put Andy to bed. He's already had his supper."

The expression on Rocky's face as he looked through the open door into the den made Kitt chuckle. "It looks like a real disaster area, doesn't it? I have to get it all cleaned up before Ellen comes home or Andy and I both are in trouble. It's against the rules for him to bring toys into the den, but he always talks me into it. I guess I'd make a terrible parent."

The amused glance Rocky shot back at her said that he wasn't surprised Andy twisted her around his little finger, and he didn't know if that disqualified her from parenthood. Feeling vaguely complimented, Kitt hurried out to the kitchen with the pizza, glad of the chance for a few moments to herself to regain her balance. It was just such sheer, unexpected pleasure having him come here tonight. The smell of pizza had never been quite this delectable before. Life had never been quite so full of undefined promise.

When she returned to the den, Rocky was lounging comfortably on the sofa, giving his close attention to five-year-old Andy as he explained in painstaking detail the make-believe war raging down on the carpet between plastic soldiers inside a fort constructed of toy logs and the marauding Indians on the outside. Kitt sat down on the floor where she could look from one of them to the other in cross-legged ease.

"If you want to play, you could shoot the cannon." Andy offered this lure to Rocky with extreme casualness.

"Boy, do you rate!" Kitt exclaimed protestingly to Rocky before she faked a scowl in Andy's direction. "You never let me shoot the cannon."

The child's urchin features beneath a thatch of carrot-red hair were liberally sprinkled with large freckles. He broke out into a grin in response to Kitt's pretended indignation.

"That's 'cause you're a girl!" he taunted and then took a backward dive in anticipation of the desired retaliation.

Kitt pounced and subjected him to a thorough rib-tickling, accompanied by his gales of laughter interspersed with phony orders for her to stop and then finally the apology that was all a part of the game.

"I'm sorry! I'm sorry!" he gasped. "I won't say it again."

Looking on, Rocky was just as glad the tickling session was over since it had presented him with an extended view of Kitt's bottom encased in soft, faded denim. He hadn't come over here with any lustful intentions, but under the circumstances he would have had to be blind not to notice that her buttocks were trim and nicely rounded.

Settling back on her haunches, Kitt wasn't aware that her lack of inhibition had caused Rocky any mild discomfort. She would have been interested in the fact if she'd known, and she wouldn't have been displeased. "It's about time you and I started cleaning up this mess, sport," she announced cheerfully.

Andy's features screwed up immediately in protest. "Not yet, please, Kitt!"

"Right now," she insisted firmly, reaching for his hands to help pull him up. "Before you know it, you'll be falling asleep on me, and I'll have the whole thing to pick up myself. That wouldn't be very fair, now would it?"

"But I'm not sleepy," Andy grumbled, even as he put his small hands in hers in unwilling capitulation to her adult's reasoning.

"Good," Kitt told him brightly. "That means you can stay up a few minutes more after we get everything picked up and watch TV with Rocky and me. Did you ask Rocky if he'd autograph your football for you?"

The reminder worked beautifully, just as Kitt had intended, to insure his ready cooperation in clearing the den of his toys. Rocky looked on as the two of them first made a game of destroying the fort and then loaded all the miniature wooden logs, plastic cowboys, Indians and horses into a cardboard box. While Andy was transporting it to his room, Kitt scooped up an armload of assorted toys scattered around the room.

"He didn't really put up much of a fight," Rocky observed, watching her total economy of movement. He was inclined to believe Betty Boudreaux's claim that Kitt could outwork her employees. Most people, including himself, had a few false starts and stops when they were doing physical tasks, but not her.

"That's partly because you're here," Kitt admitted readily. "But he's a good little boy, even if he is a little spoiled. I don't mind keeping him at all." She glanced over, caught the wry expression on Rocky's face and grinned. "I can see what you're thinking: I don't 'keep' Andy; we just entertain each other. Actually, I guess that's true. His mother sometimes accuses us of being on the same mental wavelength."

Andy returned with the football and a felt-tip pen and climbed up on the sofa next to Rocky. Kitt cast the two of them a fondly approving glance as she swept out of the room with both arms loaded up with toys.

"Do you think you ought to be picking up the rest of your toys before she gets back?" Rocky asked the small boy gravely.

Andy didn't have to give his answer any thought. "Kitt doesn't really care if I help," he explained earnestly. "She can do it faster by herself, but she just wants to make sure I don't grow up irresponsible."

"I see." Rocky managed somehow to keep from smiling at the five-year-old's astuteness.

It took Kitt one more trip between den and bedroom to clear away all the evidence that she and Andy had infringed upon the house rules. Upon her return to the den, she sat down on the sofa beside Andy and dutifully inspected the lengthy inscription Rocky had written on his football.

"Mmm. Looks like you might have had some help from Andy deciding what to write," she murmured with raised eyebrows, locking glances with Rocky and reading amused confirmation.

"Word for word," he said, deadpan.

Kitt slipped her arm around the small boy and pulled him unresistingly back against her.

"If you really are going to grow up and be a famous football player yourself one of these days, sport, I guess we'd better get you into bed so that you can do some growing, don't you think?"

Andy gave her words some reluctant consideration and then nodded his head. The sound of it rubbing against her T-shirt was audible in the room. Unexpectedly a yawn came on, and he snuggled a little closer against her, snickering.

"Guess it's a good thing we got those toys picked up when we did, huh, Kitt?"

"Guess it's a good thing we did, Andy," she agreed teasingly.

Andy twisted around to face her, and the two of them grinned at each other in total understanding. Looking on, Rocky remembered Kitt's light comment earlier: *I guess I'd make a terrible parent.* Her methods might not be the most conventional, but he'd bet she would make a terrific parent. A kid of hers would be damned lucky, he thought.

"Off to bed with you," Kitt ordered fondly. "Take your football with you. And keep the snoring down, will you? Rocky and I want to talk."

Andy got up from the couch, giggling. "Just grown people snore, silly, not children."

"How do you know you don't snore?" Kitt teased. "When you're asleep, you can't hear yourself, can you?"

Andy looked at Rocky as though for support and was visibly struck by a curious thought. "Do football players snore, Rocky? I heard my mom telling Kitt she didn't care if she ever had to share her bed with another snoring man again. I think she meant my dad, but I don't remember him much."

"Andy, it's still time for little boys to hit the sack." Kitt's reminder was amused but definite. "Tell Rocky good-night and vamoose."

"Oh, okay." Andy caught the football Kitt tossed him and hugged it close. "Night, Rocky. Thanks again for autographing my football." With an impish expression he started trudging out of the room.

Kitt turned and watched him over her shoulder until he reached the open door, his steps slowing. "Hey, you," she called at his back. "Haven't you forgotten to tell somebody good-night?"

A smothered delighted giggle was followed by a clear childish voice. "Night, Kitt. I love you."

"I love you, too, you little redheaded freckle-faced monster. Now scram."

Rocky was prepared to cover up his slight embarrassment at being party to the scene, but Kitt's quick change of mood saved him the trouble. As soon as Andy had disappeared, she slid to the edge of the couch in preparation for getting up.

"I could have answered Andy's question for you," she teased. "You know, about whether football players snore," she added when Rocky looked vaguely questioning.

"How would you—" Rocky broke off in the middle of the question, able to answer it for himself. He'd fallen asleep on the sofa the night she'd come over and watched "Monday Night Football" with him. "Well?" he prompted.

Kitt lifted one shoulder in a devilish little shrug that served warning to Rocky. "I turned up the TV as loud as it would go, and I still couldn't hear the com—" She moved with lightning quickness at the last moment to elude Rocky's lunge, which he immediately regretted since it brought reminders of cracked ribs and bruises from Sunday's game. The involuntary grunt wasn't very loud, but it earned him Kitt's concerned scrutiny as he straightened up.

"I forgot—" she began apologetically.

"How about that pizza?" he broke in before they could get off on the subject of football aches and pains, a subject he would just as soon avoid altogether tonight.

"The pizza!" Kitt threw up her hands and then headed immediately for the door. "I'll go and warm it up right now." A quick glance over her shoulder told her Rocky was getting up from the couch with far more deliberate motions. "You can stay here and watch TV, if you want. I don't really need any help," she urged solicitously.

Rocky got up anyway and followed behind her, remembering Andy's sage explanation earlier that Kitt didn't really need his help in clearing the toys from the den since she could do it faster without him. Rocky felt pretty much the same way when he came to a pause in the doorway of the combination kitchen and breakfast room. Kitt had already gone straight to work getting the pizza heated and served. For Rocky to venture inside the kitchen would be to foul up a flawless process. Instead he lounged in the doorway and watched.

The pleasure in her swift economy of movement was becoming a familiar one and didn't present Rocky with any problems since it didn't seem at all sexual. It occurred to him that a woman of her height and lanky build who wasn't so perfectly coordinated would look all arms and legs, but not Kitt. She managed to convey the impression that the lengthy proportions of her body were a fortunate departure from the norm.

With the spicy aroma of the pizza filling the kitchen and Kitt happily at work getting ready to serve it, Rocky was lulled into a most pleasant sense of well-being that was threatened by male instincts that took him unawares when Kitt reached up to pluck two plates from an upper cabinet shelf. She was standing sideways to him, and the stretch of soft cotton over her chest drew his unwilling attention once again to the absence of a bra under the T-shirt.

When she pivoted and took several strides in his direction to put the plates down on the table, Rocky couldn't convince his gaze to leave the front of the T-shirt until, sure enough, he'd made out the merest imprint of small nipples bumping against the soft cotton. Against all his inclinations, he could imagine them half in hiding, half emergent from tender peaks, shyly awaiting a man's fingertip or, better still, the tip of his tongue. Rocky banished the image savagely, disgusted with himself for having such thoughts about Kitt.

"The smell of that pizza is driving me crazy," he declared forcefully, crossing his arms across his chest and directing his gaze over at the glass door of the oven.

"Doesn't it smell wonderful?" Kitt sneaked a glance at him and then treated herself to a longer look when she saw his attention was fixed on the oven. *So this is what it feels like to swoon over a man,* she reflected with self-deriding humor. But what woman who was really honest with herself wouldn't enjoy looking at a man with a body like Rocky's? His jeans and open-throated pullover weren't tight, but they couldn't conceal—at least, not from Kitt's eyes—that superb muscled hardness or the intangible impression of leashed power. Kitt suspected that the most dyed-in-the-wool women's libber would be tempted to don an apron and take up residence in the kitchen with a hunk like Rocky looking on.

"If you can hold on a few more minutes, it'll be ready," she soothed abstractedly and was caught in the act of blatant inspection when Rocky unexpectedly shifted his gaze back to her. "I was just wondering whether you're still taped up around the chest," she ad-libbed quickly.

"I am," he replied, resisting an urge to peel off his shirt just to see her reaction. Naturally he'd felt her looking him over and wouldn't be human if he weren't at least mildly titillated. But, strangely enough, her fascination with his body only reinforced Rocky's instinct to harness his male tendencies where Kitt was concerned. She wasn't in the same league with the women he took to bed. It would be like the proverbial leading a lamb to slaughter, and every man has a certain amount of decency buried somewhere inside him.

"I'm ready to eat that pizza, whether it's hot or not," he announced, straightening to his full height and flexing his shoulders. "What about you?"

"It's probably hot enough." Dreamy echoes of *Yes, my lord; anything you say, my lord,* in her voice brought a little self-conscious grin to Kitt's lips as she slid herself into gear again and went to take the pizza out of the oven. Rocky was grateful for her speed. It meant that there was just that couple of seconds when she was bent forward with her bottom thrust out invitingly before she came upright again, the pizza in her hands.

"Hmm." Kitt breathed in the aroma, her expression rapt with genuine appreciation. "Smells wonderful. I haven't had a pizza in goodness knows when." She grinned broadly. "It's been at least a week. I'm sure glad you had this idea."

Rocky was glad, too. Any discomfort from base male reactions was eased as they agreed unanimously to take the pizza to the den and eat it there. Kitt dispensed with conversation as she devoted her full attention to devouring first one slice and then a second, murmuring fervent sounds of appreciation.

"This is delicious," she said, slumping back when she had finished the second slice and taking out the time to lick her fingers. "I hope you like it," she added anxiously, looking over at Rocky, who was eating at a more leisurely pace, using his fork. "I didn't even stop to ask you before if you liked all these toppings."

Rocky tried unsuccessfully to discipline a smile of amusement that undermined his tongue-in-cheek inquiry. "Is it just fast food that sends you into a feeding frenzy, or is it food in general?"

Kitt chuckled appreciatively. "Mostly it's fast food, because I like it better than regular home-cooked food." She leaned forward and helped herself to another piece of the pizza she'd placed on a low table in front of the sofa, positioned so that it was precisely within equal reach for both of them. Her next remarks opened up a different conversation entirely and reminded Rocky of the apology he intended to repeat with more detail before the evening was over. It was hard now to imagine that he'd ever been hostile with Kitt or would ever again take serious offense at anything she did or said.

"That was really a nice thing you did—visiting Joey in the hospital." Kitt took a bite, munched steadily and swallowed. "Betty says the difference in him—before your visit and then afterward—was like the difference between night and day. Now he can't talk about anything but visiting the Revelers' practice field and meeting all the players." She started to bite into her slice of pizza again and darted a sly look over at Rocky instead. "You know I wouldn't half mind doing that myself."

Rocky had his mouth full so that he could only grunt his discouragement until he had swallowed and could safely speak.

"Taking a teenage boy to the practice field is one thing. Taking a woman is something different."

Kitt found the refusal to her oblique request highly pleasing. "I didn't mean you had to take me in the locker room," she quipped lightly before cramming the remaining bite of pizza slice into her mouth.

"Just let me know any time you want to go to a home game, and I can get you a free ticket," Rocky offered casually. "Or make that two tickets, since you probably wouldn't be going alone." He wondered if she had a steady boyfriend who shared her avid interest in football. So far she hadn't mentioned one.

"I might take you up on that," Kitt said appreciatively. "When I lived in the French Quarter, I used to go to most of the Saints' home games, especially the year before I moved over here. I was dating a guy who had one of those fancy entertainment suites upstairs at the Superdome. Actually, it's more fun to sit in the stands, though."

Rocky found himself distinctly not pleased with this casual glimpse into her background. He didn't like the idea of her living in the French Quarter, a totally unsuitable habitat for someone as wholesome as she was, or dating some rich old lecher who could afford the high price of a dome suite.

"I certainly hope you didn't have a cleaning service in the French Quarter," he remarked so grimly that Kitt eyed him in surprise.

"Why, no, I didn't. Actually I had a number of jobs, one for a tour company." She grinned reminiscently. "The pay was lousy, but there was never a dull moment. I did about everything except drive tourists around in a buggy."

Rocky took another piece of pizza and sat back with an air of determination. "I think it's about time you filled in a little background information about yourself, Dana Kittredge—that is your real name, I believe." He knew quite well it was. He'd gone to the trouble of calling his rental agent to reinforce his memory.

Kitt shrugged her ready compliance. "Sure. I'll tell you whatever you want to know." She hesitated and made a little face. "You've just got to promise, though—"

"I know, I know," Rocky interrupted her impatiently. "I can't blow my top when you turn out to be something entirely different from what you seem. You can start with your mother and father," he prompted and then grinned. "I assume you weren't sprouted full grown?"

Kitt grinned back, but uneasiness still hovered in the clear depths of her gray eyes. Normally she had no qualms whatever talking about her background, but she didn't want to risk having this meal with Rocky end up the way the last one had.

"My mother and father are living in Maryland right now. They've always moved a lot," she began evasively. "My father's a vice president of a big corporation." In a ruefully apologetic voice, she named the huge electronic giant that was a household name.

"A vice president?" Rocky repeated unbelievingly.

She nodded.

He rolled his eyes backward and muttered, "Her father's a vice president of a big corporation, all right!"

"You said you wouldn't get upset," she reminded pleadingly.

"Go on," he ordered. "I can't wait to hear about your mother. Is she next in line for some European throne?"

Kitt had to smile at that notion. "Hardly. My mother's a true California native. She's also a child psychologist. I have no idea how she and my father ever got together because they're total opposites in almost every way. He's very organized and practical, kind of standoffish with people. She couldn't organize a one-car parade if her life depended on it and never meets a stranger. Everybody loves her, from the president of Dad's company to the—" Kitt's face took on a guilty expression as she broke off "—to the housekeeper and the garbage man," she finished apologetically.

"Go on," Rocky chided in a long-suffering tone designed to reassure her that he would keep his promise not to blow his top, no matter what revelations she made.

"I'm sure my parents' marriage would have ended in divorce if we hadn't been able to afford housekeepers," Kitt explained earnestly. "We moved every few years, and she'd never have been able to cope with setting up housekeeping over and over again. Her solution would probably have been just to live out of the boxes until things were gradually unpacked!

"Clutter doesn't bother her at all, and it drives my father crazy. He learned a long time ago that it was best not to encourage her to do anything around the house, though, because she's incredibly inept. My mother has a doctorate in psychology, but she can turn vacuuming the living room into an absolute disaster!'' Kitt shook her head fondly.

"You obviously don't take after her in that regard,'' Rocky commented dryly. "How did you manage to learn housekeeping when you grew up in a house with a maid?''

"It always seemed so easy to me, and I never minded it,'' she mused. "Maybe it was because I really wasn't expected to do anything, the way some kids are. It's strange, but my two brothers and I were actually very neat kids. Maybe we took after our father. Maybe we just picked up on the vibes of the household and realized that everything ran smoothly as long as the housekeeper was happy, so we tried to be helpful and cooperative.''

Rocky thought it was ironic as hell, considering the misleading circumstances under which he had met her, that in a way Kitt was a Dana, after all. In fact, she would have been even more out of his league if he'd known her in high school, than his own fluffy little blond Dana. Being the leading doctor in a small Louisiana city was nothing compared to a vice presidency of one of the richest corporations in the world.

Seeing his moody abstraction, Kitt glossed over the rest of her background quickly. She had moved to Baton Rouge with her family during her impressionable high school years and stayed to attend Louisiana State when they moved again. She considered herself an adopted Louisiana native now. Basketball had been her major interest in high school and college. Next had come having fun with her friends. If it hadn't been for wanting to take that trip with her friends after college graduation, she might never have stumbled upon cleaning for other people as a good source of income. Now she considered herself fortunate to be half owner of The Magic Broom.

Rocky sprawled a little deeper into the sofa cushions, subjecting Kitt to a measuring glance that made her nervous to hear whatever it was he was thinking.

"That's quite a story," he said dryly. "No wonder you seemed like the most carefree cleaning woman I'd ever run across. I guess it's easy coming from a background like yours to take a cheerful outlook on life in general."

After treading on eggshells in the hope that he wouldn't be offended by her affluent background, Kitt found that she couldn't let that final remark go unchallenged. Her background had affected her outlook, but not in the way he implied, cushioning her from reality.

"I guess I do have a cheerful outlook on life," she said crisply, sitting up very straight. "My parents deserve most of the credit. By example as much as anything else, they taught my brothers and me that everybody in society has an important role and should be treated with respect. We weren't allowed to call the housekeeper by her first name. She was always Miss or Mrs., whatever the case should be. The garbage collector, the mailman, the repairman who came to fix the washing machine or the air conditioner, the mechanic who serviced our cars—they were all important people, making life pleasant."

Kitt had never been truly comfortable mounted on a soapbox. In this particular circumstance, she gained little satisfaction in the virtues of being right, not if proving Rocky wrong meant pushing him farther away from her. Before he could make any reply, she made a swift apology, not for substance but for manner of speaking.

"Sorry, I didn't mean to get on my high horse like that." Curling up sideways facing him, she balanced her plate with its half-eaten slice of pizza on her knee. "I guess what I'm trying to say is that I don't consider any kind of honest work demeaning, and so therefore it doesn't occur to me that anybody else would. Nobody can make me feel bad about myself except me."

She eyed him hopefully, asking only for understanding, and then held her breath as Rocky leaned sideways toward her, his hard, cynical features softening into an expression she could only read as affectionate.

"I think Betty Boudreaux has your number," he mused lightly and reached out to lay his hand on her head. "You're one of a kind. I hope you don't ever change." He waggled her head gently the way he might have done five-year-old Andy.

Kitt felt incredibly complimented and yet deep down in the center of her pleasure a small hollow space opened up as he took his hand away and she knew that was the full extent of the physical contact he intended. She wanted something more intimate. For the first time in her life, friendship and camaraderie with a man weren't enough.

Not nearly enough.

Chapter Seven

Would you like me to heat the rest of the pizza up again?" Kitt offered. "It's gotten cold on us during this heavy conversation."

Rocky shook his head in refusal. "Not for me, thanks. I had enough." He sprawled a little lower so that he could rest his head against the back of the sofa.

Kitt eyed the remains of the pizza with exaggerated interest. "Looks like there's more than enough left for breakfast," she declared. "You could even take a couple of slices home with you, if you want."

Rocky groaned. "Thanks, but no thanks." He rubbed his hard, flat stomach. "If the pepperoni's finished fighting with the green peppers and Italian sausage by morning, I'll just consider myself lucky."

He made an abortive effort to get up when Kitt started clearing away the pizza and plates but was easily persuaded when she insisted he stay right where he was.

"I won't be but a minute. You'll just get in my way," she said cheerfully. "Would you like another beer?" The offer was hesitant only because he was getting that heavy-lidded relaxed look she'd seen before. She was halfway expecting him to be asleep when she came back from the kitchen.

Rocky was feeling more lazily content with every passing second. "I suppose I really shouldn't. . . ."

"No, you shouldn't," Kitt agreed before he could weaken. "You have to drive home."

"Yes, Mother." His sarcasm was good-natured.

"That wasn't a mother talking," Kitt corrected him briskly. "That was a loyal Revelers fan. I won't have you leave my house and wrap your red Ferrari—or whatever it is that you drive—around a pine tree. If you really do want another beer, you can have one," she offered, dropping the scolding tone. "I can make you a cup of coffee before you leave."

Rocky sat just a little straighter. It hadn't escaped him that Kitt didn't appreciate being cast in a maternal role, not even jokingly.

"You're right," he said easily. "I shouldn't have another beer. I'd hate like hell to put a scratch on my car, much less wrap it around a tree." He grinned. "By the way, I hate to disappoint you, but you don't have a red Ferrari parked outside. In fact, the neighbors aren't likely to be impressed at all at the sight of a 1969 Mustang. And how about a cup of coffee right now?"

"Coming right up." On the way to the door, she paused and inquired over her shoulder, "Do you take anything in your coffee?"

The impulse to tease her was fast becoming second nature to Rocky. He succumbed to it now, replying as though he assumed she was offering to prepare his cup of coffee exactly to his taste. "Two slightly heaping tea-spoons of sugar and a lot of whatever you have to change the color, milk, creamer, it doesn't matter. Of course, you don't have to wait on me the way my moth—"

"How about milk of magnesia?" Kitt shot back at him. "That would change the color and take care of your pizza digestion problem, too."

But she was grinning to herself as she left the room, with the sound of his low chuckle coming from the sofa. He was still awake when she returned, sitting with his arms crossed over his chest and watching the TV screen with an air of diligence rather than real interest.

He came alert and sat up straight to accept the cup of coffee she handed him. After noting the beige color, he smiled, lifted the cup to his mouth and took a sip.

"Perfect," he pronounced, as though awarding her a prize.

Kitt doubted that his mother had ever been tempted to take a steaming cup of coffee away from her strapping son and pour it over his crotch. But then Kitt wasn't se-riously tempted to do that, either, especially when he proceeded to drink the coffee with evident enjoyment.

"A 1969 Mustang?" she said skeptically, backtrack-ing to his remarks before the request for a cup of coffee.

He nodded. "It's a real beauty. Black with red leather interior. If you're really nice, I'll let you ride in it some time."

"Black with red interior?"

His broad grin was sheepish. "Impressed, huh? Wait 'til you hear the engine. That baby purrs like a big cat just waiting to take off."

"Big wheels, lots of shiny chrome—" Kitt broke off, her expression denying in advance the next item in her speculative description. "Not fuzzy dice..."

Rocky threw back his head and laughed in delighted appreciation. It was the first time Kitt had actually seen him really turn loose like that, and the effect on her was disconcerting. She thought she might be tempted to do or say almost anything in the future to provoke his mirth.

"No fuzzy dice hanging from the rearview mirror," he said, chuckling. "Not even a dog on the dash with a wagging head." His gaze was suddenly shrewd. "You hit right on target, though. I might have known you would. The car I'm driving now is the same one I'd have sold my soul for when I was sixteen."

Kitt was complimented at his implication that she was a person of insight, but a little wary of pursuing the subject of his car fantasy since it would take them back to that time in Rocky's past when his mother had done cleaning for other people. She thought it was too soon to open that up again.

"I guess most of us try to live out certain childhood or teenage fantasies after we're adults," she observed casually, never once suspecting where the remark would lead.

"I guess so," Rocky agreed thoughtfully.

Seeing the dawn of curiosity in his eyes as they made a slow inspection of her lanky build from head to toe, Kitt was suddenly extremely self-conscious. She could sense a question about her own youthful fantasies forming itself in his brain and felt ridiculously unprepared to answer. She talked quickly to head it off.

"Boys usually have a fascination with cars, don't they? Of course, some girls do, too. But girls are more likely to dream about being Miss America and growing up to marry someone tall, dark and handsome. Would you like another cup of coffee?"

"Yes, please."

Rocky had the feeling as he handed her his empty cup and watched her leave that she was glad to escape to the kitchen. He found her evasion most interesting, partly because it seemed atypical. She wasn't the type to evade any kind of question. Aside from that, he was genuinely curious. What kind of fantasies would a teenage Kitt have harbored in her young breast?

When Kitt returned with the second cup of coffee, she didn't give Rocky a chance to open up the conversation again. Picking up the TV remote control, she flipped the channel to a station with the evening news and turned the volume up a little louder. Rocky sipped his coffee, content to wait until another time to satisfy his curiosity. For there would be other times, he felt sure. There was no sense of urgency about learning all about Kitt, but rather a sense of leisurely expectation. The prospect of future conversations about anything and everything during casual, enjoyable evenings like tonight filled him with a quiet pleasure he'd never known before with a woman. He didn't want anything to spoil that pleasure.

They watched the news, commenting on this or that news item. During the sports segment, Rocky noted the way Kitt's concentration sharpened. He was able to smile his amusement, unnoticed, when she carried on a forceful dialogue with the sportscaster pointing out the error of his thinking on a number of points.

"Maybe you should be a sportscaster yourself," he suggested teasingly when the commercial came on. "It must be frustrating to sit and listen to all those mistakes night after night."

Kitt grinned without any self-consciousness. "Actually it's one of my favorite pastimes. No, I'd better stick to the cleaning business. I'd have a hard time getting some of those locker-room interviews anyway, where the camera never gets any lower than the waist.''

Rocky thought of a locker room full of naked athletes milling around uninhibitedly and a wide-eyed Kitt standing in the middle, taking it all in. Judging by her reaction to his own nudeness that day in his bathroom, he thought her main problem wouldn't be getting inside the locker room, but keeping her mind on the interview once she was there!

''You probably are better off sticking to the cleaning business,'' he agreed, smiling at his own mental scenario.

''Why?'' Kitt was more curious about the smile than the comment.

For a split second Rocky was tempted to tease her with the truth, but instinct told him he would be venturing into very provocative territory he would do best to avoid. Instead he gave her an alternative truth.

''Because pro football players have to be the worst chauvinists in the world. They'd never really take a woman sportscaster seriously.''

''Oh.'' Kitt was skeptical that the reason he'd given was the mental mate to his smile, but the barrage of thirty-second commercials ended and the error-prone sportscaster was back on the screen making predictions about the following Sunday's pro football games. She had to listen in order to differ with him.

When the news was over, they watched a late-night talk show. During a commercial break about midway through it, Rocky shifted as though preparing all his joints and muscles for rising and glanced at his watch. Kitt waited, expecting him to announce that it was time for him to go. She was surprised that he had stayed this long. It was almost as though he were patiently waiting for something, but whatever that might be she didn't have an inkling.

"I suppose you have to get up and go across the lake in the morning," she mused, providing him with an opening.

Rocky nodded, confirming the conjecture. By now he knew the vernacular of the area and didn't question the dual use of "going across the lake." For a resident of greater New Orleans, it meant crossing Lake Pontchartrain to either Mandeville or Slidell, while to residents on the North Shore, it meant a trip into the city or one of its suburbs.

"I don't guess I'll get to meet your business partner, Andy's mom, and her boyfriend—I forgot what you said his name was."

"Bob. Bob Bailey." Kitt supplied the name in a tone of vague surprise. So he had been waiting for something, for Ellen and Bob to get there so that he could meet them. In a hundred years she wouldn't have guessed he would have any interest in meeting her friends. The fact that he did was at once immensely pleasing. "They may be late. After the dinner, they might have gone to Bob's place in Covington."

Rocky stood up. "Well, some other time, then. I'd better get my prized black stallion home to the stable."

"Sure. Some other time," Kitt agreed promptly. "I know they'd like to meet you. Just don't expect any enthusiasm about football from Ellen. She was a cheerleader in high school and has a general idea what a touchdown is, but that's about the extent of her grasp of the game."

On the walk to the door, Kitt came as close as she ever had in her life to chattering nervously. The moment of leavetaking brought back a full-blown awareness of his physical presence that somehow was made more intense by his indication just now that he intended to see her again. Why else would he want to meet her friends? Rocky wasn't the kind to say, "Some other time, then," if he didn't mean it.

"Thanks for bringing over the pizza. I was really in the mood for one." This expression of her gratitude coming just as they reached the door sounded far too emphatic since at the ripe age of thirty she was seized by a sixteen-year-old's suspense. Would there be a good-night kiss, even a casual one? She wished there would be. She'd like to feel his mouth against hers. More than any other feature, even his eyes, which were sharply observant but guarded, his mouth seemed to betray what he was feeling and thinking: cynicism, amusement, even interest.

"Thanks for letting me invite myself over." Rocky reached for the doorknob himself when Kitt came to a standstill and didn't make a move to open the door. "I had every intention of making a fuller apology, but somehow the subject just never got around to anything unpleasant, did it?"

His smile was warm and sincere. Kitt appreciated the disarmingly attractive way it changed the hard planes of his face and involved all of his features, even the shrewd dark eyes. Still there was no warning flutter inside Kitt's breast to alert her to any intimate intention on his part, because there was no such intention. He was going to smile and walk out of the door without even a friendly pat on the shoulder. Suddenly she knew that she wasn't going to be able to let him go without first touching him.

"We really haven't talked about football at all tonight, have we?" she said slowly, feeling her impulse take hold. "I held my breath every time you carried the ball Sunday. It must have been terribly painful playing with those cracked ribs." She reached out her hand to his chest and poked it very gingerly with her fingertips. "Where are you hurt?"

Rocky felt his pulse speed up in answer to the uncertain probing in her tone as well as her feather touch. He glanced down as though drawn to watch her touch him. Her hands were totally familiar to him by now. He'd watched with appreciation her quick dexterity as she used them. He remembered the feel of their sureness and confidence that day she had given him a rubdown. These strong impressions contrasted oddly with her tentative exploration of his rib cage now. The allure of giving her free range to touch him at her pleasure was so strong that Rocky drew in his breath and grasped her fingers to still them.

"Here." He escorted her hand to the location of the injured ribs and pressed her fingertips much harder than she would have dared. Her wincing expression on behalf of the pain she imagined he might be experiencing brought another smile to his face, but one not so unguarded as that before it. Still holding her hand against his tightly bound chest, he leaned forward and bent down to give her a quick little peck on the forehead.

"Night. Thanks again."

Kitt stood there holding her hand as though it were an alien object attached to her wrist and watched him go.

"Night, Rocky." Her farewell sounded dreamy to her ears, but, spoken in that faint voice, she doubted that he heard it anyway. Breathing out a sigh that was both happiness and regret, she took several steps to bring her just outside the open door. Sure enough, there parked in the driveway was an early model black Mustang, even in the semidarkness agleam with wax and chrome polish. The sight of it brought a smile to Kitt's lips. He hadn't been kidding. He did drive the car of his adolescent dreams. She waited, inspiration broadening the smile into a grin, until he had unlocked the driver's door and glanced back to see her watching him.

"That's a *real* nice *car* ya got there, Rock-y," she sang out, in an overdone parody of a teenage girl's arch overture to a high school boy.

Rocky grinned, feeling as devil-may-care as a high school kid as he slid under the wheel and started the car. The revving of the powerful engine was music to his ears and probably would be when he was ninety. He shoved the floor stick shift into reverse and made a showy production of backing out of the driveway. Then, after a cocky toot of the horn, he peeled out with a squeal of tires that was sure to be the envy of every adolescent boy in the whole neighborhood.

He smiled most of the way home, thinking to himself that only with Kitt could he indulge himself with such an exhibition and enjoy it to that extent. There was something very special about her, some fun-loving quality associated with youth that most people tended to lose as they grew older. Rocky didn't think Kitt would ever lose it. He certainly hoped she wouldn't.

The brief scene at the door as he was leaving came back to him, and he felt the same quick tension that he easily recognized as sexual and thought he understood. Kitt wasn't the type of woman Rocky was attracted to sexually and took to bed, but he liked her very much and wouldn't be human if he weren't at least a little turned on by her acute physical awareness of him, which he considered basically innocent and wholesome, like everything else about her. He was quite confident he could control himself around her and make sure things didn't get out of hand.

After Rocky had left, Kitt resumed her thirty-year-old self and went back to the kitchen to warm up a slice of pizza. She might as well have a snack while she waited for Ellen to come home.

"Guess what?" she greeted her partner and friend when Ellen popped her head into the den door a half hour later, her expression both surprised and questioning that Kitt was still up.

"Well, I know he was here. I smell the pizza," Ellen replied, wrinkling up her petite nose. "Please tell me there wasn't any left over."

"Sorry. There's plenty left for breakfast," Kitt informed with a pleased expression.

"You had to stay up to tell me that?" Ellen answered the lightly sarcastic question for herself by taking several steps inside the room and waiting for whatever it was that Kitt was fairly dying to tell her.

"Rocky wants to meet you and Bob!"

Certain that there had to be more to bring that glow to Kitt's face and that exultant tone to her voice, Ellen made no reaction to what on the surface wasn't a revelation of the earthshaking variety.

"Is that it?" she asked dubiously when several seconds had passed.

Kitt's enthusiasm was undaunted. She nodded with a kind of eager impatience. "After we'd finished eating, I noticed that he was starting to look drowsy. During football season I gather that he keeps himself on a strict schedule and goes to bed early. Plus he takes muscle relaxants and they can make you drowsy. Anyway—" Kitt made an impatient gesture for Ellen to come closer and rushed on with her explanation while her friend cautiously complied.

"He drank a couple of cups of coffee, and we talked and watched the news. I kept waiting for him to say that he had to go, but he stayed and stayed. I got the feeling he was waiting for something. And then, finally, he said he guessed he wouldn't get to meet you and Bob tonight!"

Ellen sighed and came to sit on the sofa next to Kitt, feeling more like a den mother in a college dorm than a contemporary.

"Kitt," she began reluctantly and then sighed again, not enjoying the prospect of being a wet blanket.

Kitt was blissfully unconcerned with her friend's plight. Bringing her bare feet up to the sofa cushion in front of her, she hugged her long legs and confided cheerfully, "Ellen, I think I've finally fallen in love. All the signs I've never believed in are there." She clapped her right hand across her left breast. "My heart goes pit-ter-pat at the very sight of him. I swear it really does. And when he gets within reaching distance—with arms as long as mine, you know that's not all that close—I get all weak and warm inside. Tonight he gave me this scrawny little peck on the forehead when he was leaving, and I all but had to grab onto the door to keep from falling!"

"Kitt—"

"Come on, don't look so worried!" Kitt chided. "I thought this was what you've wanted for me all these years when you accused me of not being a normal female!"

Ellen took her responsibilities of friendship too seriously to be courted into a smile. "You're making a big joke of this, Kitt, but it may not turn out to be funny, you know," she warned somberly. "Take it from someone who's learned the hard way: falling in love is not some entertaining game. You really are deeply attracted to this

Rocky Players character, and I'm afraid you're going to end up getting hurt."

"But Ellen, what I'm feeling is great!" Kitt cajoled, throwing her long arms wide as though to embrace the world. "Being in love is fantastic; it comes close to winning the state championship in high school." That drew a grudging smile. "Notice I said almost. Come on. Be happy with me. I couldn't wait to tell you."

Ellen half rose from the sofa to give Kitt a quick little hug and then dropped down again.

"I want to be happy with you and for you, Kitt. You know that. You're my dearest friend in the whole world. In some ways you just seem so young for your age. That's all. I worry about you like an old mother hen." She gave Kitt's arm a warm pat and summoned a rueful smile. "Just please keep in mind that Rocky Players has probably been to bed with hundreds of women. He could literally have a different woman every night, if he wanted to. Just—" Ellen broke off when it was apparent from Kitt's dreamy expression that the words weren't having the desired effect. "Be careful," she implored.

Kitt squeezed her legs tighter and rested her chin on her knees. "If he makes love anywhere near as well as he plays football, I couldn't blame any woman for wanting to go to bed with him," she mused. "He's so sexy...." She smiled impishly. "With or without his clothes on." The dreamy expression on her face grew thoughtful and then pensive. "Problem is, will he ever want to go to bed with me, Ellen?"

Ellen knew they were getting down to the rock-bottom reason Kitt was still up instead of sound asleep in bed. "I don't know why he wouldn't, unless there's something wrong with him," she replied in the same bristly tone she might have used to defend five-year-old Andy from an implicit criticism. "When are Bob and I going to meet this male marvel, anyway?" she asked very casually.

Kitt shrugged. "I don't know exactly when, but some time soon, I expect."

"I see. When are you seeing Rocky again?"

Kitt stretched lazily and yawned. "I don't know that either," she admitted complacently. "Now that I've told you all, I'm ready to hit the sack. Tomorrow's a busy day, as usual." She stood up and stretched again with the same luxuriant, feline deliberateness that Ellen found strange in the person of Kitt, the perennial tomboy. It was the movement of a woman intrigued with the inner rhythms of her own body, rhythms that Ellen knew Kitt was feeling for the first time.

"So Kitt has finally fallen in love," Ellen mused fondly. "It happens to the best of us sooner or later. I have to admit I envy you a little, but I wouldn't trade places with you for anything. I'll take companionship with a nice man over falling madly in love any day of the week." She got up from the sofa, a diminutive figure next to Kitt's leggy height, even in her high heels.

The two women made a Mutt and Jeff duo as they headed for the door companionably, each absorbed in her own thoughts. Kitt was wondering why love couldn't always be mutual. All these years Bob had been so quietly and devotedly in love with Ellen and would have given her all the material as well as the emotional security she wanted out of life. He'd have made her a wonderful husband and been a good father to their children. It seemed a shame that Ellen couldn't have fallen in love with him, before she became so disillusioned with the whole notion of romantic love.

In spite of the fact that Kitt's giddy attraction to Rocky might well turn out to be one-sided, she didn't perceive any serious parallel between herself and Bob because she felt that her feelings for Rocky just weren't in the same category as Bob's feelings for Ellen. What she was experiencing was more superficial. It was a very willing kind of infatuation on her part with a pleasant mix of mutual liking and easy companionship. She quite frankly looked forward to a relationship with Rocky that wasn't platonic and shared none of Ellen's fears about the dangers of involvement.

Chances were good that Ellen knew what she was talking about when she said this zany feeling of being in love didn't last, but then what kind of high did last? As a top high school and college athlete, Kitt had known the exhilaration of competitive pressure. She'd stood at the free throw line in an overtime period when the state championship depended on whether she could arc the ball through the air and swish it through the hoop, as she'd done countless times in other less important games. She'd experienced the hush followed by total pandemonium when the fans swept out of the stands and bore her high on the wave of victory. Because the moment hadn't lasted, that didn't mean she would give up having lived it. There was still the memory of adrenaline racing through her veins, making her feel incredibly clearheaded and capable of superhuman achievement.

No, Kitt didn't waste any time in sleeplessness worrying about the transitory state of her emotions. She hugged her exultation close the way Andy hugged his teddy bear and fell asleep with a foolish smile on her lips, her last waking thought of Rocky and his flashy car.

Chapter Eight

Kitt was no novice at the dating game. She could tell if a man liked her and enjoyed her company and was able to predict whether he'd want to see her again. There was little doubt in her mind that she'd hear from Rocky within a reasonable time, perhaps as early as a week. He would probably call and suggest another casual get-together. She didn't expect him to call her the very next evening.

"I just wanted to check and make sure your neighbors weren't getting up a petition about your late-night visitors disturbing the peace," Rocky explained as soon as he had identified himself. He sounded relaxed and prepared to enjoy whatever rejoinder she would make.

"When I got home this afternoon, there was a whole crowd of teenage boys out in the street in front of our driveway, examining the tire marks," Kitt declared, taking pleasure in his answering chuckle as she settled herself on a high stool located near the wall phone in the kitchen. Bob was over tonight. He and Ellen and Kitt had been in the den talking and watching TV when the phone rang, and she had come out to answer it, never suspecting the caller might be Rocky.

"What are you doing right now?" she asked impulsively, struck by a spur-of-the-minute inspiration.

"Not much. Is there something in particular I'm supposed to be doing when I talk to you on the telephone?" The smile was still there in his voice.

"No, silly. I just thought you might want to drop over for a cup of coffee and meet Bob and Ellen—if it's not too late, that is."

"A cup of coffee's all you're offering? I take it I've passed my beer curfew."

"I've seen for myself the way one beer can affect your driving," Kitt retorted, picking up on his banter. "You can't afford to lose any more rubber off those tires." She was rewarded once again with the sound of his low chuckle.

"I guess I had better spare them tonight. Actually I'm not in Mandeville. I'm staying overnight here in the city."

"Oh." Kitt had to adjust to the news that he wasn't talking to her from his condominium, just a fifteen-minute drive away. He had called long distance from New Orleans.

"I wondered if you and your friends already have plans for Friday night. I could bring some steaks over to barbecue, early enough so that I could drink a beer or two before the curfew for pro football players with a local franchise."

Kitt was instantly sold on the idea and made no effort to conceal her enthusiasm. "Hey, that sounds like a real winner to me. As far as I know, they don't have anything special planned. I can check with them right now, if you want to hang on a minute."

"You can let me know tomorrow evening," Rocky said casually. "Just so I get the right number of steaks. By the way, how was your pizza breakfast?"

"It was great! Started my day off right!" Not even Kitt could work up that much enthusiasm about pizza for breakfast, but she needed an outlet for the gladness bouncing around inside her. He obviously assumed the two of them would barbecue steaks Friday night whether Bob and Ellen could join them or not. In order to let him know of their plans, tomorrow evening she would be talking to him again so there was the certainty of another phone conversation between now and Friday. The world seemed a good place to Kitt.

"I'm trying to imagine the kind of day that would start off right with pepperoni, Italian sausage, mushrooms, green pepper, onions and olives," Rocky remarked dryly.

"A busy day," Kitt replied cheerfully. "I ran around all morning making estimates on several big jobs. If we get them, we'll definitely need several magic brooms, not to mention some extra human hands."

"What do you mean, 'big' jobs?"

"These are onetime cleanups of new construction. For example, there's an office condo complex on Highway 190 between Mandeville and Covington almost ready to be cleaned and a new little shopping center in Covington that'll be finished in a couple of months. We go in after all the construction is finished and get everything spic and span for the new owners or leaseholders. We clean all the stickers off the glass and polish it, cart away the debris, vacuum and spot-clean any carpet that's been laid, scrub and wax floors that need waxing and so on."

"I didn't realize you did that kind of cleaning," Rocky mused. "Sounds like some pretty heavy work. Are all your employees women?"

"Most of the regular ones are, but we hire quite a few high school and college boys on a part-time basis. They don't mind climbing ladders and cleaning fixtures and high windows."

"I'll bet you don't mind that either," he predicted confidently.

"Most of the time I don't." Kitt's voice was amused as she thought of a recent incident. She had been perched rather precariously on a high ladder, cleaning a huge wooden ceiling fan when someone had turned it on. She'd grasped an oversize blade and hung on, making a full circle before she could hook her feet onto a rung of the ladder and grab on to a higher rung with her hands.

"Thank God whoever accidentally touched the switch turned the fan on low speed," she said after relating the anecdote. Just as she'd expected, Rocky was entertained by it.

"It's a good thing you're so athletic," he remarked, chuckling. He could see the whole incident vividly. "Do you think you have a good chance of getting those jobs you made estimates on this morning?"

"I'll be surprised if we don't," Kitt admitted with a candor that verged on smugness. "It's not likely that anybody will beat our price. You see, it's worth giving a bargain price just to get in on the ground floor. We show that we can be depended on to do the job fast and do it well. Chances are more than good that we'll end up with a long-term contract." Even as she made this explanation, Kitt wondered if Rocky had forgotten they were talking long-distance, not local. If there'd been any doubt that he could afford the expense, she might have reminded him.

"Very smart," Rocky approved and then asked her another question that required more than a simple yes or no answer.

Kitt talked on, giving him an insight into her business approach and her daily routine. He was such an appreciative listener that she was inspired to recount additional entertaining anecdotes that came to mind. It seemed to have become one of her primary goals in life to make him laugh. Once during the conversation Ellen came to the kitchen door looking for her, peered in curiously and then returned to the den.

When she hung up the phone some time later, after promising that she would call him about eight o'clock the following evening, Kitt stayed right where she was on the stool for a minute or two longer, basking in a schoolgirl complacency. He'd called long distance to pave the way for seeing her Friday night and then kept her talking a full hour. Yes, the world was definitely a good place.

As she slid from the stool with a languid motion and ambled off to the den, Kitt was frankly torn between hoping that Ellen and Bob would be free Friday night and hoping that they wouldn't. She was eager for them to meet Rocky and get to know him, but she didn't in the least mind the thought of spending Friday night alone with him. This ambivalence lingered even after the issue was settled and communicated itself in her tone the following night when she called Rocky.

"Ellen and Bob didn't have plans for tomorrow evening. They're looking forward to meeting you."

Rocky was aware of a cheerful resignation underlying the pleased note in her voice and found that he shared her feelings. "Good. I'll be there about seven, if that's okay, with four thick ribeyes. Or should I make it five and bring one for Andy, too?''

"No, when we grill steaks, Andy usually has a hot dog or a hamburger. I'm glad you're coming early, though, so that he'll get a chance to see you before his bedtime. You've been a big topic of conversation with him the past two days. He took his autographed football off to kindergarten yesterday."

The unself-conscious loving quality in Kitt's tone when she spoke of the small boy roused that same faint envy that Rocky had felt a couple of nights ago. Perhaps it was being able to express affection so naturally and casually that he envied. Rocky lacked that ability himself, probably because of his background. There had been love between him and his mother and his four brothers, but even she wasn't a demonstrative person, perhaps because her life was so filled with worry about day-to-day survival. Rocky hadn't grown up in a household where there was frequent touching and casual expression of love. Physical contact in his youth had consisted almost entirely of rough and tumble play with other boys, including his brothers. Then there had come the disciplined contact of football and almost simultaneously his first close association with girls. That had been a more subtle kind of assault with a different kind of "scoring," but still definitely physical. The kind of simple, outgoing affection that Rocky had seen Kitt lavish upon Andy, Rocky had never known. He thought the kid was damned lucky, no matter what kind of mother he had.

"How was practice today?" Kitt's question, calling for a drastic change of subject, required a quick adjustment on Rocky's part.

"You don't really want to know," he warned her with grim humor.

"That bad, huh? You're playing Los Angeles this week, too. That'll be a tough game."

"We're going to have some serious problems getting through their frontline defense, especially with Cafferty on the bench. We don't really have a backup who can take his place at right tackle. I'm sure I don't have to tell you the team is weak in offensive blocking."

"Does that mean you'll just have to take to the air and pass?" To her amazement Kitt noticed that she didn't even sound hopeful. What a change there had been in her whole attitude toward the game of football since she'd met Rocky Players! Not too long ago, she'd been of the opinion that giving the ball to a running back was just a break in routine to keep the opposition guessing. The game would be won or lost by a team's passing game. That was before the 38 emblazoned on the back of Rocky's jersey had become the most important number in her life.

Once again they stayed on the phone a whole hour, but this time Rocky was the one who talked. He discussed in depth the game plan for that Sunday and pointed out the various offensive and defensive problems she could expect to see if she watched the game. Kitt listened with rapt interest, made intelligent comments and asked knowledgeable questions that told him she was following him. It never once occurred to her that the conversation she was having with Rocky was a first in his life and a giant step in their relationship.

Rocky had discussed football with numerous women on numerous occasions, some exceedingly intimate and taking place in bed, but he'd never had this same kind of straightforward, technical football conversation with a woman before. Afterward he was amazed on several counts. One was that he didn't have a single qualm about the wealth of personal insight he'd given her, raw material for any number of hot sports news items on Rocky Players's opinions about his Revelers teammates. Another was that it had felt so plain damned good to talk it all out with her. Having spoken aloud his pessimism for the team's chances of winning the upcoming game that weekend did nothing to change things, but he felt more positive in his outlook than he had since coming to New Orleans.

And there was no need, none at all, to make any real or pretended apologies about boring her with man talk, no call for thanking her for letting him get things off his chest. He had needed to talk and she had listened because she was interested. That was the simple, momentous extent of it.

"Hey, I'm looking forward to tomorrow night," he told her when they were exchanging final, casual remarks. "I'm glad I'll get to meet Ellen and Bob." What he really meant was that he wanted to be a part of Kitt's world. He wanted to enter the privileged ranks of those near and dear to her.

"Good heavens, Kitt, you were on the phone a whole hour again!" Ellen exclaimed when Kitt came back into the dining room, which they used as a home office. Ellen sat at the table with papers spread out in front of her. When Kitt had gone to make her phone call, the two of them had been working out a schedule for the next quarter in order to decide whether they would need to hire some new permanent employees.

"I think you're regressing to your high school years," Ellen added. "Remember when we used to talk on the phone for hours with the guy we'd seen just thirty minutes before and would see again first thing the next morning?"

Kitt sighed dreamily as she slid into her chair. Resting her elbows on the table she linked her fingers to form a flat-topped steeple and propped her chin on it.

"Not me, Ellen. I had basketball practice after school and was pooped by the time I got home and still had homework to do and tests to study for." She smiled, remembering. "There were calls from guys, of course, including a lot of other girls' boyfriends who wanted answers to math problems."

"What on earth were you and Rocky Players talking about for a whole hour?" Ellen asked curiously.

Kitt sighed again. "Football."

"Football?"

Kitt nodded and then grinned teasingly. "Sorry, I can't tell you any more than that, Ellen. Rocky told me all about the game plan for Sunday and asked me to be sure and keep it confidential."

Ellen made a snorting sound and rolled her eyes ceilingward, but she couldn't keep from smiling. "Then be sure and don't tell me, because you know I'll tell everybody I know. Football's such a major topic of conversation in my life." She shook her head and then briskly changed the subject back to the work at hand. She was curious to meet Kitt's pro football player but was afraid the evening would turn out to be a god-awful bore. He'd probably expect them all to sit around and ogle his muscles admiringly while he regaled them with macho football stories.

Well into the following evening, Ellen thought fleetingly of her glum expectations and admitted to herself how wrong she had been. Even someone like herself who detested football and was especially cynical about the male of the species in general, couldn't have denied that Rocky Players was a prime physical specimen of a man.

Dressed conservatively in jeans and open-throated shirt with a V-neck pullover sweater, he still had a superb physique with a rugged appeal that would have qualified him to mount a horse and act as a stand-in for the Marlboro man, and yet there was no male swagger. Quite the opposite, in fact. He was reserved and seemed slightly ill at ease at first. It was understandable since he was walking into the midst of old, close friends so thoroughly comfortable with each other that they didn't pull any punches with their joking banter.

When he was introduced, Bob Bailey offered Rocky his hand and then went into a vaudeville routine immediately after the handshake, pretending permanent injury to the hand.

"Good thing I'm an attorney," he gasped in mock pain. "I don't really need this hand anyway. All an attorney needs is a devious mind and a gift for gab."

"You're definitely qualified, then," Kitt declared, draping her arm around Bob's shoulder, her lanky height easily topping his five and a half feet, even with the thick-soled shoes he wore. "Don't mind this little shrimp, Rocky. I saw the gleam in his eye when I told him you were coming tonight. You know these attorneys—always on the lookout for a big lawsuit."

Bob assumed an injured expression and made an elaborate production of shrugging off Kitt's arm. "That gleam in my eye was relief, not greed, beanpole," he declared, flicking imaginary lint off of his bright red velour pullover. "Seriously, I was glad for you, honey. After all these years of trying, you finally managed to drag home a football player." He looked from Kitt to Ellen and then to Rocky, his expression friendly but rueful. "Now that we've all met and done our opening routines, why don't we sit down? I'm getting a complex just standing here. How about a beer, Rocky?''

Rocky accepted gladly and turned over the package of steaks he still held tucked under one arm. It was silly but he'd felt a little nervous coming here tonight and meeting Kitt's friends, as though he were being put to some sort of test. He was definitely the outsider in the group and because he was a public figure, he would probably encounter some prejudgments, whereas he didn't have any idea what to expect of them.

The first sight of Bob Bailey had triggered warnings. A man that short and slight of build would have to have a lot of self-confidence not to be threatened by a Rocky Players. The smaller man's wit and intelligence were immediately obvious, though, as was the fact that he had long ago come to terms with his physical size. He had the assurance to joke about it in such a way as to admit honestly that he *did* feel defensive. Rocky admired the honesty.

Ellen came as a surprise to him because she was a total contrast to Kitt in every way. A tiny brunette with a petite, lush figure, she was exquisitely made up to emphasize her natural prettiness and yet there was a cool, look-but-don't-touch challenge to her poise as she greeted Rocky. It was reinforced by her ironic manner of speaking. Rocky sensed at once an anti-male hostility that he'd encountered before in attractive women who'd been disappointed by men. It had always seemed inconsistent to him that those women continued to make themselves desirable in a man's eyes and then resented the man's natural male response. By the time the evening was over, he was fairly certain his insight into her personality was sound, but there had been glimpses into the underlying warmth and wry intelligence that explained Bob and

Kitt's devotion to her. Rocky would have had to be blind not to notice that Bob Bailey's feelings went much deeper than friendship. The man was nuts about her.

The evening went quickly and pleasantly for Rocky. Andy was allowed to come into the den and visit with the grownups after he had finished his dinner. During this time some talk about football was unavoidable, but when the boy had been dispatched to his room, Rocky made a point of getting the subject off on something else. He'd decided in advance that he didn't want to sit around and talk about football tonight. Accidentally he hit upon the perfect topic.

"I understand that you were in on the original Magic Broom business yourself," he remarked to Bob.

The comment was like the opening line to an entertaining stage show. Bob, Ellen and Kitt recounted the whole story of how they'd formed the cleaning business in their senior year of college to earn money for a post-graduation trip around the country, and then they told highlights about the trip itself. They interrupted each other to take over the narrative, to differ on a detail or to prompt the remembrance of some hilarious anecdote. If they hadn't been such marked individualists, each with his or her own distinctive brand of humor, the story might have been boring to an outsider, but Rocky wasn't bored at all. He sat back, relaxed and amused and more than a little envious.

"I'd like to have been along on that trip myself," he mused with utter honesty when the story was finished.

Bob made a hooting sound. "Who're you kidding, man? Your first year out of college you were probably earning your first million in the pros, right?" The remark wasn't rude now that the polite barriers had been lowered. Rocky interpreted the openness as it was intended: an indication of acceptance.

"I wasn't earning a million," he denied, "but you're right—I was headed straight from college into pro football." His next remark, again directed to Bob, hit shrewdly on target as he second-guessed what was in the other man's mind. "I did graduate, too, in case you're wondering. I have a degree in business administration with a minor in mathematics."

Bob immediately held up both hands to ward off imaginary bullets. "Don't shoot! Don't shoot!" he implored and then grinned a more candid admission. "You can't blame me, can you? The least a guy like you can do to make the rest of us male mortals feel better is admit that you're a little dumb."

Rocky was struck again with admiration for the smaller man's honesty. It called for a similar candor. "I don't think 'dumb' is the right word. The statistics are hard to argue with, though. I heard recently that slightly over seventy percent of the players in the pro league don't earn college degrees. There are reasons other than lack of intelligence, of course. Big conference college football takes an enormous amount of time and concentration and energy."

The two men continued the discussion as they got up and went out to put on the steaks. Ellen and Kitt stayed behind in the den since the salad was already made and in the refrigerator and the table in the kitchen, where they would eat, was already set informally with bright-colored placemats, stainless steel flatware and paper napkins. They weren't putting on any show of elegance for Rocky tonight but were giving him a sample of their casual enjoyment of life.

"What do you think, Ellen?" Kitt asked with a contented sigh. "Isn't he gorgeous?"

"He is that," Ellen admitted. "He seems very nice," she added. "You do realize, though, that you look at him like he's some male model and you'd like nothing better than to rip his clothes off. Honestly, Kitt, I'm surprised you don't embarrass the man! Probably he's used to that kind of reaction from women."

Kitt made a feral sound. "I would like to rip his clothes off, Ellen. What woman wouldn't?" She giggled at her friend's efforts to look disapproving. "I think he does get a little uncomfortable." Her sigh this time was more of the wistful variety. "I know he likes me, Ellen, but I'm probably not his type."

"You're right about one thing, Kitt. He does like you," Ellen mused. "That's pretty obvious from the way he looks at you." She was about to say more, but obviously thought better of it and got up briskly from her chair. "I'd better check on Andy and make sure he's in bed by now."

"Ellen!" Kitt wailed disconsolately. "You don't think I'm Rocky's type, do you? You think he likes me as a person but doesn't find me sexy at all. You won't come out and say it because you know the truth will hurt like the dickens!"

Ellen's large brown eyes were soft with understanding as they met Kitt's despairing gray gaze. "I don't know, Kitt," she said with quiet reluctance. "I just really don't know. But you have to keep in mind that I've been one of the world's prize fools in judging men myself. You're just going to have to let Rocky answer that question for himself."

Kitt was left alone in the den with this new feminine anxiety for only a minute or two before the two men returned and shortly thereafter, Ellen. Lively conversation quickly resumed and suffered only a short lull during the early portion of the meal when they all paid some appreciative attention to the thick steaks Rocky had brought.

Kitt looked up to find him watching her with amused interest. "I see you do like steak, even though it's cooked at home," he remarked teasingly.

She nodded and chewed gustily at the same.

"Anything cooked on the grill comes under the same heading as fast food," she explained after she'd swallowed.

"I see," he said as though making a note of her revelation for future reference.

Warm pleasure seeped through Kitt. The exchange seemed to go far beyond the words, which were actually of little consequence. Rocky's teasing attention to her eating habits made her feel unique and interesting in his eyes. Gone for the moment were any worries about whether or not he found her sexually desirable.

When Rocky left at eleven-thirty, the parting remarks were all sincere. He had genuinely enjoyed meeting Ellen and Bob and looked forward to seeing them again. They reciprocated his sentiments.

Kitt walked with him to the door, but this time she opened it and followed him outside. "I've got to see that car up closer," she declared.

"You can look but be sure and don't touch it," Rocky warned lightly. "I don't want fingerprints. Say, I really enjoyed this tonight," he added in a more serious vein. "I like your friends."

"They like you, too," she assured him and then offered no further word on the subject. With her hands thrust out behind her in an exaggerated heeding of his warning, she examined the black Mustang from front to back, while Rocky stood near the driver's door, watching her with a grin.

"Nice car, eh?" he prompted.

"It is a nice car." She dropped her hands and her pose and came up close to him. "I had a good time tonight. I'm glad Bob and Ellen liked you and you liked them. Good luck Sunday. I'll be watching the game."

Rocky had little advance warning of her intention. Before he knew what was happening, she had put her arms up casually around his neck and uptilted her face in the confident expectation of a good-night kiss. Feeling his heart suddenly pick up its tempo, he kissed her quickly on the mouth and then gathered her close for a hug that served two purposes. It gave him the pleasure of feeling her in his arms and allowed him the couple of seconds he needed to muster his defenses.

"Good night, Kitt." He released her and took a step back, reaching for the door handle. "Let's get together for some fast food next week, okay?" She had to move farther away to avoid the opening door.

"Sounds good," Kitt managed to get out, still feeling the power in his arms and shoulders as he'd squeezed her close against him, the contact limited to their upper torsos. The little peck of a kiss had been disappointingly swift, but she had finally felt his mouth on hers and was filled with an ache for a harder, lingering kiss.

He lowered himself into the bucket seat, slammed the door and rolled down the window with one hand while he started the engine with the other.

"Maybe Monday night, if I'm not in too bad a shape."

The wheels were beginning to roll backward on the last word. Kitt just waved and smiled and stood there watching him back out of the driveway and accelerate forward along the street.

"Sure thing, Rocky," she murmured with a wistful sigh. "Maybe Monday night . . ."

She turned and trudged slowly back toward the house. Instead of joining Ellen and Bob in the den, she went into the kitchen and started cleaning up the mess from dinner. Even though she was making an effort to be quiet, Ellen must have heard her because she came out to the kitchen and subjected Kitt to a closely questioning look.

"Well?" The inquiry was halfhearted. Ellen could read for herself the droop of the strong, slender shoulders, the mechanical movements of the usually quick, eager hands.

"I'm afraid we both were right, Ellen. I'm just not his type."

"No good-night kiss, I take it."

Kitt filled the soap compartment of the dishwasher and then closed the door. Deftly she set the knob and then answered Ellen over the sound of rushing water.

"Just a little one, and it wasn't really his idea. I sort of forced him into it. He jumped into his car and drove off so fast you'd have thought I attacked him or something." Kitt glumly crossed her arms across her chest. "He wants me to come over Monday night, if he's up to it after the game Sunday."

Ellen's face lost most of its sympathy. "The man is leaving here tomorrow morning for Los Angeles, playing ball there Sunday, coming back here probably on Monday morning and wants to see you Monday night, and you're moping around?" She made a disparaging motion with one hand.

Kitt unfolded her arms, spread them wide and braced her hands on the counter on either side of her, a long-limbed tragic figure.

"I'm probably the only woman in the whole world he'd even think of inviting over on a Monday night," she said morosely. "You haven't seen him on a Monday night. I have. He told me himself the sexiest woman in the world would have a hard time getting him to seduce her on a Monday night. What kind of a chance do you think that gives me?"

"He told you that?"

"He sure did. The first time he invited me over to his place, immediately after I'd walked in on him naked in his bathtub."

"At that point the poor man was probably fearful of rape. I've seen the way you look at him with his clothes on."

Grudging humor lit the gloomy gray eyes and then initiated the beginnings of a smile at the corners of Kitt's mouth. The two women stood there and looked at each other, grins breaking out over their faces. Next came muffled snickers that grew into loud howls of laughter that brought a curious Bob scurrying from the den.

"What's so funny?" he wanted to know.

"Just woman talk," Ellen managed to get out.

He looked from one to the other. "Sounds more like it was 'man' talk to me," he conjectured shrewdly.

That brought on a fresh flurry of chuckles by way of admission. Then Kitt shooed them both out of the kitchen and finished cleaning it up in short order, humming a cheerful little tune while she tried to decide what kind of fast food she'd like on Monday night.

Maybe they'd have chicken again....

Chapter Nine

On Sunday the Revelers surprised everybody, including their highly favored opponents, when they lost by only one point. The game was one of the most exciting of the season, the TV commentators declared. Rocky Players had been superb. He was always a fine football player, one of the best running backs ever to play the game, but today the commentators had been reminded of Players that first year he broke into pro football and was everybody's unanimous choice for outstanding rookie. His physical and mental toughness had made him awesome. No defense could stop him. He would go around, through or over the solid wall of his opponents.

Kitt thrilled to every praise of Rocky. She was tuned into a sports talk program that evening when Rocky called from Los Angeles. He didn't bother to identify himself.

"Hi. See the game?" The question was purely rhetorical. It was the first time Kitt had ever heard that undertone of exultation.

"Did I see the game! Rocky, you were unbelievable! I was so proud of you. The commentators couldn't talk about anybody else the whole game."

"I'll bet. They were probably making predictions about how many more years I can hold up at this pace." His cynicism was cheerfully matter-of-fact, not bitter.

"They say the same sort about a first-year player, though," Kitt pointed out reasonably. "It's just all a part of the hype to build a player up and then question whether he can ever play that well again. You should be used to that by now."

"You're right, I should be," Rocky agreed, taking pleasure in her honesty and her positive outlook. It wouldn't even occur to her to deny the discussion of his age on the air that day, even while he played as high a level of football as any younger man could have played. But it also wouldn't be possible for her to shrug aside the negativism of those remarks unless she really felt that way.

"They said you're at your peak, Rocky. You've kept yourself in tremendous physical condition and whatever you might have lost in years is more than made up by experience." There was the slightest pause. "They also said nature gave you the perfect body for a running back along with lightning reflexes." Kitt was tempted to add her own personal agreement to the "perfect body" sentiment, but there was the inhibiting memory of his reaction Friday night when she forced him into a good-night kiss. She didn't want to make him uneasy and hurry the long-distance conversation to an end.

The unvoiced compliment brought a smile to Rocky's lips and stirred a familiar pleasure in a body that would be stiff and sore tomorrow, despite all the expert ministrations of a trainer. It wouldn't be a pretty sight tomorrow night with all the bruises, that was for sure, but then he had no intentions of taking his clothes off for her. He could enjoy her company and she could look him over to her heart's content, and they both would be quite safe from any risk that he would get turned on and take advantage of her. What he felt for her was too new and valuable to endanger with sex.

"How about tomorrow night? You want to come over to my place?" The invitation was casual but not indifferent. He wanted her to accept, expected her to accept. When she did, without any hesitation or female dissembling, he was amazed at how downright good he felt.

"Of course, if you feel up to having me over. How about fried chicken? I can stop on my way and pick some up."

"Sounds good. After all, it's Monday, right?"

"Right." A pause. "I haven't had any for a while, either."

"Not since the night you left me with the mess to clean up and went off hoping I'd choke myself on a chicken bone?"

"No, not since then. I'll clean up this time."

"That's a deal. I'll pay this time. Actually, I don't mind helping you clean up, either, but I'd probably just get in your way, like Andy." Rocky's chuckle was the sound of a happy man. "He explained that night I brought the pizza over that you just let him help you pick up his toys to keep him from being 'irresponsible,' his word, I swear."

"That little character! He's too smart for his own britches."

The fondness in her voice awakened the familiar envy in Rocky's breast, only now it was stronger than before. He was seized by an absurdly competitive urge and wanted to say something to wipe Andy out of her thoughts completely and take full possession of them for himself. The temptation was there to tell her something glib and flattering: *I played for you today, sweetheart.* He'd said things like that to other women many times. But he couldn't say it to Kitt. The irony of it, too, was that he had thought of her during the game today, not during the actual plays, of course, when total concentration on time and place was required. Still, there had been the knowledge somewhere in the background of his consciousness the whole time that she was back in Mandeville, watching the game, plunging herself into every play, shouting at the screen, slapping her thighs, groaning her disappointment and hooting her approval. In a way, he thought perhaps he *had* played for her today.

"Tell Andy hello for me," he told her.

"I'll do that. He'll be tickled." Kitt read the signal that he was about to close the long-distance conversation and knew it was silly to feel such poignant regret at breaking the connection when she'd see him tomorrow night. It wouldn't do to blurt out her feelings, when he obviously enjoyed their relationship on a light, friendly level.

"Thanks for calling. Guess you're probably invited to some big party with a lot of movie stars tonight, huh?"

Rocky heard the wistfulness but gave it the logical and wrong interpretation. "There are several parties, but I'll probably pass on all of them tonight. Movie stars off the screen are like football players out of their uniforms, just people you either like or you don't like." There had been a time when he hadn't been so blasé about being in the company of film and television celebrities, of course, but that was many parties ago. Right now he'd rather stay right where he was and talk to Kitt long-distance on the telephone.

Which was exactly what he did. He told her about some of the big parties he'd attended in the past and his impressions of big stars he'd met. She was full of curious questions and spontaneous reactions that amused and delighted him. When he finally hung up the phone more than an hour later, he had that same revitalized feeling he always had after he'd been in contact with her. As he thought of boarding the plane the next morning and flying home to New Orleans, there was a new element of anticipation. Rocky really felt like he was going home. It was a warm, good feeling.

Kitt hung up in a state of mixed happiness and despair. "I must seem so ordinary to him!" she lamented to Ellen later that evening, after she'd given a recounting of the conversation. "He lives in a whole different world from you and me!"

"That's right," Ellen agreed. "He can afford to spend a fortune talking long-distance to an ordinary, dull person and never miss the money. Obviously, he just enjoys being bored. That's the only explanation I can give."

The droll irony drew a grateful smile from Kitt. "We must have talked at least an hour and a half. That is pretty expensive, isn't it?"

"Damned right it's expensive. And you said he's going to pay for the dinner tomorrow night, too, didn't you?"

The two women smiled at each other, sharing an appreciation of their mutual support and friendship that they didn't need to voice and cause each other embarrassment.

"I think you enjoy food more than anyone I've ever known before," Rocky observed the next evening when they were seated at the table eating. It sounded like a compliment.

Kitt was too happy to be genuinely apologetic as she disparaged her table manners. "I eat like a pig, don't I? Just say 'Down, Fido' every now and then. That's what Bob and Ellen do when I start gobbling everything in sight."

"No, I like it. Food tastes better when I'm eating with you."

It was hardly the equivalent of "You look ravishing tonight, my dear," but the expression in Rocky's dark eyes was warmly approving, and Kitt had never known how to accept romantic compliments from men, anyway. Rocky was telling her that he liked her the way she was. That was the kind of compliment she could deal with.

There wasn't a single awkward moment during the meal, not even a brief lapse in conversation when either of them was conscious of having to think of something to say. Kitt might have been coming over to his place on a regular basis for the past two years, so comfortable were they with each other's company. They ate nearly all the food she'd brought, enough for the two of them and at least one more healthy eater. Kitt pumped him about Los Angeles and the game. He answered all her questions, revealing a recall of every single play that amazed her. There was no false modesty on his part. He gave himself credit where it was due. He had played some outstanding football, knew it and was pleased.

"I don't know how many more games like that I've got left in me," he mused, pushing back from the table.

Rubbing his stomach, he grinned at her. "Many meals like this one, and I'll be too chubby to run."

Kitt's look was scolding. "You're sounding like those announcers now."

"Are they predicting I'll get fat if I eat too much fried chicken, too? How did they know?"

"*Silly!* I meant the first part." Her expression grew serious. "Do you worry about losing it, Rocky? This special genius for the game or gift or whatever the sports people all call it."

Rocky nodded. "Sure do. Of course, I don't really buy the genius and gift notion. There's some inherent ability, but mostly it's years of training and hard work and determination that make a successful athlete. I guess it's the mental part of the game that can really fall apart, more so than the physical. I'm just hoping I can keep the spark alive this year and two more. After that my contract with the Revelers will be up. I'll be thirty-five, and it'll be time to hang up the helmet."

Kitt got up and started clearing the table. "You can play that long for sure," she declared with utter confidence. When Rocky started to get up, she reached over and gave his shoulder a little downward push. "Just stay where you are. Remember, I'm cleaning; you're paying."

"I was just getting up to get my wallet," Rocky teased her, settling contentedly in his chair.

"Don't worry. I won't leave without collecting. I thought maybe you'd like some coffee."

"I'd love some coffee. You think that might keep me awake a little longer or what?"

"You're a smart man—for a football player."

His laughter affected Kitt as it always did, making her feel that place and time had hit upon some perfect partnership. She was glad to be where she was, doing what she was doing.

Rocky enjoyed watching her as she cleared away the dishes with that effortless efficiency she had developed to an art. He was in too good a mood to give more than fleeting thought to the fact that he'd actually bared one of the most secret compartments of his soul to her a minute ago, admitting the fear of losing his football-playing ability before his contractual responsiblities ended. Her blithe refusal to believe that could happen made the possibility suddenly unlikely to him, too.

Kitt made coffee and they carried their cups over to the sofa. A pregame talk show was in progress on the TV screen, with the volume turned down low. Rocky sat sprawled sideways in the corner of the sofa, giving her his full attention and ignoring the TV set.

"What was the magic broom up to today?" he inquired. "It didn't turn up any closet-type skeletons, I hope."

Up until she started giving him a rundown on her day, Kitt thought that it had been fairly routine, but then he chuckled over her handling of a personality conflict between two of her workers, and she was inspired to entertain him further. The quick summary turned into a humorous saga with Kitt acting out parts and imitating the voices of the other people involved. Almost without realizing it, she missed the whole first quarter of the football game.

They drank second cups of coffee, but Rocky still found himself getting drowsy during the latter half of the game. It was a combination of lack of interest in the game and contentment. By stages he managed somehow to end up lying full length on the sofa with his head in Kitt's lap, facing the screen but actually not focusing upon it. With her denim-clad thigh under his cheek and a smile on his lips, he drifted off to sleep, unaware that he'd done a thorough job of destroying Kitt's ability to concentrate on the game. The intimacy might be enjoyable on a completely asexual level for him, but it wasn't for her.

With her heart quickstepping, Kitt looked longingly at the masculine length of him, within such tantalizing reach of her hands. She let herself think about touching him, imagined placing her hand on that powerful shoulder and then just taking it from there. The thought made her so weak and shivery that she had to bite her lips to assert control.

Minutes passed and she tried to concentrate on the game, but really she was concentrating on Rocky's breathing. When it was regular and deep, she leaned forward and peered down into his face to confirm that he was fast asleep. Ever so slowly she brought her fingertips to his face and caressed the hard bone structure of the cheek exposed to her view. It was as exhilarating and nerve-racking as anything forbidden she'd ever done. Lifting the fingers, she paused, waiting, her heart pounding in her chest now, but apparently she hadn't disturbed his sleep.

Emboldened, Kitt just couldn't resist availing herself of the further sensory pleasures there for the taking. Again slowly and very lightly, she settled her palm in the curve of his neck and shoulder, felt the pulsing warmth through his shirt, the hardness of muscle and sinew. Increasing the pressure ever so slightly, she moved her palm outward toward his shoulder and rested there, enjoying the solid feel of him and suffering indecision about which of the several delightful paths she would next take, his back, chest and arm all beckoning, *Come feel me..*

If she hadn't hesitated, if she'd slid her hand forward to Rocky's chest and tested his heartbeat, she would have known that he wasn't fully asleep and oblivious, after all. He'd felt the feather-soft touch of her fingertips on his face and been torn between the danger of it and the sheer pleasure. Pleasure had won and was still campaigning strongly, but he couldn't allow the exploration of his supposedly sleeping body to continue. He wasn't that strong, and he knew it. Not even on a Monday night.

"That tickles," he lied gruffly and reached up for the hand on his shoulder, feeling her tense and go still with the knowledge that she'd been discovered in the act of touching him. He brought her hand to his lips and kissed the palm, hearing her sharp little intake of breath. It stirred him more than anything else had, shattering the remaining fragments of complacency. His groan was exaggerated as he got himself upright again.

"I guess I bothered you." There was a breathless quality and not much apology in Kitt's tone. "I didn't know you were ticklish."

Rocky sat back next to her and met her gaze. The uncertainty in it was totally disarming and brought a flood of protectiveness.

"I'm not—always," he said gruffly, putting his arm around her shoulders and pulling her over so that she was leaning half on his chest. "Watch your football game." He caught both her hands and held them imprisoned in his against her lower abdomen. His cheek rested against her head, and he could smell the faint herbal scent of her shampoo.

Kitt was still and silent a long moment, her gaze directed toward the TV set, as though she were following his order. There were fates much worse than this one. She thought she could stay right here imprisoned in his arms, feeling the hard thump of his heartbeat against her back for an awfully long time. Here there was such strength and warmth and closeness that she felt a little dizzy with the goodness of it, but still not content to let things lie.

"Did it ... tickle, Rocky? When I touched you?" she asked forlornly.

Rocky sighed. "No, it didn't tickle. It felt good. Okay?"

Kitt read the rest of the answer without any trouble: *So let's just drop the subject, shall we?* During another long pause when she didn't see anything but a colorful blur on the TV screen, she honestly tried to drop it, but some subjects at some particular times just didn't drop easily.

"Then why did you say it tickled, Rocky?" For an awful second, Kitt thought she'd really blown it when Rocky sat up straighter and the hardness of his cheekbone left her head, but to her immense relief, he still held her. As much as she wished that she could see his expression right now, she didn't dare try to twist around and look up at his face.

"Kitt, it means a hell of a lot to me to have you come over here like this tonight. It meant a lot to me yesterday to know you were watching the game ... watching me. After we talked on the phone last night, I looked forward to coming home today and seeing you tonight."

There was no doubting the sincerity behind the carefully worded evasion of her question. That and his obvious desire not to hurt her brought a huge lump to Kitt's throat. She swallowed at it so hard that tears came to her eyes, but she had no intention of giving in to self-pity. It wasn't Rocky's fault that he liked her as a friend and not as a lover. She wouldn't want to make him feel bad and ruin what they had.

"I looked forward to seeing you, too, Rocky." She cleared her throat of the huskiness and blinked the mist away from her eyes. "Especially after you said it was all right to bring dinner over."

Those same magic hands the sports commentators raved about squeezed Kitt's hands hard, so that she winced against the pain even while she welcomed it.

"So what you're telling me is that this is just a free meal and a good TV set." Underneath the fake gruffness, he was clearly relieved. Releasing her hands, he slid over a small distance, ostensibly to give himself room to sprawl out more comfortably. His near arm rested along the back of the sofa, but it didn't touch her shoulders now.

"I've always liked your TV, but you never have any goodies to munch on," Kitt grumbled, purely in the spirit of cooperation.

"Just tell me what kind of goodies you like, and I'll stock up on them tomorrow," he declared.

She scowled at the screen, glad that a play was in progress. "I like things that crunch and make lots of noise—atta boy, Jericho! Great throw!" She clapped her hands and felt a little better, hearing the vigor of her own voice. The tension between her and Rocky dissipated quickly as she concentrated her attention on the last minutes of the game. After it was over, she demanded the money he owed her for the chicken, told him good-night and then left.

"I had a wonderful time," she told Ellen later on in answer to her routine-if-you-want-it-to-be-routine inquiry and then added, "He as much as told me that he likes me an awful lot."

The pensive tone might have struck someone else as odd, but Ellen understood and just nodded. Kitt showed no inclination to discuss the matter further, and Ellen didn't press. She had a lot on her mind herself. Soon she and Kitt were going to sit down and have a real heart-to-heart talk about a decision Ellen was about to make that would affect both their futures, but not tonight.

The next evening Kitt called Rocky to tell him the good news that The Magic Broom had gotten those big contracts she'd recently told him about. He seemed glad she'd called, and they ended up talking on the phone for almost two hours.

"My arm's about to fall off from holding this receiver," Kitt finally complained laughingly.

Rocky invited her to come over for dinner the next evening. He'd barbecue something on the grill if she'd agree to making a salad.

"I think I can handle that," Kitt replied promptly, liking the idea.

The next day she mulled over the question of how she could make herself physically desirable to Rocky. Obviously he already liked her personality. Perhaps she should change her hairstyle, wear exotic makeup, dress in a more feminine or sexy style? The problem was that the way she looked fit her personality because basically she liked to be comfortable and have a good time. She'd never enjoyed spending hours primping in front of a mirror or whole days shopping for clothes. But almost anything was worth a try if it could get Rocky to look at her in a different light.

It was just as well that she didn't come to any decisions, because circumstances made her late getting home that afternoon, and she had to rush to shower and change clothes. There wasn't time to blow-dry her hair, and shampooing it had been a necessity. She tied a fine ribbon around her hair, little-girl fashion, letting the sandy, wet strands hang free down her back, and wore her usual jeans, pairing them with a dove-gray velour pullover that matched her eyes.

A quick inspection of her appearance in the mirror reflected a dissatisfied expression on a fresh-scrubbed face she'd imagined transformed into various stunning looks by expert applications of makeup during the day. She knew she'd feel silly and self-conscious arriving all painted up with wet hair stringing down her back. Besides, there wasn't time. On her way she had to detour by the supermarket and pick up salad makings.

By the time she arrived at Rocky's place, her hair was partially dry and fluffing out. Not accustomed to wearing it down, she was aware of it only in an apologetic sense as she bustled past Rocky when he opened the door, her arms around her grocery bag.

"Hi, sorry I'm late. Busy day," she declared briskly, sailing past him.

"I'm glad you said something so I could recognize you," he commented in a surprised tone, following her to the kitchen. "I didn't realize you had so much hair."

Kitt wasted no time unloading her grocery bag on a section of countertop adjacent to the sink. "I had to wash it tonight and there wasn't time to dry it. I was thinking today about getting it cut. I need a big bowl." Right in the middle of this last comment, making it more noticeably extraneous, she was opening the logical cabinet and getting out the bowl she needed.

"Why would you do that?" Rocky sounded disapproving. "I like your braid." He liked everything about her looks and wasn't at all in favor of any change.

Kitt jerked her shoulders upward in a quick shrug and caused a sway in the long, fair tresses. She bounced the iceberg lettuce smartly on its axis and then plucked out the stem.

"Just for a change, I guess." She ripped the lettuce into halves, the two halves into four quarters, and then started in on the quarters. "Everybody gets tired of looking the same old way. It gets boring looking at yourself in the mirror. I could get my hair cut short in a punk hairstyle and wear glittery eye makeup. What do you think?" She was terribly conscious of the fact that he had come up close.

"I think you're making enough salad for an army." Rocky stroked one hand down the length of her hair and then took a hank of it and tugged gently. "You look fine to me just the way you are. I vote no on the haircut and the makeup."

Kitt briskly wrapped the two unshredded lettuce quarters in the original cellophane wrapper and then picked up a tomato and cucumber in one hand and turned the water on full blast with the other hand. The dousing she gave the salad vegetables made it seem that they had done something to offend her.

"I'd better go check the ribs. We're having ribs tonight. Did I mention that?"

Rocky's only answer was a swift, accusing glance from stormy gray eyes. He had only a glimpse of the combination of belligerence and hurt in an appealingly fresh face that glowed with health and natural color.

Rocky eased out an inaudible breath. "Is something wrong, Kitt?"

Kitt heard the male reluctance beneath the concern and wished that she could load her grocery bag up, go outside and come in again, starting out fresh. She hadn't meant to act stupid and emotional like this, over absolutely nothing.

"Nothing's really wrong, Rocky…well, yes, I guess you'd say something *is* wrong, but…why don't you check the ribs and let me get this salad made?" She moderated the flow of water from the sink faucet, set down the thoroughly cleansed tomato and cucumber and broke off a stalk of celery.

Rocky was relieved at this seeming return to normality and wanted nothing more than to take her suggestion. "You sure you don't want to tell me what's bothering you?"

The shake of her head played havoc with the tresses streaming down her back, causing some of them to slide forward over her shoulders. Kitt tilted her head back and shook it hard.

"This is why I wear it braided," she said irritably. "It gets in my way."

"Here, let me." Rocky stepped behind her and gently lifted the offending tresses and returned them to the luxuriant mainstream of hair that was drying more all the time and growing in mass. "You have very pretty hair." He gathered all of it in both hands at her neck. "No wonder that braid you wear is so thick." He made the heavy mane sway from side to side, then he flipped it and set off ripples, admiring the pale sheen and enjoying the feel of it.

"Do you like it better braided or hanging down like this?"

It was the odd, stifled quality of her voice more than the question itself that brought Rocky to his senses and made him realize how sensuously involved he had been, standing there, playing with her hair. He hadn't even been aware that she had stopped her salad preparations and was standing utterly still.

"I like it both ways." He freed her hair and retreated to the doorway. "I'd better check those ribs. They're probably burned to a crisp by now."

Kitt had gone back to slicing mushrooms. "I like mine a little burned," she announced in a secretive, pleased voice.

"Well, I don't."

Soon afterward she heard the sound of the sliding glass door leading out to the patio. Gazing down at the salad ample enough to feed ten, Kitt grinned.

"Well, I'll just be darned," she murmured and tilted her head far back, waggled it slowly sideways and felt the heavy swish of her hair against her back.

"I'll just be darned," she said again.

Chapter Ten

It's a good thing you like your ribs burned," Rocky grumbled, bringing in the platter of charred ribs.

"They are burned, aren't they?" Kitt found it difficult to sound sympathetic in her state of mild euphoria. "At least there's lots of salad."

Rocky couldn't maintain his irritation in the face of her good humor. Whatever had been wrong with her earlier had vanished.

"It's actually all your fault," he accused with a grudging smile. "What were you upset about, anyway?"

Kitt tried to look mysterious and ended up looking like a cat who'd finished up a sumptuous dish of cream. "I'll tell you about it later. It's not exactly good dinner conversation."

Rocky eyed the platter of ribs with a disgruntled expression. "The conversation had better be good to take our minds off the burned taste."

"The ribs aren't that burned," Kitt soothed, sitting herself down at the table.

Her air of satisfaction intrigued Rocky and made him vaguely uneasy. Somehow it, as well as her earlier display of temperament, was related to the business of cutting her hair and changing her appearance.

"Come on and sit down," Kitt urged, helping herself to the ribs. Rocky was about to comply when the telephone rang. Kitt stopped midmotion, a startled expression on her face. "Do you know, that's the first time..." she said thoughtfully, more to herself than to Rocky since he had gone over to answer the call on the extension in the living room area.

Kitt didn't even pretend not to listen in on his end of the conversation. She could tell somehow that it was a woman from the way Rocky spoke, even though he wasn't what you'd call friendly to his caller and made the conversation very brief.

"I wonder how she got this number," he mused, frowning as he returned to the table.

"Don't look at me, I didn't give it out," Kitt quipped jokingly. She took a bite from the rib she held in both hands and crunched on it while she watched Rocky made an unenthusiastic selection from the platter.

"Is that why you have an unlisted number? To keep women from calling you? Ellen said you could probably sleep with a different woman every night if you wanted to."

The rhetorical tone of the first two questions hadn't prepared Rocky for the follow-up comment. It was one of those Kitt-type conversational offerings that never failed to take him aback and amuse him. She left intriguing gaps in the continuity of her thoughts, but circled back later and filled them in.

"Ellen said that?" He took the two least charred ribs from the platter. "I'd say that's probably a slight exaggeration." He ate a bite of salad. "Hmm. This is good. Ellen doesn't like men very much, does she?"

Kitt shook her head vigorously and was suddenly reminded of her cascade of free-hanging hair again when Rocky's gaze was drawn to it. "She doesn't trust men. You know, that's the first telephone call you've ever gotten when I was here. Don't you give your number out to your friends?"

Rocky made the adjustment between Ellen's distrust of men in general and his lack of telephone calls. "I haven't made many friends here. I've been busy and there hasn't been much time." He meant to leave the matter there, but the expectant look in Kitt's eyes made him probe a little deeper into his own motivations. "I guess I haven't really been that open to making new friends. Maybe I just wanted to see what it's like spending some time alone." He shrugged to emphasize the indefiniteness of his explanation.

"I guess most of your friends, your close friends, that is, have all been football players. Probably teammates."

Rocky nodded, aware that she was honing in upon some truth in her instinctive fashion. "You're right. They have been."

"Maybe you don't want to get close to your Revelers teammates because you're planning to retire in three years. But three years can be a pretty long time."

"You might be right." Rocky judged from her tone and her expression that her thoughts were already leaping on.

"You remember that first night you invited me over, you said that most of the pro players' reputations were pretty true to life. Well, so far your reputation hasn't seemed all that true. You don't drink a lot. In fact, you hardly seem to drink at all. When you called me from Los Angeles Sunday night, you said you weren't going to any big parties you were invited to."

"I didn't go," Rocky put in. He thought he saw her direction now. "A lot of my so-called reputation goes back to the first couple of years I played pro ball. I was kind of a hell-raiser, along with some of my teammates. But football players grow up, like everybody else."

She didn't respond to his placating tone but met his gaze thoughtfully. Rocky took a bite of salad, aware that she was deciding how to approach what had really been her main interest in his media reputation from the beginning: his purportedly numerous affairs with women. He was utterly unprepared for the drastic personal turn of the conversation.

"I'm not a virgin, you know. You did know that?"

Rocky choked on his bite of salad, managed to swallow it and then dropped his fork and sat back, abandoning the danger of any further efforts at eating.

"What does that have to do with anything?" But he knew, and so did she. "This is the conversation we were to have later, not over dinner, isn't it?"

She nodded, her expression rueful. "I didn't mean for us to have it now. It just kind of got started, on its own."

"Kitt, this is damned awkward—what do you expect me to say—" Rocky threw his napkin down on his plate.

"I'm sorry, Rocky. It's just that I think you ought to try to look at things from my point of view, too."

He stared at her, irritated and yet fascinated in spite of himself to hear what she would say next. "Okay, I'm listening. I guess this all has something to do with your wanting to cut your hair and wear punk makeup."

She nodded again, sending waves through the canopy of hair covering her shoulders. The warmth and heaviness of it gave her much-needed courage, but she still had to fall back on her old standby in tough emotional situations: humor.

"I don't guess it's even occurred to you what a blow it is to a woman's ego to spend evening after evening with a man who's known for all his affairs with women and have him treat her like a sister or a nun or something. I know I'm not sexy and beautiful, but I'm not *that* bad, am I?" She held her arms wide and made a production of looking down at herself. When her hair slid forward, forming a screen, she flipped it back impatiently. "It's the same old story. Always a good friend of the big jocks, but never the date at the Homecoming Dance. The whole problem started when I couldn't hold up a strapless dress in high school. And I guess I still can't."

She'd have done better not to try for the light treatment, since it wasn't successful and struck a false note. Rocky wasn't in the least amused.

"It's the same old story, all right," he said grimly and got up from the table. Jamming both hands into his jeans pockets, he took several steps away and stopped, with his back to Kitt. "Speaking of seeing things from someone else's point of view, did it ever occur to you that I might be a little tired of having women treat me like Secretariat, just a stud to be trotted out of the barn? Frankly, I expected something different from you." Contempt was underlaid with genuine disappointment and a tinge of defensiveness that made Kitt think that all was not lost.

Her deep sigh was audible in the charged atmosphere of the room. "I'm sorry," she said miserably. "I guess I should have kept my big mouth shut. I guess I'm just like all the other women who pester you, like that one on the phone tonight. You know, I saw Secretariat one time, at the farm in Kentucky where he lives. He's really a gorgeous animal.''

She saw a jerky movement in Rocky's back, heard a muffled sound and flinched involuntarily when he wheeled around. Her eyes widened with surprise at the expression on his face. He didn't look angry or contemptuous, as she'd expected him to look, but incredulous as he searched her face and then grudgingly amused.

''You are really impossible, did you know that?'' he said, slowly shaking his head. ''Secretariat's a gorgeous animal.'' The last was muttered under his breath as he came back to the table and sat down.

''Impossible'' sounded like another of those left-handed compliments to Kitt, but she was relieved that he wasn't angry. The way he was looking at her made her extremely nervous, though.

''I guess I've spoiled everything, now, haven't I? Bringing things out in the open this way just makes both of us self-conscious. You'll probably feel like you have to come on to me sexually now, and I'll—''

''You'll probably just keep talking, whatever happens,'' Rocky cut in. ''Do I get a chance to speak, or what?''

''Sure.'' She flipped her hair back again and waited anxiously.

''Number one, there's nothing wrong with the way you look. For the record, I like you just the way you are.'' Kitt sat stock-still while his gaze moved over all of her that was visible, including the bosom that wouldn't hold up a strapless gown. Her lips parted and she drew in her breath when he leaned over and lightly stroked his fingers along a sandy tress of hair. "I like your hair like this, and I like it in the braid down your back, too. I like your long arms and legs, your hands—" He reached for one of the latter, and she numbly gave it to him and watched in rapt suspense as he examined it with apparently the greatest interest, squeezed it and then held it while he continued.

"I wouldn't like to see you change anything about your appearance any more than I'd like to see you change your personality. My not coming on to you sexually was something mental on my part, not physical. I guess it was pretty stupid of me not to realize that you might feel—" he frowned, searching for the right word "—slighted."

Kitt visibly pondered his words, her face doubtful. "I don't understand what you mean when you say it was mental. A man and a woman are either attracted to each other, or they aren't, especially when they get to be our age. We're not a couple of high school kids, and this is an age of sexual liberation. A man doesn't have to feel guilty about not marrying a woman he's been to bed with."

Rocky looked uncomfortable with her words. "Maybe I do have a moral hangup and unconsciously put you in a nice girl category," he said skeptically. "I just don't know. It was just a strong instinct not to let sex mess up a relationship I could see I was going to enjoy. Could we just leave it at that for now?"

"I guess we could." Kitt plainly was reluctant to drop the subject. Her glance took in the table with the uneaten remains of their dinner and then swept around the room before it came back to him. "What now?"

Her heart started to pound as he got up slowly from the table and drew her to her feet. They stood facing each other, their bodies not quite touching except for the clasped hands. The thought widening her gray eyes brought a smile to Rocky's lips.

"Why don't I take you for a ride in my fast car?" he suggested, releasing her hand and smoothing her hair back over her shoulders.

"Sure, sounds like a good idea," she said, sounding mesmerized. Her eyes held his as he framed her face in both hands and started bending his head to hers.

"You really don't have to do this," she murmured. "I don't want you to—just for me...." She closed her eyes on the last word and left her lips parted.

"Okay, I won't—just for you."

The low, amused words were spoken tantalizingly close to her lips. Then what Kitt had wanted for untold centuries, since that first time she'd met Rocky Players in person a few weeks ago, finally happened. This was no peck on the forehead or the lips, but a real kiss, one that was unhurried and exploratory, a first-time happening between her lips and his, not a practiced possession.

With the first touch of his mouth on hers, Kitt's concerns about his reasons for kissing her pulled a vanishing act. With a soft little moan of surrender, she slipped her arms up around his neck and hung on for dear life. It wouldn't have surprised her in the least if music had begun to play or bells to toll in the background, because this was cinema stuff, watery knees, pounding heart, the whole bit. His lips were firm, as she'd known they would be, searching and warm and playful at first, then more aggressive, more demanding.

At first Kitt was a receptacle of purest, deepening pleasure with a boundless capacity. Her only purpose in life was to stand there and be filled. This delicious patience deserted her, though, when the pressure of his mouth grew harder and his tongue plunged them into devastating intimacy. Pleasure took on a more tempestuous nature that brought sounds to her throat, and she kissed him back and pressed herself against him so that he had to close his arms around her to keep his balance.

Then there was added bliss as she felt herself encompassed in his strength and the full length of her body was stamped with the male imprint of his body. Kitt knew at last what all the romantic hoopla was about. This was the subject matter of every love song ever written. This was the poignant emotion behind those swelling finales of love stories in the movies. She hadn't ever believed in any of it before, but now she knew for herself that it was real, with Rocky. It was true. It was wonderful....

When Rocky brought the kiss to an end, that was just right, too. Not abrupt and not too gradual, but giving her enough time to descend from the clouds. Still, she was very much under the spell of the kiss and mesmerized with the wonder of her discovery.

"That was really unbelievable...." she murmured, looking into his eyes, her arms still tight around his neck. She sighed dreamily. "Just unbelievable...."

Rocky studied her enraptured expression without any show of approval. He loosened his arms, reached up behind his neck for Kitt's hands and held them as he took a half-step backward.

"Glad you liked it. I liked it, too."

Kitt held on tight to his hands while she got her foothold on reality again, adjusting to the fact that Rocky's feet had probably been planted solidly on the earth for the duration of the kiss. It hadn't affected him the way it had affected her, but then he was a man, and not just any man, but one with lots of experience making love to women. She felt no sense of embarrassment, and her natural instinct was to share her feelings with him.

"Rocky, that was just like a love scene in a movie, I swear—"

"I don't want to hear about it, Kitt. I was there, too, remember?" His interruption was curt and shattered her lovely aftermath.

"I'm sorry. I just wanted to tell you...." she mumbled, tugging her hands to free them.

He let one of her hands go and kept the other one. "So why don't we take that ride now, okay?"

She shrugged defensively. "Okay. I'm just sorry you're upset with me. I wish you'd tell me why."

"Come on. Let's go." He forbade her with his grim expression and with the terseness of his words to pursue the subject. Kitt was intimidated into obeying, at least for the time being.

She had looked forward to the first time he would take her for a ride in his adolescent dream car, which had served as a stimulus to conversation and been a handy vehicle for letting him lower his guard with her. Now what should have been an event was spoiled by the constraint between them. Kitt still made a valiant attempt at salvaging the situation.

"Hmm, smell that red leather," she declared when she settled into the bucket seat on the passenger's side.

"Fasten your seat belt" was Rocky's brief response. She wondered if that was a dire warning when he backed out of the garage with a great surge of engine power that snapped her head, but then he headed toward Causeway Boulevard at a more sedate pace.

"Oh, we're going to New Orleans," she said with mild interest when he pulled across the two northbound lanes at the boulevard intersection and took a sharp left turn toward the causeway tollgates. Rocky didn't make any reply until after he'd stopped at one of the gates, paid the one-dollar toll and then accelerated through the progression of gears with brisk precision.

"Some people don't like driving the causeway on a regular basis. They find it monotonous and boring. I find it soothing, especially at night. Twenty-four miles of straight highway with just the sky overhead and the lake on both sides. There's nothing to do but sit back, hold on to the wheel and think." He didn't sound hostile anymore, but he was still tense.

Kitt thought there was probably a pointed message there for her just to sit quietly and hold her tongue. She folded her hands in her lap in an attitude of patience and nibbled at her bottom lip to combat the frustration of silence. There was so much to say, darn it! She'd never been one to keep everything all bottled up inside her.

"You and Ellen are very close, aren't you?"

Rocky's question wasn't exactly rhetorical. It required a reply, but nothing more than the simplest affirmative.

"Yes, we are." Kitt managed only with the greatest effort not to append her gut reaction to his apparently irrelevant choice of subject: *So what does my friendship with Ellen have to do with you and me?*

"I gather that you confide in her, talk things over with her, even very personal things."

Kitt vented her impatience in an audible sigh. "Ellen and I can talk to each other about anything. We've known each other practically forever. I don't see—"

"You've known Bob a long time, too, and you're around him a lot. You probably feel comfortable telling him almost anything."

Rocky's air of iron determination intrigued Kitt as much as his purpose eluded her. She felt like a two-year-old being propelled along to some unknown destination by a stern adult, who wouldn't be deterred by any amount of kicking and complaining.

"Bob and I go way back. In high school, he referred to himself as my mascot—"

"How much have you told Ellen and Bob about you and me?" The interruption was a firm tug on the hand. *Sorry, little girl, we don't wander off in that direction.*

"What do you mean?" Instinct bade Kitt to drag her feet and gain a little time.

"I mean exactly what I said."

"This is silly. Well, naturally I told them about the Sunday night you walked in on me in your condo, when I was supposed to be cleaning it and was watching TV instead. And I also told them about the afternoon *I* walked in on you in your bathroom. Is that what you mean?"

"With your knack for storytelling, I'm sure your friends were highly entertained. What else?"

Kitt stared at him a little resentfully. The storytelling remark smacked of criticism, and she wished he would go ahead and make his point, whatever it was. "There hasn't been that much else to tell," she said crossly.

His gaze probed hers in the semidarkness, and suddenly she knew they had reached the "unknown destination." Kitt couldn't believe she had been so obtuse not to see his point from the beginning.

"Did you discuss with Ellen and Bob the fact that there wasn't much to tell?"

Kitt's silence proclaimed her guilty before her qualified defense served as a confession of her sin.

"Not with Bob. Only with Ellen."

Rocky held the wheel steadily with both hands and looked ahead into the uncompromising straightness of the two-lane span opened up by his headlights. His attitude was plainly of the just-as-I-expected variety, but never had a man looked any less pleased with being right.

Kitt felt awful. She'd let him down without meaning to, and there was nothing she could to do to undo the damage. Before now, she hadn't stopped to think that her openness with Ellen might be a violation of Rocky's privacy.

"I'm sorry if that embarrasses you, and I can see that it does," she said contritely. "Ellen and I are just really close friends. We share almost everything. Actually, I guess I tell her more about my feelings than she tells me about hers. It helps me somehow to say things out loud. Good feelings are even better, and bad feelings don't seem to hurt so much. I'm sorry." She sighed. "I guess I'm just not a private person." It was a lament, an admission that her tendency to verbalize feelings was a serious flaw in her character, but one she probably couldn't change.

Rocky took his eyes from the road long enough to glance over at her and verify her total dejection. The moment was a delicate one for him because he was struck by the tragicomic element in the scene. Kitt was so totally wrong for a villain's role and guileless of any awareness that she might be overplaying it. Tenderness washed away most of Rocky's irritation and hurt pride.

"At any rate, it's not the end of the world," he said, reaching over to give her clasped hands a squeeze. He disengaged her left hand and carried it over to his thigh, where he smoothed it out and covered it with his hand.

"It's not?" Kitt wasn't about to argue. She was instantly cheered by his overture and ready to drop the whole thing, if he was. The delightful situation her hand was finding itself in was of far more interest to her than talking about what couldn't be changed. It had no more than settled on his hard muscled thigh and curved to its contour in a custom fit than it wanted to wander.

Rocky had practiced, quick reflexes and clamped his hand down harder when she made her first testing movement, but he was too slow to cut off some basic male responses she'd already triggered. The glance they exchanged cleared away the old tension and replaced it with a new stimulating variety.

"Ticklish?" Kitt inquired with puckish humor.

"That all depends."

"On what?"

"On how many people you intend to tell about it."

Kitt curled her hand around and linked her fingers with Rocky's. "I promise that from now on I won't tell anybody anything that happens between you and me, unless you say it's okay. There's just one condition."

They exchanged another quick, penetrating glance, both of them startled by the "till death do us part" fervor that had crept into Kitt's voice quite of its own accord.

"What condition?"

Kitt totally empathized with his caution and hastened to reassure him with an explanation, only to get bogged down in awkwardness. "I just mean that the only way I'll be able to keep my promise is if you'll let me tell you the way I feel about . . . you know, certain things at certain times. Otherwise, I might just bust wide open. Once a blabbermouth, always a blabbermouth."

Rocky was reassured by her runaway panic more than anything else. He was also amused and titillated at the prospect of being Kitt's lover-confidante. One thing he could depend on. Making love to her was going to be different from making love to any other woman because so far doing anything with Kitt was different from doing it with anyone else, sometimes disconcertingly different, sometimes irritatingly different, often delightfully different, but *different*.

"Okay," he told her, and apparently it was answer enough.

Kitt rubbed her knuckles against his thigh.

"So, does this tickle or not?"

In answer to her question, he brought her hand to his crotch, where his jeans definitely fit too tight for comfort.

"Oh," she said in an awed, interested voice, but kept her hand very still. "It's a long way across and back to Mandeville, isn't it?"

"Yes, it is. And I don't know about you, but I could use something to eat." Right on cue, Rocky's stomach growled, and they both laughed.

"I'm starving," Kitt declared and then smiled over at him teasingly. "Those ribs were a little too crisp, even for me. There's a Jerrie's right over here at the end of the causeway. How does a stuffed potato sound? I'm thinking cheddar cheese and chili filling." She had to swallow at the saliva collecting in her mouth.

Rocky had actually been thinking more along the lines of a real restaurant somewhere over in the Fat City area, just across the causeway, but at the enthusiasm in her voice, he reconciled himself to Jerrie's and didn't mention the reason he usually avoided eating out at fast-food places.

"Jerrie's, it is," he said indulgently.

Kitt casually disengaged her hand from his and returned it to his thigh, where she savored the easy intimacy of touching him and enjoyed the sensation of power and speed as the racy Mustang took them through the night. Conversation was casual and effortless, skimming off in different directions. When the south toll-gates were visible up ahead, she gave his thigh a little pat and sat straighter in her bucket seat.

"Now isn't it also kind of nice," she inquired compla-cently, "to have someone to talk to?"

It took Rocky a few seconds to supply the connection for himself between her remark and his own some twenty minutes earlier, when he'd stated his pleasure in solitary drives across the causeway. That seemed much longer ago now. They'd progressed much farther than twenty-four miles in their relationship. He picked up her hand and carried it to his lips.

"Sometimes it is kind of nice," he agreed, his smile carrying over into his voice.

Chapter Eleven

In the brightly lit Jerrie's, Rocky was immediately recognized. Kitt found all the attention highly novel at first. As Rocky's female companion, she came in for her share of curious stares. It didn't even seem so bad when the first autograph-seeker approached them, a self-conscious boy of about twelve bearing a napkin over to their table after much egging from his parents.

Rocky put down his cheeseburger and good-naturedly signed the napkin, while everybody in the chain restaurant watched. After that, it was a steady stream, made up of both sexes and almost every age group. Kitt readily discovered that the female fans were bolder and harder to discourage than were the males. The former wanted to linger and flirt. After a measuring glance at Kitt, they tended to ignore her so that she at least was able to eat her meal in comparative peace, but she didn't enjoy it very much. Rocky was lucky to get two consecutive bites without interruption.

"I'm sorry I suggested that," Kitt declared with feeling when they were back in the Mustang and pulling out of the parking lot. "Is it always like that when you go out?"

"Fast-food places are especially bad. I think the atmosphere encourages a lack of privacy."

"Imagine what a rock star has to put up with," Kitt mused.

"I'd rather not."

"You certainly are good-natured about the whole thing," she observed as he pulled up to a causeway tollgate and paid the dollar toll. When he accelerated and changed gears, she watched him, a smile of exhilaration on her face at the surge of engine power and the cool blast of air through his open window.

Rocky grinned over at her. "The getaway car."

"I was thinking that same thing," she marveled.

They settled back with the causeway ride in front of them, enveloped by a sense of peaceful leisure. Kitt reached her left hand over and reclaimed its rightful place on his thigh. Her touch was intimate but not provocative.

"I like your car," she told him in a tone so serene that it drew a questioning look. She smiled at him. "Tell me about when you were a little boy in Shreveport."

Rocky didn't speak for at least a minute, but there was nothing resistant in his silence. It would have been like resisting the natural order of things not to try to share with her his past. He was simply making the journey back in time and deciding where to begin. It seemed easier just to start at the very beginning with a description of his mother and father and then take it from there, being as honest and fair as he could.

He knew at the outset that there was a lot of pain in his childhood story, a lot of shame, a lot of resentment, a lot of guilt. What he didn't expect was to dig up so much that was humorous and good to remember. He knew it had something to do with his rapt and totally patient listener, who let him tell his own story with only now and then a comment or a question. It was as though he had taken her by the hand and was leading her up the steps of the shabby frame house in the old neighborhood and then back down them again, to the playground ringing with boyhood voices and after that a tour of the schools he'd attended. Through her eyes he saw things as they had been, and it hadn't been all bad, after all.

Almost unconsciously Rocky drove slower once he began telling her about his background and added an extra five or ten minutes. There still wasn't time to dwell on any one incident or person, but by the time the north tollgates came in view up ahead, he'd given her a good insight into his home and neighborhood environment and taken her up to his high school adolescent years.

"You know more about me now than anyone else who wasn't there," he told her. "I don't make a habit of talking about my background." He paused reflectively. "I guess I must be ashamed of it. I know I'm ashamed of what I'm about to admit. After I was drafted into pro ball and became well-known, I had invitations to go back to the old schools in Shreveport and talk at assemblies— you know, the 'return of the successful graduate' sort of thing. I've never been able to make myself do it. I don't even like to visit my mother and brothers and their families there. I don't, very often."

Kitt's pat on Rocky's thigh was reassurance that there was at least nothing wrong in honest admissions. "It's a shame you don't talk about your background," she mused. "People would find it interesting. I know I do. They'd also admire you for how far you've come. You were lucky, though, weren't you, to have a mother like yours and also to have some of the teachers and coaches that saw so much potential in you and steered you right when you were heading off in a wrong direction."

Rocky covered her hand with his on his thigh. "You're right there. I was lucky. Damned lucky." He felt damned lucky at the moment, too, to have her sitting there next to him. He felt lucky... and yet deeply uneasy now that they were across the causeway and would soon be pulling up at his condo. His reservations about sexual involvement with her were back full force, but he knew he probably would make love to her tonight. The idea excited him even as it filled him with an undefined fear. It was like dreams he'd had of hurtling along full speed in his precious Mustang, totally out of control, endangering himself, the car and anybody else who was unfortunate enough to be in his path. It was exhilarating and scary as hell.

Kitt felt his tension as they drove along the residential streets in Mariner's Village on the way to his condo. She thought ahead to arriving there, going inside with him, and her heart began to beat faster.

"I'm getting nervous," she told him as he pulled into his driveway and opened the garage door with a remote control.

Rocky looked over at her. "So am I," he said, shifting into low gear. She drew her breath in with a soft gasp as he accelerated forward so fast that she expected them to drive right through the garage, but before that happened he braked sharply and brought the Mustang to a safe stop, exactly where it'd been before.

It was suddenly very quiet with the engine dead. The sound of Kitt's sigh of relief that they hadn't crashed was loud and so was the click of her seat belt as she unfastened it. She wasn't sure whether she could actually hear her own heartbeat or whether she was just feeling it pounding in her breast.

"You should have warned me about your Batman and Robin routine," she declared in a breathy voice. "Remember how they always zoomed into the secret garage with the Batmobile and closed the door behind them? You ought to feel my poor heart. I swear it's running away a mile a minute." She put her hand over her heart and took in a deep breath as she looked over at Rocky. There wasn't much to read on his face, but she got a closer view of it as he leaned over toward her.

Deliberately he picked up the hand on her breast, carried it to his own chest and deposited it there, then brought his hand back to the space he'd cleared, only he wasn't just checking out her heartbeat. He was cupping her breast, and his touch was definitely sexual. Kitt was aware now of more than a runaway heartbeat, and she knew he was, too. Through the material of her blouse, he was surely able to feel the peak of her breast contracting and hardening against his palm.

"Your heart is beating fast, too," Kitt whispered and closed her eyes as Rocky answered by bringing his lips to hers. She didn't close her lips, and it was just as well she didn't because this kiss omitted the exploratory stage and got down to basics fast. It was a kiss that blatantly admitted experience and intention. The hand on her breast squeezed and kneaded in a devastating little circle as his tongue went immediately inside her mouth and coiled around hers in a straightforward proposition that did nothing to restore a normal heartbeat, to either of them.

"Let's go inside," Rocky said in a voice that matched the abruptness with which he ended the kiss and left her with her head swirling.

Kitt obediently opened her door and was marshaling coordination back into her long limbs while Rocky got out and came around to her side. She wished he would take her into his arms and kiss her again, right there by the car, but he didn't. He opened the door leading into the kitchen and waited for her to enter ahead of him.

It seemed terribly quiet inside, too. She was suddenly filled with a strong sense of misgiving about what was happening or maybe it was the way it was happening that bothered her. For the first time, she considered the risk of what she was about to do. It wasn't the thought of forging emotional bonds that broke her out in a sweat, but something more realistic. What if she were a total disappointment to Rocky in bed, after virtually forcing him to make love to her? Thought of all the gorgeous, sexy women he'd taken to bed made her horribly self-conscious at taking off her clothes for him. He would think her breasts too small, her arms and legs too long, her body too skinny.

"Do you think we ought to clean this up?" she stopped to ask on their way toward the stairs. The dining table over near the patio sliding doors was still littered with soiled dishes and the remains of their uneaten dinner.

Rocky didn't answer, letting the eloquence of his silence bring her gaze to his, which was uncompromisingly direct. "You haven't changed your mind, have you? I thought this was what you told me earlier that you wanted." His glance over toward the table and the plate of charred ribs was a pointed reminder of the conversation they'd had there earlier, culminating in the first real man-woman kiss between them.

Kitt gnawed at her bottom lip. "But not if you don't want it, too. I was wrong to force the issue. I've already admitted that."

Rocky's eyes narrowed on her face. "Come on, Kitt. Don't play games with me. You know damned well a man *can't* make love to a woman if he doesn't *want* to. Make up your mind."

"You know what I mean," she murmured stubbornly. "Do you really want to?" Before he could answer, she turned her back to him. "This certainly isn't very romantic."

The toss of her head played havoc with the mass of fair hair streaming over her shoulders and down her back. It brought back to Rocky her uncharacteristic display of temperament at the very outset of this evening. He understood now that it had been provoked by a feminine need for reassurance, and he supposed the very same need was behind this present behavior. The impulse to go to her and soothe away any self-doubts was undermined by his own ambivalence about taking her to bed. She had forced the issue of sex against all his better judgment and now she apparently wanted him to seduce her.

"You haven't mentioned before that you wanted romance, Kitt. I thought you just wanted raw, primitive sex with a pro football player. That's what most women want. They want to check out Rocky Players's equipment and see if sex is any better with a super jock than with an ordinary guy." Rocky saw her shoulders stiffen under the heavy mantle of hair and felt like a super jerk. He prepared himself for anger, hurt pride, possibly even a physical attack and thus was utterly unprepared for her true reaction, which he should have known would be different from any other woman's.

Kitt turned around, guilt written all over her face. "But that was before I got to know you," she said defensively. "Now you're more than just a famous football player. You're a person I like a lot. And I definitely don't want romance. One of the things I really like about you is that you don't say phony things that we both would know weren't true. I just got cold feet, that's all." Her smile was tentative and coaxing. "Maybe we should just forget the whole thing for now and clean up the dishes, okay?"

By now Rocky's initial surprise and relief had changed to irritation, both at her frank admission and at being caught so offguard.

"Maybe we'll forget the whole thing, *period*," he said curtly.

Kitt sighed and crossed her arms over her chest. "You're mad, aren't you? I really have a way of messing things up."

Rocky knew "mad" was an oversimplification of what he was feeling, but it would serve the purpose until he'd decided just how he wanted to deal with this situation, which was definitely a first in his relationships with women.

"Of course, I'm mad. How'd you feel if the situation were reversed and I told you I just wanted to get you in bed because I was curious to see what it would be like? Isn't that one of the main complaints women are always harping on—being a sex object to men?"

Kitt's rueful grin spelled trouble with staying irritated with her. "If you told me that and I believed you, I'd probably be flattered. Being a sex object hasn't been one of the great problems in my life, believe me. If it were, we probably wouldn't be standing here having this discussion, would we?"

With any other woman, that last remark could have been a provocative challenge or an ultimatum, but not with Kitt. It was just rueful candor at first and then, spoken aloud like that, an inexorable kind of truth that hurt too much to stand around talking about it anymore. With every passing second she was more achingly disappointed that things weren't different all the way around, but she wasn't surprised. Hadn't she known from the first that she wasn't Rocky's type? All those teenage girls had known that tonight at Jerrie's after just a glance. Up to this point in her life, she'd never wasted time in futile anguish over what couldn't be changed, and she didn't want to start now.

Rocky watched her in amazement as she went calmly over to the table and starting clearing it. "I guess I'll just have to throw all this away," she mused sadly. "The ribs were too burnt, anyway, and that salad's all limp now."

He stood there, torn between the urge to laugh in disbelief and the urge to go over and shake her. As far as he was concerned, their discussion wasn't over. He was strongly dissatisfied with what had and hadn't been said by both of them and frustrated as hell. It only increased his annoyance that she apparently could stop on their way to his bed and turn her attention to cleaning up the dinner dishes without feeling any of what he was feeling. Her instant recovery seemed further proof that she had been acting out a fantasy with the Rocky Players of her imaginings, not responding to the flesh and blood man.

"If you'll excuse me for a few minutes, I think I'll run up and take a cold shower," he said sarcastically. "That's what we men are supposed to do when we're sexually frustrated, isn't it?"

Very slowly Kitt put down the stack of dishes she held in her hands. Her eyes were wide and stricken as they held Rocky's hard gaze, and then she closed them as she brought her hands up and covered her face. Rocky stared, caught up between his own complex need to mete out punishment and a sudden deep concern for her.

"I don't think I can stay and finish cleaning up," Kitt said in an odd stifled voice from behind her hands. "I really think I've got to go now—" She turned around and started out the same way someone who is suddenly violently ill rushes for the bathroom.

Rocky had never moved faster on the football field. He caught her before she'd made more than a few steps and held her from behind by the arms.

"You can't just leave like this—" The harsh, baffled anger in his voice was meant for himself as well as for her.

He encountered no resistance. Kitt was like a rag doll as she turned around into his arms. "I'm so sorry," she whispered as she slipped her arms around his waist and leaned into him. Wave after wave of misery washed through her, each one too deep to allow for tears. She hadn't ever been besieged by such black despair like this before. It had come upon her unexpectedly and frightened her with its awful intensity. Nothing so serious had happened, had it? Why did she suddenly just want to die?

Holding her close in his arms, Rocky was more unsure than ever of how to deal with the situation. She was such a puzzle to him, always reacting entirely true to her open, impulsive nature and yet managing to do the unexpected and take him off balance. One second she infuriated him with her imperturbable calm and the next she aroused this savage tenderness with her total vulnerability.

"I just don't know what the hell it is that you want, Kitt," he said in a voice still vaguely angry and baffled, but gruff with concern. The sound of it did nothing to soothe Kitt's misery, but it roused her out of her total absorption with herself.

"Don't worry, Rocky, I'll be fine. Just fine," she told him dully, the words muffled against his chest. "None of this is your fault. It's all mine." He felt the deep sigh like a giant bellows cruelly at work in her slender body. "I just wish there was some way I could undo tonight. It was all wrong, right from the start…except for the ride back across the causeway, when you told me about yourself as a little boy. I wouldn't change that."

Kitt interpreted Rocky's silence as agreement, but it wasn't. He had to run fast forward through the evening from the start to the present to see if he felt the same way, and he discovered that he didn't. No, he *wouldn't* wipe out tonight if it were in his power to decree that it had never happened at all.

"Tonight wasn't all that bad, was it? We had our good moments." The gruff tenderness in his voice matched the feel of his hands on her back.

Kitt's answer was to hug him tighter around the waist. Her sigh wasn't so much like a shudder this time.

"You're wrong when you say that none of it was my fault," he went on. "It was a lot my fault. I could have handled things different when we got back here tonight."

"Please don't feel bad, Rocky." Kitt's voice was faraway and sad. "It's not your fault or mine that we like each other an awful lot, but I'm not your type of woman."

Once again his silence seemed an unhappy confirmation, but he was giving her words some thought. On the surface what she said was true. She wasn't like any of the other women he'd ever been involved with, or at least sexually involved. In high school and college there'd been some girls he could liken somewhat to Kitt, wholesome and outgoing, whom he'd liked as friends, but not as girlfriends. It was strange because he actually enjoyed their company more than the campus queen types he dated and made every effort, mostly successful, to score with.

But it wasn't true that Kitt didn't appeal to him physically. He'd wanted her a few minutes ago, and he wanted her now, but because the physical attraction was so different from what he'd felt for other women, he was uncomfortable with it, had been uncomfortable with it from the first. Sexual attraction had been complex before, but always his relationship with the opposite sex had been adversarial, and his women had all been skilled opponents in the game of the sexes. The problem with Kitt was that somehow she'd reached feminine adulthood without learning the necessary skills of waging sexual battle with a man or else she just refused to play the game. One way or the other, it put Rocky in a ticklish situation. Taking her had seemed as sportsmanlike as tackling a kid in junior high school. He certainly hadn't intended his constraint to be a source of pain to her.

"Why don't you let me make up my own mind about whether you're my type of woman, or not?" he chided her.

"Okay." It was plainly an effort at humoring him and getting them both past this bad moment. "I still think I'll go now, if you don't mind." She loosened her hold around his waist and patted him on the back as she drew back a little.

Rocky studied her face anxiously and saw that she was completely dry-eyed. Somehow that was disturbing. He'd almost rather have seen tears. The expression on his face drew a wan smile that was another effort at reassurance on her part.

"Don't look so worried. I'm fine. Honest. I'm not going to drive my car into a lamppost or jump off a bridge or anything desperate like that." She took her arms from around his waist and would have stepped free, but he didn't let her go, and she looked at him solicitously. "I'm okay."

"But I'm not okay," he said softly, lifting her up off the floor and holding her against him, hip to hip. "I'm not okay at all."

The startled expression on Kitt's face just inches away from his own quickly changed to chagrin. "Rocky, I wish you wouldn't do this—"

"I wish you would stop talking. Put those long arms of yours around my neck, woman, and kiss me."

He watched the idea instantly take on appeal, but there was reluctance in the way she put her arms around his neck. "I must be awfully heavy," she murmured, looking longingly at his mouth.

"You are heavy, especially for a beanpole." Her total abstraction in watching every movement of his lips as he answered her in a tone that was deliberate sex language aroused him, and his anticipation was keen as she tightened her arms around his neck and brought her lips to his.

"Here goes..." she murmured. Her kiss wasn't shy, but it was soft and encompassing, taking in the hard shape and texture of his mouth, which always drew her attention. It seemed such a barometer of his emotion even while it registered his control. From Rocky's point of view, the kiss was tantalizing as hell, deepening his hunger for pressure and depth, but he managed to keep himself from taking over.

"Hmm, not bad," he murmured when she ended the kiss and pulled back a few inches to look at him. "Now try it again, this time with some tongue."

Kitt obliged him, and the deep, plunging intimacy had devastating effect on both of them. They were out of breath when she twisted her lips free of his.

"Wow," she murmured dazedly, and her face matched her tone. "Kissing you makes me feel so *strange*. It's like I'm out in space or something. I can't put it into words. I know it's probably not the same for you."

"No, I *can* put it into words. Kissing you makes me hurt right *there*." Rocky rubbed her hips against his and watched her reaction to the blatantly sexual contact. She was pleased and excited at his arousal. "It's a good hurt, and we both know exactly what to do about it, don't we?" Inch by inch he slid her down the front of him until her feet touched the floor, and her lower abdomen pressed against the location of his pleasurable discomfort.

"I think we both do," she agreed, smiling into his eyes.

"Then why don't we make another try at getting up those stairs over there? Do you think you could get past the dirty dishes this time?"

Even with the humorous undertone, the suggestion was pure seduction, aided and abetted by the desire in his eyes. It acted upon Kitt like a milder version of her reaction to his kiss.

"I know I can," she said with a soft little sigh. "This time is different."

"Yes, I guess you're right. It is different this time."

Rocky still had his arms loosely around Kitt. He brought his hands up to her shoulders and held them while he kissed her again, making the contact brief, hard and deep. The kiss did more than intensify the ache in his groin. It made him feel a little strange, too. Not "out in space," but like that sensation in his runaway car dream: panicky, highly exhilarated, out of control.

Chapter Twelve

None of Kitt's earlier fears proved well founded. She wasn't embarrassed when the time came to take off her clothes. For one thing, passion created an urgency, and it wasn't just her stripping down, but him, too. She was too interested in Rocky's nakedness to be self-conscious about her own. It came as no surprise that his body was magnificent. Already she'd seen most of it without any clothes, but tonight was a different matter altogether. He was nude and aroused and *her* lover.

The reality of having him make love to her far surpassed her fantasy. There was no denying his skill and experience, but as far as she was concerned he might have been in training up until now just to give her this consummate pleasure as he took his own. His hands as they caressed her breasts, hips and thighs were not too rough and not too gentle. His kisses demanded that she be all woman and yet they weren't brutal. He became Samson shorn of his power when Kitt's delight in touching him brought her to an inevitable knowledge of his most intimate manhood. He groaned as she stroked gently at first and then took him in her hand.

"I've always wanted you to touch me like that," he said. "You have such great hands. I love to watch you do things with them."

But he did the very thing that would make her hands go still when he brought his fingertips up between her thighs. She held her breath as he found her moistness and then she arched her back and opened her legs wider for him in an instinctive confirmation of her readiness that Rocky was prompt to accept.

He was careful entering her, but when the uncertainty in her eyes reinforced his own dissatisfaction, he withdrew and entered her again, this time with a thrusting power that took him deep within her and made her gasp with the shock and the pleasure. The exhilaration and the urgency in her voice as she spoke his name was his exhilaration, his urgency, too.

Rocky put everything he had into making love with her and sharpened the fine edge of his own pleasure with the sheer enjoyment of hers. He used his power to thrill her, his finesse to drive her wild, his control to delay climax so that when it came it was cataclysmic, for both of them. Her sharp cry followed by the first involuntary convulsion was the signal he'd waited for before he let go. All two hundred and twenty pounds of hard muscle collapsed on top of Kitt, but she didn't make a single complaint.

When Rocky summoned enough strength to roll over to one side, she rolled too and ended up lying pressed full length to him, her arm circling his chest, her head nestled on his shoulder. The disorientation that kissing him brought upon her was nothing compared to what she was feeling now. Her sense of marveling had a touch of panic to it.

"That was *unreal...*" she murmured, groping for reality. "Just *unreal*. I never believed it could really be like this." She took in a deep breath and waited for her head to clear and her heart to slow its wild pounding. The insensible quality of Rocky's silence and the thundering beat of his heart were flattering evidence that he was undergoing a recovery, too. As they lay there together with normalcy making a leisurely return, Kitt found the closeness too comfortable and sweet, the relaxation too deep, too disconcertingly a matter of the mind and spirit as well as the body. She was compelled to break the spell with humor before either of them could spoil it. "I think I'll get a bumper sticker," she said, chuckling. "One that says It's Better With Football Players. What do you think?"

Rocky drew in a contented breath. He didn't know if he ever wanted to move from right where he was at this moment. "It would be immodest of me to say for sure," he said lazily, pretending to misinterpret her question. "Most of the football players I've known say it's better. I'll have to get a bumper sticker myself, one that says Take Your Cleaning Lady To Bed."

He expected a chuckle and probably a humorous reply of some kind. When there was neither, just a brief silence he couldn't read, he wondered what was going on in that head now.

"What do you think?" he asked, mimicking her own light query.

She rose, her long tumbled hair falling like a screen over her shoulders and down her chest, partially hiding her breasts in a way Rocky found quite provocative. The ends of several tresses rested against his shoulder and chest, and when she absently moved her head from side to side, the silken slide against his bare flesh tickled and stirred immediate interest farther down his body. Rocky was surprised at wanting her again so soon and complacent at the idea of making love to her in a more leisurely fashion this time. Mistakenly he assumed that she was telling him with her actions what was on her mind, only to have her take him by surprise once again.

"I'd better be going," Kitt announced and started at once to get up from the bed. Rocky grabbed for a handful of hair to stop her, not sure whether she was teasing him or not.

"Why do you have to go? Why don't you just stay all night with me?" There was as much challenge as honest urging in Rocky's voice because mentally he hadn't even gotten around to whether he wanted her to stay all night with him.

"It's late," Kitt explained patiently. "I'd have to call Ellen and tell her I was staying, and I might wake up Andy. If she should happen to wake up some time in the wee hours and find me not there, she'd be worried to death that something had happened to me."

Rocky loosened his fingers and let the handful of hair slide through them as she pulled steadily free. He couldn't argue with her reasons for leaving. They were so typically Kitt and thoughtful, but it irritated him that she wasn't even making a pretense of wanting to stay with him.

"Can't you spend the night with a guy without getting Ellen's permission?" He reached down and pulled the sheet across his loins, then lay back with his hands behind his head and watched her while she dressed, growing more aroused by the second despite the absence of any efforts at provocation on her part. She was simply getting dressed the way she performed any task, without a single wasted motion, so that there was no impression of hurry, but Rocky was familiar with her speed by now and knew that if he didn't delay her somehow, she'd be gone in seconds.

"Don't you ever spend the night with a man after you've gone to bed with him?" The subtle aggression invited her to make either a defense or a counterattack. Naturally, Kitt did neither.

Kitt was tucking her blouse into the waistband of her jeans and her hands didn't falter as she looked over at him with a shy questioning that Rocky couldn't understand because he didn't know that Kitt felt horribly self-conscious dressing under his gaze. Her earlier fears about measuring up to comparison with the other women in his life were back and much worse now than they had been before.

"There haven't been that many men." She shook her hair back, all for naught, because it slid forward again as she looked down and watched her feet step into her moccasins. "None the last three years since I moved here to Mandeville and started the business with Ellen," she added. "I've been very busy." She was fully dressed now and poised to leave.

Rocky tensed with the suspense of not knowing what she would say or do next. Surely she wouldn't leave without a good-night kiss or a parting touch, and he didn't know what his reaction was going to be to either. Was he going to be cool and proud and let her go if that's what she really wanted or was he going to present her with the male argument he was concealing under the sheet?

"It won't take me but a minute to stick those few dishes in the dishwasher and throw away the food," Kitt told him. "You don't need to get up. I'll just make sure the door is locked when I leave." She smiled. "Oh, and don't worry. I always keep my promises. I won't say a word about any of this to Ellen or anybody else." She hesitated for a split second and then headed for the door so that her "Night now," drifted to him over her shoulder.

Rocky really couldn't believe it was happening. Sure, he'd had women get up out of bed and leave him before, but never like this. Either they had somewhere they had to go or they were playing some game with him. He wasn't convinced Kitt had to go, and yet she didn't play games, so where did that leave him? What was he supposed to do?

It was easily in his power to stop her, especially since she intended to stop and play housemaid on her way out, but he didn't go after her and didn't call out. He lay there with every muscle tensed and stared at the ceiling, listening to her quiet movements downstairs, knowing that she wouldn't take long, just as she'd said.

When the sound of the front door opening and closing signaled her departure, he still didn't relax. He thought of the silken feel of her hair pulling through his fingers and fought the disappointed sensation that something important had eluded him. He was just frustrated, that was all. Kitt had reawakened his sex urge, which had seemed to be slumbering the past five or six months.

He got up and took the cold shower he'd made sarcastic reference to earlier, but he succeeded mainly in killing the possibility of falling asleep any time soon. Thinking through the evening brought back the physical frustration and increased his dissatisfaction with the way it had ended. When he finally fell asleep, he didn't rest well because of disturbing dreams that were still fresh when he awoke the next morning. In one of them Kitt had taken his Mustang without his permission and was driving away in it, her long hair floating out of the window. Rocky ran after her, shouting for her to stop, but was helpless to stop her on foot. He was angry at her and frustrated at his own powerlessness.

Upon waking it annoyed him to think that while he was putting in a hell of a bad night, all on her account, she was probably home sleeping like a babe. He decided that he was strictly going to cool it where she was concerned. If she wanted to see him again, it was going to be up to her to make the next move. Then he went downstairs to make himself a cup of instant coffee and, since he was down there anyway, checked to make sure the Mustang was parked safely in the garage.

It was, of course, and he felt foolish. His immediate thought was what Kitt's reaction would be when he told her about his dream. No sooner had the thought of her amusement improved his foul mood than he remembered his resolution not to call her and wasn't at all sure she'd call him. After one swallow of the coffee, he dumped it into the sink and stalked on back upstairs to get dressed and drive into the city. He was grimly looking forward to a workout. It would ease this urge he had to smash something.

Actually Kitt hadn't put in a good night either. Her promise to Rocky not to confide in Ellen had robbed her of her usual outlet for confusion and worry. Never had she needed to verbalize her fears and thus make them inconsequential the way she needed to do that now. The power of her own responses to Rocky that evening had frightened her silly. It was one thing to revel in the superficial euphoria of falling madly in love with Rocky Players, macho answer to every woman's sensual fantasy, and quite another thing to have the emotional props knocked out from under her.

She'd known from the first that he had a more powerful appeal for her than any man had ever had before.

His masculinity excited her and made her feel like a woman. Ellen's warnings combined with the whole beguiling legend of the dangers of falling in love had added a risk factor that heightened her sense of heady adventure. The risk hadn't seemed real, not until this past night.

A broken heart was no more real to Kitt up until now than a cute valentine. She'd flirted with the notion of ending up with one eventually when her relationship with Rocky ended, but she hadn't bargained for the range of pain, despair, joy and tenderness she'd felt that evening. They had all come upon her because of the interaction between Rocky and herself. She had realized his inadvertent power to make her happy and to hurt her, and it had frightened her to comprehend, for the first time, that a deep, lifetime commitment like Bob's feelings for Ellen might be *involuntary*. Kitt's sympathy for Bob's unrequited love all these years had always been undermined by the assumption that he had invested his affection unwisely and was unwilling to admit he'd made a mistake. She'd never looked upon love before as an invading force that could move in upon a person unawares.

Kitt knew without any doubt that she didn't want to feel for Rocky a permanent, committed kind of love like the love Bob had for Ellen. For one thing, she just didn't like the idea of being that vulnerable where any other person was concerned. Even if she were willing to take that risk, there wasn't a chance in the world that Rocky Players was going to fall in love with her the same way. Sure, he liked her and thought she was fun and entertaining, but she wasn't the type to knock a man like Rocky off his feet and make him think he couldn't live without her.

Sometime in the middle of the sleepless night, Kitt decided she'd had a close call and had better be awfully careful from here on out, not to fall any deeper in love with Rocky than she might already be. Maybe she'd better just not see him anymore. That would be the safest thing to do, she realized, and what she thought Ellen would advise. But the thought of not seeing Rocky ever again made her so incredibly miserable that she wondered if it was too late for caution, after all. She decided not to decide anything one way or the other that night.

The next morning when she wandered sleepily into the kitchen, still in her robe and not at all her usual alert morning self, Ellen raised her eyebrows questioningly.

"Bad night?"

Kitt yawned and nodded. "Terrible. I don't see how people put up with insomnia," she grumbled, pouring herself a cup of coffee.

Ellen waited for her to come over and sit down at the table. "Did you and Rocky have a fight?"

Kitt took a sip of coffee. "No, not exactly a fight," she said glumly. "But even if we had, I couldn't tell you about it. I promised Rocky last night that I wouldn't tell anybody anything that happened between him and me." She held up her hand to stave off an imaginary avalanche of questions. "That's all I can say. Not another word. And anybody in his right mind could see I had to at least tell you that."

Ellen nodded, managing to keep back a smile. "I see. Well, I'll be sure and not ask you any questions about Rocky in the future. Since you can't tell me anything about last night, I'll tell you some good news. I'm pretty sure it'll cheer you up. Bob and I are going to be married. I know that doesn't come as any great surprise—" She broke off, staring at Kitt in surprise and consternation as Kitt's eyes welled with tears that spilled over and ran down her face, one great drop splashing into her coffee. "What's wrong? I thought sure you'd be so happy."

"I am happy, Ellen," Kitt declared sadly. More tears welled up and followed the wet tracks of the first ones. "I couldn't be happier for you *and* Bob. All these years he's loved you. I just hope you finally love him back, at least a little."

"Kitt, I do," Ellen assured her softly. "I wouldn't be marrying him if I didn't. I hope you're not worrying about having to move out of this house," she added. "Because you won't have to move unless you want to. We can work out something where you can buy out my equity. You'll still be seeing Andy and Bob and me every single day, you know. It's not as though there's going to be a big change. We'll still be like a family."

The anxiety in Ellen's face and voice made Kitt pull herself together and realize she was being terribly selfish in letting her jangled emotions cast a pall over Ellen's good news.

"I'm not worried about any of that," she told Ellen with a determined sniffle. "I've had my fingers crossed for ages that things would work out for you and Bob. It'll be good for you and Bob and Andy and probably for me, too, in the long run. I'll probably be forced into working on my social life. Not that it's going to be an easy adjustment because I'm going to miss living in this house with you and Andy and having Bob always coming in and out. From a purely selfish point of view, I hate to see things change." She took a sip of her coffee and made a face because it was lukewarm and salty from her tears. "Yuk," she said, getting up to empty the cup in the sink and then refill it with hot coffee.

"I just had a bad night," she continued, leaning against the counter. She thought for a moment, a frown of concentration cutting lines across her forehead.

"When I couldn't sleep last night, for one reason or another that I can't talk about, I thought about Bob and you, along with a lot of other things, of course. It's only very recently that I've been able to kind of put myself in Bob's shoes, and I have to admit I felt sorry for him. Last night the way he's been so hung up on you all these years seemed sad to me, unfair and... scary. Then I come dragging in this morning and you tell me that you and Bob are going to get married. I can just imagine how happy he is. It was... well, just too much. I know this doesn't make much sense."

Ellen's smile was both discreet and wise. "It makes a lot of sense, Kitt, and you haven't told me a thing, so don't worry that you've broken your promise to Rocky. Why don't you go and wake up Andy and see about getting the two of you dressed while I make some breakfast?" She got up from the table. "The world will probably look like a much brighter place after you've finished that cup of coffee and had something to eat."

"It's a brighter place just thinking about something to eat," Kitt replied on her way to the door. She was feeling more cheerful just having had that oblique exchange with Ellen that hadn't really betrayed any confidence. "Last night wasn't the greatest as far as food was concerned, that's for sure. First, we had burned ribs—" She stopped and turned around to meet Ellen's glance guiltily. "You don't think he meant I shouldn't even tell things like that, do you?" she demanded defensively.

Smiling, Ellen returned to her task of getting food out of the refrigerator. "Maybe you'd better clear it with Rocky before you say any more," she suggested. "By the way—" she deposited a jug of milk and a carton of eggs on the counter "—you can tell Rocky that he's definitely invited to the wedding, which will be after Christmas."

The pause drew a look from Ellen, who noted the strained expression on Kitt's face. Kitt cleared her throat. "When and if I see Rocky, I'll tell him that," she said carefully. "And that's all I can say on the subject."

Ellen looked after her vanished figure, grinning and shaking her head fondly. As much as she was sure that she was making the right decision for everyone concerned by marrying Bob, she was going to miss living in the same house with Kitt, and so would Andy. That consideration along with Bob's patience had undoubtedly kept her from marrying Bob sooner.

Even though she and Kitt were the same age, Ellen's sympathy for Kitt now, as the latter ventured for the first time into a serious man-woman relationship, was similar to what a mother would feel for a daughter. Kitt had managed to convey quite a bit just now without spelling anything out. She apparently was getting in deeper territory emotionally than she'd ever intended, and it disturbed her to perceive any parallel between herself and Bob. The fact that his devotion was finally being rewarded with what he wanted was only adding to Kitt's confusion as she tried to figure things out for herself.

As Ellen broke eggs into a bowl, added milk and salt and pepper, she wondered why Kitt's state of upheaval this morning hadn't worried her any more than it had. Why wasn't Ellen more fearful for her friend? The answer wasn't long in coming. Somehow the restriction that Rocky had put upon Kitt was reassuring. His wanting Kitt to keep whatever transpired between them confidential could well be a hint of jealousy or possessiveness, maybe both. It also indicated his intention to pursue an intimate relationship with Kitt. After all, if nothing happened, Kitt wouldn't have anything to tell. And if he didn't anticipate something more than just a casual fling, why should he care whether she confided in her close friend? Ellen didn't think for a moment that Rocky was concerned about Kitt's mentioning that he'd burned the ribs or even the mere fact that they were sleeping together. He wanted Kitt's private emotions about him and his about her to be kept private.

As Ellen briskly prepared breakfast, she thought about the fact that Kitt had always seemed so much more vulnerable than herself and yet she was the one who'd ended up hurt and disappointed. Kitt had breezed through life, living far more adventurously than herself, and been virtually unscathed. In that open, impulsive nature there had to be some survival mechanisms at work. Maybe this realization was partly responsible for Ellen's optimistic outlook about Kitt's involvement with Rocky. Whatever happened, Kitt would be able to handle it.

As for Rocky, well, Ellen didn't know him well enough to be truly concerned on his account. He'd undoubtedly had a lot more experience with women than the ordinary man. Ellen hadn't really believed at first that Kitt could be his type of woman, but he certainly was paying her a lot of attention. If he was falling for Kitt seriously, he just might find that he was playing a whole new ball game, different from any he'd ever played before, one without any printed rules.

By the time Kitt was dressed and had helped Andy dress and make up his single bed, she was feeling almost her normal self. She ate the breakfast Ellen had prepared with appetite and chatted naturally with her and Andy about the day ahead. Last night was seeming more and more remote from her real world, a figment of her imagination, especially her sleeplessness and anxiety.

Her day was busy, as were all her days, and she put her customary vigor and enthusiasm into her work. The thought of Rocky and the previous evening were there, either in the foreground or the background of her mind all day. She made no effort to avoid thinking of him or of anything that had happened, but it all took on a make-believe element that relieved her recall of any uneasiness. Without breaking her promise to Rocky, she could tell the whole tale to herself mentally and see the humor and entertainment in it.

During the afternoon she checked in with Ellen at The Magic Broom headquarters and inquired about her plans for that evening. "You and Bob go out somewhere and have a romantic evening," she insisted. "Andy and I will stay home together. After not sleeping worth a darn last night, I'll be in bed by the time he is, anyway." Ellen didn't question and she didn't argue.

Kitt enjoyed playing with Andy during the couple of hours between his supper and his bedtime. She wasn't holding her breath waiting for the phone to ring and wasn't disappointed that Rocky didn't call. It was just an ordinary evening. Everything was reassuringly the same as it had been before last night and before she'd met Rocky Players. The only difference was this consciousness of sameness and relief at finding it intact.

After she put Andy to bed, she got ready for bed herself, putting on an old, oversize Louisiana State football jersey that she wore as a nightgown. Then she settled down comfortably on her bed and dialed Rocky's number on her phone extension. He answered on the second ring.

"Hello."

The combination of guardedness and aggression he managed to convey in that one word didn't bother Kitt in the least. He had sounded much the same way when he had answered the phone in her presence as they were sitting down to dinner the previous night. It was probably just the way a man beleaguered by females answered the phone.

"Hi. It's just me," she said cheerfully. "I hope you slept better than I did last night. The way I tossed and turned, you should be glad I didn't stay. It must have been the combination of burnt ribs and eating at Jerrie's with all those jealous girls glaring at me and wishing they were in my place. I got up growling like a bear this morning and Ellen hit me with the news that she and Bob have decided to get married. Frankly, it's good news and bad news. I'm happy for them, but it's going to bring about some changes."

Unlike Kitt, Rocky had been tensed in readiness for the phone to ring and considerably in suspense about what she would say if she did call and how she would sound. All day he'd thought about the way she'd gotten out of his bed and gone home, and it kept seeming like some kind of flight. He'd thought, too, about making love to her. Driving home, his resolution not to call her himself was shaky.

In his own mind the telephone conversation they would have, no matter which one of them did the calling, would have an element of confrontation. It would be unavoidable, he thought, for them not to get down to the *why* she had left and the *why* he had let her go. He might have known better than to try to guess what would happen where Kitt was concerned. Here she was blithely skipping over the whole incident by touching upon it so casually, telling him with the light, cheerful tone of her voice: *Nothing serious has happened between us. We're great pals having a good time.* He was incredulous, relieved and angry, all at the same time.

"I'm glad to hear you didn't sleep well," he said with irony. "I didn't sleep worth a damn myself. For one thing, I dreamed you stole my Mustang." The sound of her laughter brought a grudging smile to his lips. "I got up first thing this morning and checked the garage," he added.

"No wonder you didn't sleep well," she said, chuckling. "I know what that car means to you. Your dream was probably some kind of omen. A mustang is a horse, and I've had the notion in the back of my mind all along that when Ellen and Bob got around to marrying each other, I'd buy myself a little place out in Folsom and have a horse or two. The only time I ever came close to getting married it was to a man with a horse farm out there. He was a nice man and I liked him fine, but I was crazy about his farm and his horses."

Rocky knew that her mention of that "nice man" that she'd "liked fine" wasn't intended to make him jealous, but it did. He didn't like to think of her with another man.

"Well, at least I know what it takes to entice you. Maybe I should think about buying a horse farm out in Folsom. Then maybe you'd stay all night with me."

"Why don't you?" she demanded gaily. "We'd be neighbors and could swap horse remedies. I'm really looking forward to the idea of living out there. I love the hilly, rolling country with all the pastures and big oak trees. If you want, you could ride out there with me some time when I'm looking around for a place to buy. Oh, but that's right, I'll probably be going on weekends, and you'll be tied up, traveling and playing games. By the way, what do you think about the game on Sunday with Minnesota? You'll be playing your old teammates, won't you?"

Rocky let her change the subject and then keep it rolling along. She had the ball and was running. He either had to follow her lead, take the ball away from her, or drop out of the game. If he took the ball, he'd have to have a game plan, which he didn't have. It was hard to know how to play an opponent who wouldn't admit to being an opponent. The only thing he knew for sure at this point was that he wasn't dropping out.

"Can I see you tomorrow night?" he asked before they hung up.

"Sure. That'd be fun," she agreed at once.

"Would you like to go out to dinner or a movie or something?" Rocky offered with the hope that she would refuse. He'd rather just have her come there to his place where they could be alone.

"A movie might be fun. There's a comedy playing that I want to see." She mentioned the name. "People don't come up and bother you in the movies, do they?"

"Not once I get inside and sit down. Do you want me to pick you up at your place?"

"That's not necessary. It would make more sense for me to drive over to your place and then go from there."

"Fine, if that's the way you want to do it."

The sound of Kitt's yawn came to him over the phone.

"Now that we've settled that, I'm going to sleep. I'm dead."

"I'm tired, too, but I still wish you were here," Rocky told her softly and would have told her more, but she didn't let him.

"No, you don't. You should see me the way I look right now. I look awful." She described herself in comic, unflattering detail.

He could see her clearly, but the picture didn't change his mind. He still wished that she were there with him.

Chapter Thirteen

The next evening Kitt and Rocky both were aware that she was working too hard at casualness. He wasn't sure if she was trying to convince him or herself that everything was still basically the same between them as it had been before that night when they'd made love and she had rushed off afterward.

Of course, it wasn't the same. There was a new intimacy that Rocky didn't find at all unpleasant. When he looked at her and touched her, he felt blatantly possessive and saw no reason to keep his feeling from her or anyone else. It amused him that she acted embarrassed when he put his arm around her shoulders in the line outside the movie theater, where currents of recognition were stirring the other moviegoers.

"What's the matter?" he murmured in her ear. "Not ashamed to be seen with me, are you?"

Kitt fought the weak, warm sensation his closeness, even in public, brought to her body. "I do wish you weren't so fat and homely," she joked, trying to shrug free of his arm without making a big production of it.

Rocky accommodated her by taking his arm from around her shoulders, but he only slipped it down to her waist instead and pulled her closer. Partly he enjoyed teasing her and partly he just liked feeling her close to him.

"Try to act a little fascinated," he cajoled in the same low murmur that played havoc with her pulsebeat. "Think of my reputation as a womanizer."

"Believe me, I am thinking about it," she retorted.

With the help of that remark, Rocky was able to interpret her reticence as uneasiness at being in the public eye. Apparently she was still hung up on the business about not being his type. He'd thought when she showed up tonight with her hair in the thick braid and wearing the usual jeans and low-soled shoes that her insecurities had been laid to rest. She had seemed her easygoing self.

The line was short, and it didn't take them long to get into the theater lobby. With his arm back around her waist, Rocky ushered Kitt up to the concession counter.

"Butter on your popcorn?" he asked Kitt in a tone so blatantly proprietorial that hot color suffused her cheeks. While he didn't call her "sweetheart" or "darling," he might as well have.

"Please," she replied, feeling as though everyone around them was waiting for her answer. It was impossible not to be aware of all the curious glances in their direction. Fortunately, they managed to get served and get into the theater without anyone approaching Rocky openly.

"Where do you like to sit?" he asked her as they started down the aisle, his free hand staking casual possession to her back.

"Not too far back," Kitt replied, marching ahead of him and taking a sharp right turn into the row she chose. As soon as she'd plopped down, she slid low in her seat, her knees coming up against the back of the seat in front of her. "Why are you doing this?" she demanded of Rocky in a fierce whisper as soon as he'd sat next to her.

"Doing what?" he whispered back loudly.

"You know, making a...a scene in front of people when you know good and well they recognize you." She fixed her scowling gaze on her cup of buttered popcorn as though the answer would rise up out of it.

"So what if they do?" Rocky sprawled a little sideways to accommodate his long legs and bumped his shoulder deliberately up against Kitt's. "Why do they make these damned seats so small and put them so close together?" he complained cheerfully. "It makes it tough on us long-legged people, doesn't it?"

He waited patiently while Kitt turned her face toward him. "Doesn't it?" he repeated coaxingly and bent forward to kiss her lips, his intention at first just to wipe away the pout. But once he'd tasted the softness, a deeper, harder kiss gradually developed, and there seemed no stopping it until he was short of breath. He had little awareness of an audience until several whistles, catcalls and hand claps accompanied the reluctant parting of their lips.

"Atta boy, Rocky!" a young male voice called out from half a dozen rows back.

"My turn next!" followed a feminine voice of the same high school vintage.

Kitt went rigid and sat straighter in her chair, facing forward. Guessing that she was embarrassed, Rocky put

his arm loosely around her shoulders in a gesture of pro-
tection and made an abortive effort to cross his legs in
order to relieve his newest physical discomfort. He gave
up for lack of space and resigned himself temporarily to
the tightness of fabric across his crotch. Kissing Kitt, even
in a movie theater with other people around them, was
bad for the fit of his jeans. The thought put a smile in his
voice as he spoke close to her ear.

"I guess we'd better stay at least long enough to eat the
popcorn, hadn't we? If we get up and leave now, we'll
really cause some excitement."

Kitt's only response was to start wolfing down her
popcorn, two or three kernels at a time. As the movie
started, she crunched steadily, staring at the screen.
Rocky wondered if she were actually taking any of the
movie in, but finally she smiled at one of the gags and a
short time later laughed out loud. When she'd finished
her popcorn and he offered her the rest of his, she took
it and ate every bit of it, too.

To anyone observing him, Rocky would seem to be
enjoying the movie. Any other time he probably would
have been more entertained by it, but tonight other
keener pleasures were temptingly close at hand and yet
forbidden in these circumstances. He tried to keep from
thinking about how much he would like to reach over and
unbutton Kitt's blouse and slip his hand inside to play
with her breasts. The most he could permit himself in the
way of touching her was to slide his fingertips up and
down her arm and give it a little squeeze now and then.
Even that slowed the easing of the tightness of his jeans
brought on by the kiss. Not since he was a teenager had
sitting next to a girl in the movies been such slow sensual
torment. Relief came several minutes sooner than he'd
expected when Kitt turned to him right in the middle of

a hilarious parody of a police chase scene to suggest that they might want to leave a couple of minutes early.

"Good idea," he said when they'd made their exit from the theater. "How'd you like the movie?"

"It was okay," Kitt replied, getting into the passenger seat of the Mustang. Holding the door open for her, Rocky took pleasure in the unstudied ease of her movements. Kitt had only to do something once to figure out the best way to do it again.

"How did you like it?" Kitt asked him when he slid behind the wheel.

Rocky smiled at her as he inserted the key into the ignition. "I have an idea it was a very funny movie," he replied lazily, leaning over toward her. "I just happened to have a lot of distractions, like wanting to do this." Still smiling he undid the top two buttons of her blouse and slipped his hand inside to cup her breast. "And this..." He brought his lips to hers. As the kiss quickly became deep and hungry, the hand caressing her breast became impatient with the barrier of her bra and thrust inside the cup to find the naked warmth of her skin. When thumb and forefinger pinched the hardened peak, Kitt arched her back and moaned helplessly.

"No," she whispered as Rocky lowered his head to her breast. Whatever his intention had been, he merely pushed aside her blouse enough to kiss the curve of her breast and then took his hand out of her bra.

"You mean 'no, not now,' don't you?" he asked huskily, rebuttoning her blouse. It was more lover's talk than a real question. Her response was all the answer he thought he needed.

Kitt slumped back against the seat, her eyes briefly closed as she took in a deep, unsteady breath. "I don't know what I mean," she said, her voice troubled and uncertain. "When you touch me like that, I can't even think straight." Urgent to get them back to his place where they could do more than talk, Rocky had started the car and was backing out. Kitt was talking more to herself than to him as she added, "I don't like it."

"What do you mean, you don't like it," he chided as they moved smoothly forward. "What does thinking have to do with it, anyway?" He reached over for her hand and brought it to the bulge in his crotch. "See what keeping you from thinking straight does to me? I might have to start wearing looser pants." He made a sound of pleasure when Kitt's hand rubbed gently.

When they were out on the highway, Rocky glanced over at her several times in quick succession, noting the somber expression on her face. It didn't cause him serious concern because he was confident that making love to her would soothe away whatever feminine fears plagued her.

"The best movie in the world couldn't have kept my attention today, you know that?" The sexual message in his voice was explicit even before he reinforced it by reaching out and sliding his hand up the inside of her left thigh. When he reached the vee cradle between her legs, he rubbed his forefinger up and down the bulky seam of her jeans crotch. Her quick intake of breath and the reflexive opening of her thighs brought a pleased male smile to his lips as he looked over at her again.

"There's nothing to worry about, Kitt. I promise you that," he said coaxingly, and curved his hand around her feminine mound, taking complete possession of her womanhood. She placed her hand over his in a kind of acceptance, but there was still the deep shadow of worry in her gray eyes as she met his gaze.

"Okay, out with it," he ordered lightly. "Remember, you can tell me anything at all that's on your mind. Isn't that the agreement we made? So what's the big problem?''

"The big problem is that whether I want to be or not, and I don't want to be, I'm afraid I might be in love with you," Kitt blurted out vehemently.

Rocky stared at her as long as he dared keep his eyes off the road. He withdrew his hand from between her thighs and returned it to the wheel.

"There's a big difference between love and sex," he said irritably. "And why would it be such a damned tragedy to fall in love with me, anyway?"

"I should think that would be very obvious," she replied reproachfully. "Nobody wants to love somebody who isn't going to love them back. That kind of thing might make a great song or a hit movie, but I can do without it."

Rocky glared over at her but was silent as they neared the entrance of Mariner's Village over on the left. The force with which he pushed down the turn signal lever expressed some of the emotion he was keeping firmly repressed. Braking to a halt, he had to wait several seconds before he could cross over the two northbound lanes, which he did with a great surge of engine power. Slowing his pace once he was driving along the residential streets, he hit the wheel hard with a balled fist as though to compensate for the loss of speed as a release.

"Damn it! I just don't understand why you always have to mess things up!" he said angrily. "First, I just want to be friends, but, no, that's not enough. You want sex as well as friendship. Well, okay, I go along with you, against my own better judgment. Now suddenly you aren't satisfied with friendship and sex, you're afraid you're going to get serious about me, and you don't want that. *Goddammit—*" He hit the wheel with his fist again, hard enough that it hurt and then blew out his breath in a sigh of frustration as he looked over at her. "Just what the hell do you want out of me now, Kitt? What is it that I'm supposed to do or say to fix things?" The total lack of any defense on her deeply apologetic features only heightened his frustration. "Now I suppose you're going to tell me how sorry you are and how it's all your fault and you'll take the blame, right?"

Kitt shook her head sadly. "I *am* sorry, terribly sorry, that things got all messed up between us, Rocky, but I don't think it's anybody's fault that I started feeling the serious kind of love for you." She paused while he swung the Mustang into his driveway and came to a sharp stop. It was just another evidence of "wrongness" that he didn't open the garage door, but sat there behind the wheel a moment and then turned off the engine with a savage twist of the key. She thought he probably intended to hear her out and then send her home.

"All these years I've been under the false impression that a person had some control over falling in love with another person," she continued with the same fatalistic thoughtfulness. "I couldn't understand why Bob let his feelings about Ellen affect his whole life. He has a super high IQ, you know, and had all kinds of offers from big law firms, but he came over here to St. Tammany Parish because Ellen was here. There wasn't much of a chance that they'd ever be anything but friends, she was even married when he first moved here, but that was better than nothing for Bob. He was here to pick up the pieces after her divorce, and now, finally—but that's not my point. I just finally understand that Bob couldn't help the way he felt all those years. It wasn't his fault, and it wasn't Ellen's fault. It was just rotten bad luck."

Rocky swiveled a little more sideways in his seat and rested his elbow on the wheel. "And you've decided that you might have a touch of the same rotten bad luck," he said with heavy irony. It was hard to believe that she was really serious, but she was.

"I'm afraid so," Kitt agreed worriedly.

"What do you have in mind doing about it?"

She sighed. "When I'm not around you, I can make the whole thing between us into a story in my mind and laugh at it, but when I'm with you, it all suddenly becomes real, and I get scared. Rocky, it's not that I think you would ever deliberately do anything to hurt me. Please don't think that," she implored. "Even though you told me not to say it, none of this is your fault."

Rocky's eyes narrowed. "You still haven't answered my question, have you? Is this all your way of telling me that you don't want to see me anymore?"

"I don't not *want* to see you," she contradicted earnestly. "But don't you see that it would be best if I don't? Maybe I'll get over being in love with you. I know I'm certainly going to try."

Rocky stared hard at her and then slowly shook his head. "I keep thinking this has to be some game, and I'm the biggest dupe ever to sit here and try to figure out some way to talk you out of this foolishness. But you're really serious, aren't you? If I can't convince you that you won't be hurt, you'll break everything off between us, even though we have a hell of a good time together." He rubbed his hand roughly along the side of his face.

"Dammit, Kitt, I don't know if what I feel about you is love or not. All I can tell you is that I like you an awful lot. I enjoy being with you more than I've ever enjoyed being with another woman. When I'm not with you, I'm constantly thinking about telling you this or that little thing that's happened to me. If the night before last was any indication, we're definitely compatible in bed, and I wish that's where we were right now instead of sitting here talking. Hell, it's even been going through my mind ever since you called me last night and told me about Ellen and Bob getting married that you could move in with me." He stopped to get some reaction to his words and was disappointed to see they hadn't made any noticeable impression. She looked every bit as troubled and yet every bit as resolute as before.

In desperation Rocky dispensed with words. Leaning over toward her, he curved one hand along the side of her face and kissed her lips very gently, coaxing a response and getting it. "Let's just drop this discussion for now and go inside and make love," he murmured and took a deeper taste of her lips, this time seeking out her tongue. "I want you," he told her in a voice resonant with his need.

"I want you, too," Kitt whispered back.

Rocky ignored the fatalism in her voice and opened the garage door. But this time he pulled into the garage at a sedate pace. Mentally he was already practicing the control he was going to need. After being aroused off and on all evening, it wasn't going to be easy to prolong their lovemaking, and he wanted it to be long and good for her. For the time being, it was the only answer he had for her fears.

He took his time undressing her when they were upstairs in his bedroom, and he told her in frank, lover's language what he liked about her body. "Your breasts are so delicate and shaped like perfect cones with a satiny tip." He kissed the peak of one breast and then the other one, and then made wet circles with his tongue that brought the shy nipple quickly out of hiding. "Ah, there you are," he murmured with male satisfaction, cupping the breast in his hand as he sucked the one lucky peak and compensated the other one for its neglect by caressing it with the fingers of his free hand.

Kitt looked down at him, feeling the delicious weakness pervade her whole body. She stroked her hands across the width of his powerful shoulders and wished they weren't still covered by his shirt.

"I was afraid you'd think they were too small," she murmured.

"They're perfect," Rocky assured her, unsnapping her jeans and sliding down the zipper. The slender form he revealed pleased him as much as her breasts and upper torso, and he told her as much while he crouched in front of her and helped her step out of her jeans and then her bikini panties.

"I thought about doing this during the movie...." Clasping her behind the thighs, he planted slow, deliberate kisses from one knee up to the pale vee. Kitt moaned his name softly, feeling her knees buckle at the warm, rough intimacy of his tongue's bold exploration.

"I can't stand that," she warned him, grabbing his head as her knees gave way enough to make her even more vulnerable to invasion.

"No?" Rocky slid his hands up to her buttocks and caressed the rounded firmness. "I wanted to do this the night you were tickling Andy down on the floor," he informed her.

"You did?"

"Don't pretend you didn't know." He stood up in front of her, unbuckling his belt.

"I didn't have any idea." Kitt put her hands over his and shoved his aside. Her smile was teasingly reminiscent. "I wanted to do *this* that same night, and you definitely knew it." She unbuttoned his shirt and slid it down his arms, revealing his smoothly muscled upper torso. Her hands caressed his broad shoulders and the concave hardness of his chest before they slid across his flat stomach. "You're the one who's perfect," she told him as she unsnapped his jeans.

It was delicious torture for Rocky to let her take her time about undressing him. He managed to withstand her close attention to every detail of his body accompanied by the light touch of her hands. Then she took him in her hands and brought her face closer to him. As much as he yearned for the intimacy she offered him, Rocky didn't dare risk it, and he told her as much.

"Another time," he said regretfully, drawing her up to her feet. "Now I want to make love to you."

If possible, it was even better than the last time. Perhaps the threat of losing her added the new urgency for Rocky. He wanted to raise her to the highest plane of pleasure and keep her there for eternity, safe from doubts. Her abandoned response seemed the source of his own pleasure, his very reason for being. Until her climax heralded his own, he didn't realize he was climbing higher and higher with her the whole time and was there himself on a pinnacle of sensation more dangerous than any he'd ever leaped from before.

Afterward he felt more devastated than satisfied and was glad at first when she lay quietly in his arms and didn't require him to talk before he had recovered. After a while, though, he grew impatient with waiting for whatever she was going to do and say and broke the silence himself.

"What are you thinking?"

Her reply came without any hesitation.

"About how in spite of everything I'm still glad I got to know you. You're a fantastic lover just like you're a fantastic football player—and a nice person, too. You're fun to be with, and you have a great sense of humor."

There was something about the speech, full of accolades, that reminded Rocky unpleasantly of an epitaph.

"Sorry I asked. If I ever need a recommendation, I'll be sure to give your name."

Kitt raised her head and looked into his face. Her rueful little half-smile had a forced humor but no joy. "At least you can be the one who's sorry for a change." She grimaced to acknowledge that it was a pathetic attempt at lightness. "I hope you'll be glad you got to know me, too, Rocky," she said wistfully. She kissed him very tenderly on the forehead and sat up.

Rocky felt every muscle go tense. "Kitt, you're not planning to get up and walk out on me again tonight, I hope. Because if you do..." He left the threat open-ended as she looked at him with the same kind of tender reproof she might have shown when she was scolding Andy.

"Rocky, please don't this hard...."

She slid off the bed, but this time instead of putting her clothes back on in front of him, she gathered them up and went into the bathroom. Rocky lay there several moments, feeling like a victim of all the emotions battling inside him: disbelief that she really intended to break everything off between them, anger and disappointment that she was spoiling what was so obviously good for both of them, resentment of the fact that she could just walk away from him. What the hell was he supposed to *do*?

Kitt had fled into the bathroom because she didn't want to make a spectacle of herself trying to get dressed with hands that trembled. Their unsteadiness disturbed her deeply. It was just another evidence of her powerlessness to control her own emotions and body where Rocky was concerned. Her hands had never trembled before, not even in big championship basketball games with thousands of fans looking on, all holding their breath.

When she came out of the bathroom, Rocky was sitting on the side of the bed, waiting for her. His face was hard, the same way it had been the night he walked in on her in his living room, but she knew him well enough now to read his emotions. She didn't blame him for being angry and resentful and disappointed. He had every right to feel all of that. She just wished he wouldn't look at her so accusingly as though this were all her fault. And even more than that, she wished she weren't able to glimpse the hurt in his dark eyes, not quite hidden behind the pride. His unexpected vulnerability shook the foundations of her certainty and spread the trembling, not just through her limbs but deep inside to her internal organs. Kitt was seized by fresh panic at what was happening to her. She wanted to run as fast as she could, perhaps all the way home, to force strength back into her legs, to make air pump through her lungs, to make her heart pound with an everyday, normal function. She wanted to be her recognizable self again. Couldn't Rocky understand that?

"I suppose you'd rather I didn't call you." Rocky's terse words conveyed the complex blend of what he was feeling.

"Please don't," Kitt begged him. "It'll make things so much easier." She drew in a deep breath and took the venture of walking on her unsteady legs. It came as an enormous relief that they worked, and she dared not push her luck by stopping. On the way past Rocky she swept him a look of deepest apology and managed a wan smile. But no casual farewell words drifted back to him over her shoulder this time.

Rocky slumped forward, resting his elbows on his knees, and stayed in that position a long time, trying to take it all in. Why did she have to go and spoil everything? That's what he just couldn't comprehend. As angry and disappointed as he was over the evening, he still had no feeling that what was between them was over. It wasn't. She lived here on the North Shore and so did he. They were just minutes apart. Hell, she might be calling him the very next evening, and it would be back on again between them.

This time, though, Rocky intended to set some ground rules. He was sick and tired of thinking everything was great and then having the rug jerked out from under him. Enough was enough.

When Kitt didn't call the next evening, he settled into a state of grim patience, determined to outwait her. After all, she had asked him not to call her. When a week passed and she still hadn't called, he got furious and told himself, "This is it, I've *had* it." He started accepting invitations to parties and made the social pages of the New Orleans newspaper, hoping that she'd read about what a good time he was having and see the pictures of him with women she'd consider his type.

It was all empty, though. He didn't enjoy the parties and was bored by the women he squired to them. The extra drinking and late hours took their toll on his physical conditioning. He played some of the worst football of his entire career and was soundly criticized by the press. When even that brought no communication from Kitt, he felt truly betrayed. Didn't she even care that she was ruining his life?"

As the weeks passed and Kitt didn't call, Rocky began to realize that she wasn't going to call. She hadn't been playing a game. She'd been dead serious. For her, it was really over between them. The knowledge chilled him, and for the first time in a long while he faced life without Kitt. What would it be like never to hear that eager undertone in her voice, never to hear her laugh when something delighted her? And so much of life did delight Kitt. What would it be like never to see her grin, never to see her gray eyes light up with amusement, gladness, surprise and all the other volatile emotions that they broadcast, even the sad ones? What would it be like never to eat fried chicken with her again, never to put his arm around her, never to kiss her again or make love to her?

When the answer to all these questions came to Rocky after several days of soul-searching, he got in his Mustang, drove out to Folsom and started looking at horse farms.

Chapter Fourteen

Kitt was up on a ladder attacking a very stubborn sticker on a transom window. She didn't see Rocky enter the newly constructed office building, but several other members of her cleaning crew did and recognized him.

"Hey, Kitt, you got a visitor," a brawny young man in his late teens called out. It was obvious from the way Rocky had sought her out and stood watching her that he had come looking for her.

Kitt glanced down over her outstretched right arm and went perfectly still while she registered Rocky's presence. He read the swift succession of reactions in her eyes: shock, a wild leap of joy and then doubtfulness.

"Hi," she said cautiously, dropping the hand grasping the scraping tool down alongside her body.

"Hi," Rocky answered and just stood there looking up at her. The smile taking slow possession of his face was a gauge of the pleasure and relief seeping through him.

He'd seen enough in that first glance of recognition to give him hope. The sight of her confirmed what he already knew: he didn't want to live his life without her. His job was to convince her that *she* didn't want to live hers without *him*.

"Coming down?" His voice gave her a choice. Either she could come down the ladder or he would come up there with her.

Kitt started backing down the ladder on her traitorous, rubbery legs. She tried to muster indignation over the fact that he had broken his promise and come here to prove once again his power over her, but she succeeded only in being dreadfully self-conscious about her appearance. In her pink kerchief, overblouse and jeans, she couldn't have been any less competition for the glamorous women he'd been dating. And instead of French perfume, she smelled like cleaning solution.

At the bottom of the ladder, she dropped the scraper and wiped her hands nervously on her thighs. Intensely aware that Rocky's eyes were following her every movement and her curious workers in the same room were watching both of them, she clapped her hands smartly and called out, "Okay, everybody, back to work!" To the sound of good-natured moans and complaints about working for a slave driver, she walked over to Rocky.

"Hi," she said again, because she didn't know what else to say. The warmth in his eyes made her giddy and intensified her self-consciousness. "If you'd given me some warning, I'd have worn one of my new uniforms...." She picked up the hem of her Magic Broom overblouse at each side to call disparaging attention to it.

"You look good to me in that one," Rocky told her softly and had to fight the temptation to give her employees a scene they'd really enjoy. It wouldn't bother him in the least to kiss her in front of the whole world, but it probably would bother her.

"Oh, sure," Kitt retorted. Clutching at skepticism at this close distance was like grabbing at a piece of driftwood when you were being swept downstream, out to sea, but it was her only hope. "I've been seeing your picture in the paper a lot lately. You must have decided to get out and make some friends, after all."

"I was lonely," Rocky told her in the same soft undertone. "I missed you a lot, Kitt." He reached down and took her hand. "But we can talk about that later on, in private. Could you take off for a couple of hours? I want to show you something."

Kitt let him lead her outside and seat her in his Mustang. Her submission was mental as well as physical. What was the use of fighting a battle she had no chance of winning? After long, hard weeks of separation when she'd driven herself mercilessly with work so that she'd be too tired at night to want to do anything other than sleep, her reaction to his nearness was as powerful as it had been before. Her cure hadn't worked. She was every bit the victim of love that Bob had been all these years, and she might as well accept that.

Rocky's attitude as he got in beside her was "so far, so good." When they were driving along, headed north, he wanted to know what she was thinking but didn't dare ask.

"I guess you know I've been playing some pretty lousy football lately," he ventured, staking out what seemed dependable conversational territory.

"It's probably all that partying," she replied candidly and then smiled over at him. "Maybe you'll get offers to do beer commercials yet."

Her good humor had a little forced quality, but it warmed him nevertheless. "God, I missed you," he said, reaching over for her hand. He smoothed it over his thigh and then put his hand on top of it. "It's all your fault, you know, that my game's gone to hell. I got mad when you didn't call me and set out to prove that I could get along fine without you. I was hoping you'd read about the parties and see the pictures of me in the paper and think I was having a good time."

"I saw them and I did think that. Weren't you?"

The hopeful note in her voice pleased him enormously.

"Hell, no," he said cheerfully. "I'd have traded all the fancy hors d'oeuvres at those parties for one good offer of a chicken dinner or a pizza 'heartburn special' with pepperoni, Italian sausage, mushrooms, green peppers, onions and black olives."

The hand on Rocky's thigh made a little caressing movement. He made no effort to stop it despite the discomfort he knew it would cause.

"I haven't had much taste for fried chicken or pizza lately," she said. "Or Jerrie's, either."

"What about burnt spareribs? Had any of those lately?"

She shook her head, meeting his smiling glance with an answering smile. "I guess you pretty well destroyed my diet." She relaxed back against her seat and looked contentedly out of her window.

"Aren't you going to ask where we're going?" Rocky prompted her curiously.

"I assume we're going to Folsom. I heard you'd bought the Bordelon place. I happened to run into Jock Bordelon about a week ago. When it came up for sale, I wished I could afford it, but I can't. I really love that place."

Rocky was sorely taken aback and disgruntled to learn that she already knew what he'd meant to reveal as a big surprise. Her words jogged his memory unpleasantly.

"Jock Bordelon's not the man you mentioned to me once—"

The threatening tone of Rocky's voice drew a surprised look from Kitt. "He's the man I told you I almost married because I liked his horse farm so much," she told him matter-of-factly.

Rocky glared at her in disbelief and then muttered a string of curses as he fixed his gaze back upon the road. Kitt studied his grim profile with puzzlement.

"I don't see why that makes any difference—" she began.

"If you had a particle of sense, you'd see why it does," Rocky cut in angrily.

"You mean it upsets you that I spent time there before I even knew you?" she asked skeptically.

"What upsets me is that I bought the place as a goddamned *bribe* to talk you into marrying me, and now I find out you slept with some other guy there." He subjected her to another accusatory glare and then looked grimly ahead. The thigh beneath Kitt's hand was rigid. "Well, don't you have anything to say?" he demanded furiously.

Kitt was turning the most vital component of his revelation over and over in her mind the same way she would turn a precious jewel so that all its facets could catch the light.

"I just can't *believe* it...." she murmured, a smile spreading over her face.

"Well, believe it. It happens to be true."

They were outside of the Covington city limits now and on the two-lane highway heading to Folsom. It was a mild, sunshiny November day. Kitt rolled down her window to take in a deep breath of pine-scented air and then rolled it most of the way up again.

"You're not going to change your mind, are you?" she asked him happily.

Rocky shot her a probing look and had to follow it up quickly with another when he saw her blissful expression. "How can I change my mind? I've already bought the damned farm."

"I'm not talking about the farm, silly." She spanked his thigh playfully. "I'm talking about the marrying part. Did you mean that?"

"Of course, I meant it."

The confirmation was grudging, but it came promptly enough for Kitt's satisfaction. She unclipped her seat belt and climbed up in her seat on her knees to hug him hard around the neck.

"Careful, or you'll get us into a head-on collision," Rocky admonished her, but he rubbed his cheek against hers.

"I just feel so *happy* knowing you would marry me," Kitt told him. "You don't have to, though. I decided today when you showed up that there was no use fighting it anymore. We can live together for as long as it lasts, either in your condominium or on your horse farm, where, by the way, I never did sleep with Jock Bordelon. I never slept with him anywhere, for that matter." With a lingering kiss on his hard cheek, Kitt sat back down in her seat again, but she left her arm up around Rocky's shoulders.

"Well, I'm certainly glad to know that," he told her, surprising her with the absentness of his tone. It had seemed such a big deal just minutes ago that Jock Bordelon might have been her lover.

"You don't not want to get married, do you?" he asked several moments later.

"Of course not. I just meant we don't have to get married as some kind of condition to being together. That's all."

"Well, in that case, we'll go ahead and get married. This is still pretty rural over here on the North Shore, you know. No matter how discreet we might try to be, the news would leak out into the papers. It might not be good for your business."

"I hadn't thought about that, but you're right," she agreed. "We could just have a small, quiet wedding with our family and close friends." Riding along with him in his special car with her arm along his broad, solid shoulders, Kitt was amenable to almost anything.

"Oh, what the hell, we might as well have a big one," he suggested casually. "It's the only time I ever intend to get married, so we might as well make a party of it. I'll invite the whole National Football League. Maybe we could rent the Superdome."

"Why not?" Kitt countered gaily. "We'll probably need it once my mother gets in on the action. I guess between us we do know a lot of people. Now that you mention it, a big wedding could be fun."

They smiled at each other and held hands, both of them aware that they were skirting around expressions of deeper feelings. Rocky wanted her to know he was proud of her and would marry her in front of the whole world. Kitt was deeply touched that he wanted a permanent commitment between them, but shyness kept her from telling him that, just as it kept her from putting into words the love that was welling up inside her until she thought she just might burst from pure happiness.

Lighthearted discussion of wedding plans preoccupied them until they arrived at Rocky's new horse farm. The pleasure on Kitt's face and in her voice as she exclaimed over the gently rolling pastures, well-kept buildings and the house itself made the six-figure sum he'd paid for the place not a penny too much.

"The house is really too big for the two of us," he said as he unlocked the door. "But who's to say that in a few years there might not be more than two of us?"

They were both intrigued with what he was obliquely suggesting, but again cautious with spoken intimacy.

"I love kids," Kitt declared. "I think I'd like to have a little boy one of these days." What she meant but didn't say was that she'd love to have a little Rocky.

"I like kids, too," Rocky mused, a teasing smile on his face as he slipped his arms around Kitt but held her off a little so that he could look down at her stomach.

"Don't you dare say it!" Kitt threatened, giggling. "You're thinking I'll look like a pregnant beanpole."

He grinned broadly and hugged her closer. "I think you'll look cute." The laughter in his face changed to passion as he bent and kissed her on the mouth. The kiss was deep and hungry and addressed openly the need each had for the other. Kitt was clinging to him with her arms around his neck when it finally came to a breathless end.

"Not a thing has changed," she murmured dazedly. "Kissing you still makes me feel strange . . . like I'm taking off into space. The only difference is that now it doesn't scare me, because I know you're going to be right here until I get back."

Rocky's smile was tender. "Kissing still makes you want to talk, I gather."

Kitt looked deep into his eyes. "Sometimes it's just easier to talk than to say things that you really want to say." She took a deep breath and spoke in a soft, urgent rush. "Rocky, I not only love you an awful lot, I'm even *glad* now that I do, even though it's still scary. I can't bear to think of what I would do if something happened to you. And it makes me very happy that you want to marry me, even though you wouldn't have to. And I would love for us to have children together. A little boy who looked like you would be adorable. And—"

Rocky cut her off with a kiss. "My turn now before I lose my nerve," he teased. "I've got a bad case of your love virus myself, and I don't want to ever recover from it. I'm looking forward to living with you, Kitt. I just know that life with you is going to be an experience I wouldn't want to miss. I want to marry you so that the world knows you're mine." He smiled to give them both an escape valve for the intensity of their emotions. "Besides that, I'm determined that you're going to sleep in the same bed with me if I have to chain you down."

Kitt blinked furiously and gulped to keep back tears. "Gosh, that was beautiful, Rocky. Just like something in the movies."

He hugged her tight, binding her to him with his strength and the force of his emotions, which he hadn't even begun to express adequately.

"You know what I'm thinking?" Kitt mumbled against his chest.

"I wouldn't dare to guess, and I'm not even sure I want to hear."

She pulled back from him a few inches and grinned up into his wary face. "I'm thinking there isn't a stick of furniture in this house, but there's hay in the barn."

Rocky shook his head. "Hay in the barn, huh. In a thousand years I'd never have guessed." He grinned and released her, taking her hand in his. "Sounds a little scratchy, but, what the hell, let's give it a try. I've never made love to a cleaning lady in a barn before. Have you ever made love to a football player in a barn?"

"Never have," Kitt declared.

Hand in hand, they started for the barn, laughing and reveling in a picaresque sense of adventure. The hay was scratchy against their bare skin, and they carried on a mock argument about who would take the bottom position. Once their skirmishing flamed into passion, though, there was no discomfort. They wouldn't have traded their love nest for any other. The sweet smell of hay added to their sensory pleasure. From that day on, the scent would always have a happy association for Kitt. Her lungs were full of it when Rocky spoke for the first time those three precious words that every woman wants to hear from her special man: *I love you.*

Actually he said, "I love you one hell of a lot," but then he was a big man, a macho pro football player, with emotions to match his size and strength. He was happy in the knowledge that the woman in his arm was uniquely suited to him and not disturbed that he'd more than met his match in a contest whose rules he'd never figured out, where winning and losing were one and the same.

"I love you, too, Rocky," Kitt told him. The words still had a touch of newness that made them all the more thrilling to his ears.

"Good," he said. "In that case, I'll buy you some lunch. I'm starving."

"Me, too!" Kitt gave him a hug that matched the enthusiasm in her voice and then jumped up to start getting dressed. They picked wisps of hay off each other and discussed lunch options while they dressed.

"There's this little place in Folsom that serves the best barbecue in the whole world," Kitt confided in that reverent tone she reserved for her favorite fast food.

"Why don't we drive into Folsom, then, pick up some poboys and a six-pack of beer—"

"—and bring them back here to have a picnic!"

Hand in hand they left the barn and started at a fast walk toward the Mustang, the two pairs of long legs in step with each other. Kitt was first to break into a trot, just because she felt so darned good.

"Come on," she shouted, tugging at his hand. "Let's hurry before they sell all the barbecue!"

Rocky was caught up immediately in her energy and in the elation ringing in her tone and floating out over the pastures of their horse farm. He matched her trot and when she quickened the pace to an all-out run, he raced along beside her, incredibly hungry, incredibly happy, incredibly... *complete.*

The Silhouette Cameo Tote Bag Now available for just $6.99

Handsomely designed in blue and bright pink, its stylish good looks make the Cameo Tote Bag an attractive accessory. The Cameo Tote Bag is big and roomy (13″ square), with reinforced handles and a snap-shut top. You can buy the Cameo Tote Bag for $6.99, plus $1.50 for postage and handling.

Send your name and address with check or money order for $6.99 (plus $1.50 postage and handling), a total of $8.49 to:

Silhouette Books
120 Brighton Road
P.O. Box 5084
Clifton, NJ 07015-5084
ATTN: Tote Bag

SIL-T-1

The Silhouette Cameo Tote Bag can be purchased pre-paid only. No charges will be accepted. Please allow 4 to 6 weeks for delivery.

Arizona and N.Y. State Residents Please Add Sales Tax

If you're ready for a more sensual, more provocative reading experience...

We'll send you
4 Silhouette Desire novels
FREE
and without obligation

Then, we'll send you six more Silhouette Desire® novels to preview every month for 15 days with absolutely no obligation!

When you decide to keep them, you pay just $1.95 each ($2.25 each in Canada) *with never any additional charges!*

And that's not all. You get FREE home delivery of all books as soon as they are published and a FREE subscription to the Silhouette Books Newsletter as long as you remain a member. Each issue is filled with news on upcoming titles, interviews with your favorite authors, even their favorite recipes.

Silhouette Desire novels are not for everyone. They are written especially for the woman who wants a more satisfying, more deeply involving reading experience. Silhouette Desire novels take you *beyond* the others.

If you're ready for that kind of experience, fill out and return the coupon today!

Silhouette ❤ Desire®

Silhouette Books, 120 Brighton Rd., P.O. Box 5084, Clifton, NJ 07015-5084 *good*

Silhouette Special Edition

COMING NEXT MONTH

THIS LONG WINTER PAST—Jeanne Stephens
Cody Wakefield was a temptation that Assistant District Attorney
Liann McDowell vowed to resist. He was intelligent, charming
and attractive . . . but he was a cop.

ZACHARY'S LAW—Lisa Jackson
Zachary's law partner was against him taking the case, but when
Zachary looked into Laura's eyes and saw the pain that so closely
mirrored his own soul, he knew he had to help her.

JESSE'S GIRL—Billie Green
Ellie had always been his "Little Peanut." Even when the trouble
started and Bitter, Texas, turned against him, Jesse didn't realize
that the girl standing beside him was becoming a woman—and
she was in love.

BITTERSWEET SACRIFICE—Bay Matthews
While searching for the surrogate mother who was now denying
him his child, Zade Wakefield found Lindy. Neither of them
knew that the bond they felt was the child they shared.

HEATSTROKE—Jillian Blake
Ten years had passed since Carey had been introduced to rock
star Tony Miles. Now she could discover if the sparks ignited that
night meant love, or were merely a flash in the pan.

DIAMOND IN THE SKY—Natalie Bishop
Taylor couldn't just walk away. Jason had transformed her from
an ex-model into a box-office smash. Now he needed help, and he
was going to get it . . . whether he wanted it or not.

AVAILABLE THIS MONTH

LOVE'S HAUNTING REFRAIN
Ada Steward

MY HEART'S UNDOING
Phyllis Halldorson

SURPRISE OFFENSE
Carole Halston

BIRD IN FLIGHT
Sondra Stanford

TRANSFER OF LOYALTIES
Roslyn MacDonald

AS TIME GOES BY
Brooke Hastings